MW01253450

Swiss

Conspiracy

Spencer Hawke

3

Copyright © 2012 Spencer Hawke
All rights reserved.
jamieshead LLC
Spencer Hawke
www.spencerhawke.com
ISBN: 10: 1525391884
ISBN-13: 978-1515391883

CONTENTS

1 ENTER THE RAVEN

Bay of Naples, Sorrento, Italy
Night, October 24, 2014

Ari Cohen stood behind the wheel of a 46-foot cigar boat he found waiting at slip C107 at the Sorrento Yacht Club, just as Colonel Tom Burke had promised. The motor rumbled gently in neutral, the deep throaty growl of its dual engines reverberating as if charged with testosterone. It was floating, partially hidden, in the shadows of a much larger boat, with a 150-foot luxury yacht anchored off the port bow in the distance.

It was a quiet night, and music from the Hotel Excelsior Vitoria floated across the bay toward him. Ari was invisible, blending into the moonless dark night.

Some slight movement in front of the yacht off the bow prompted him to put his night-vision camera lens to his eye. He had not noticed before, but a nondescript 12-foot skiff was pulling up alongside the yacht he was targeting. One person was manning the oars, his stroke so symmetrical he did not even raise a splash as he approached. He wore dark clothes with a hood or cap obscuring his face, and it was definitely too dark to see who it was. He secured the skiff to the landing deck and started up the ramp to the main deck.

Ari focused his camera on the stranger and started clicking, taking as many photos as he could. Digital images were sent instantly to headquarters at the Eyes of Athena as Ari followed the stranger up the gangway through his lens.

Then he turned his attention and his camera to the person on board greeting this new guest. Getting a full facial photo, Ari noted the man on the yacht was taller than the visitor, wearing a navy blazer over a light-colored polo shirt. That bronzed face, gleaming smile and hook nose were unmistakable to Ari; that was the Raven, his image burned into Ari's subconscious.

Ari was wearing his headset and mic. He tapped his unit. "Tom, did you get that?"

Burke was not only receiving the photos from Ari's camera, but had a live satellite feed coming overhead on the 62" monitors in the Athena

OPs center.

Many people thought the U.S. National Security Agency or the CIA had the greatest state-of-the-art equipment in the world. If they were ever lucky enough to be privy to the inside workings of this centuries-old agency run outside of government bounds, they would have been shocked. The level of sophistication at the Athena Operations Center just outside of Bethesda, Maryland was top notch. It managed to run an efficient operation without ever abusing the privacy issues plaguing many governmental groups.

"Yes, Ari, running facial recognition now."

"There's no doubt that's the Raven." Ari was on point, waiting for input. He continued to scan the yacht as the two men went inside.

"Ari, no ID on the stranger. The other person on board is confirmed as the Raven. Can you get a full-facial for us on his visitor?"

No sooner had Burke finished speaking than the music from the Hotel Excelsior Vitoria was drowned out by a chopper taking off from the hotel helipad. Ari looked over at the top of a 100-foot sheer cliff face. At beach level, the hotel's nightclub was ablaze with colored lights, and from there the stairway, cut into the rock face, zigzagged its way up the cliff to the top and the hotel's rear entrance.

The stairway was already full of tourists going in both directions, many descending the steps for a romantic after-dinner stroll along the beach.

Ari was motionless behind the wheel of his cigar boat watching the chopper make its way across the bay to the Raven's yacht, where there was a sudden burst of activity as deckhands ran out to the yacht's helipad to await the chopper's arrival.

On the bridge of the yacht, the Raven was unmistakable in his dark blazer, but the stranger seemed to constantly avoid being seen. Even now, he was standing with his back to the bridge windows, talking from the side-on to the Raven. Both men moved toward the far-side door as the chopper landed on the yacht.

The Raven escorted his guest down the gangway. When he reached the bottom, he handed a small case to the stranger, who accepted it with one hand and reached for the chopper door with the other. Once inside, the rotor speed increased again and the chopper took off, heading back toward the hotel, but for all that time the stranger avoided looking out the window, wearing a dark cap pulled down as low as possible.

Burke was monitoring the scene through a satellite feed as well as listening to Ari on his headset. As the situation unfolded, he bellowed at Ari, "Follow the stranger... Follow that bag!"

Ari was not only visibly shocked by the volume of the order coming through from Burke, but also with the order itself. Matching Burke's tone, he roared back, "But he's in a bloody chopper!"

At the same time Ari responded indignantly to the rather absurd order, he jammed his cigarette boat into gear, taking off at high speed toward the shore.

The Mercury racing twin-turbocharged, quad-cam, 4-valve engines kicked Ari's boat into top speed almost immediately, creating a massive wake, slicing through the surf like a killer whale hunting a seal. Ari had his hands full steering the 1,350 horse power monster and didn't have time to comment on Burke's next order.

"Ari, get that rum-runner moving!"

The boat was approaching shore at a frightening speed, zigzagging as it went, and controlling it this close to shore was challenge enough. Ari was consumed with avoiding the smaller boats and yachts anchored close to shore as he raced by startled passengers enjoying the Mediterranean. He ignored the rude gestures and curses he provoked as he blazed by, rocking some boats so much they nearly tipped over. He continued his quest without altering his speed, roaring toward shore.

Ari had his eyes on the chopper as it circled the Excelsior Hotel, descending to land. He drove the boat straight for the beach at full speed and hit the sand with enough momentum to continue careening up the beach toward the rock stairway, scattering romantic holiday-goers and local guests alike. They took on shocked expressions as Ari jumped out of the boat before it had stopped moving. In two or three paces, he was at the stairway, racing up three steps at a time.

The stairs leading to the hotel on the sea side had a thick rope-type handrail anchored by metal stakes impaled into the outside of every fifth step. Ari grabbed the rope as he rushed up the steps. His noisy arrival on the beach had alerted everyone that an intruder was now barreling up the stairs. People turned to look at him, most motionless, some on the rock-face side, some on the rope side. Consequently, Ari had to dodge from side to side to avoid running into the indignant and gawking climbers.

As he got closer to the top, some of the guests were either too tired to have taken notice or did not hear the commotion caused by his boat making its unusual landing on the beach. Almost totally out of breath he shouted, "Make way!"

Startled tourists dropped coffee cups and after-dinner drink glasses as he pushed by. Others, further up the stairs, now heard the noise and stood to one side.

Ari finally arrived at the top panting and sweating. A crowd of guests still stood by, silently watching him. He was beat and had his hands on his knees trying to get his breath back. After only a few moments of rest, he saw or maybe heard the chopper toward the front of the hotel, the pitch increasing again as if it were about to take off once more.

Ari ran at top speed through the tall, elegant, double-door back entrance to the hotel. He didn't stop until he went flying across the lobby and out the front entrance, where a large gathering of tourists waited for taxis. He finally skidded to a stop in front of a formally dressed doorman wearing green tails and sporting a matching top hat.

The doorman looked around at Ari as he came to a teetering stop. He twirled one side of his handlebar mustache in a gesture of surprise as Ari paused, totally out of breath, bent over again with his upper body supported by his hands on his knees.

Ari looked up and over at the doorman, shouting out between labored breaths, "Where did the passenger in that chopper go?"

Another crowd of gawkers waiting in line for a taxi looked on incredulously.

The doorman responded in heavily accented English, "He got into a limo, Signor."

Ari was beginning to recover and was almost standing upright, although still breathing heavily.

"Did you hear where it was going?"

"The Salvador Dali Exhibition, Signor."

On hearing this response, Ari whistled and put his hand up to signal for a taxi. The doorman shrugged his shoulders at the waiting crowd, as if this behavior was totally unexpected. Seeing that they were beginning to get agitated, he decided to intervene before he had a mutiny on his hands.

"I'm sorry, Signor, there are people in front of you," he said gesturing to the line, his tone suggesting he felt sorry for Ari's predicament.

Ari stopped trying to hail a cab and looked around for the first time, noticing the long line of guests waiting for a ride. He dug into his pocket and pulled out some money, handing the doorman a 50 euro note. The doorman accepted the tip as a big smile spread across his face.

Then, to totally diffuse the situation, he said conspiratorially, "The quickest way to get there is to run down the Corso Italia. The taxi has to go all the way around town."

The doorman shrugged his shoulders again, still talking in a low voice, as if sharing a secret, "Italian Roads...Signor"

Ari looked in the direction the doorman pointed toward the Corso Italia Road and took off running again at full speed. Corso Italia, in this part of town, was mostly retail shops with few people on the sidewalk, so he moved fast.

Suddenly, from the distance, the loud noise of a police siren broke the silence. He took a right to follow the police car. As he got closer, he saw a policeman securing an area with yellow tape bearing the words, "Polizia de Stato." The building being cordoned off was the Villa Fiorentino, and above the entrance was a large yellow sign advertising the Salvador Dali Exhibition.

Ari slowed, regaining his breath as he approached the taped-off area. He headed for a policeman and, in fluent Italian, asked, "Cos'è successo?" What happened?

The policeman, still sitting astride his creamy-white motorcycle, only replied after seeing the flash of Ari's old Mossad badge. "Il ministro delle finanze è stato assassinato." The Minister of Finance was assassinated.

The Villa Fiorentino buzzed with police activity. Ari moved back from the cordoned-off line and found a better vantage point from the hood of an old Fiat truck. He scanned the area, and on the far side of the villa, outside the taped-off section, he spotted a limo stopping by the assembled crowd. Ari sought any anomaly among the people and saw a man with a black cap pulled down over his face. The man had his eyes to the ground, trying to avoid being seen as he walked toward another limo. Ari lifted his phone to use the camera to photograph the scene.

"Tom? Are you getting this? I think it's our man again."

"We're following you, Ari. I agree. We're trying to match up his physique with the photos from the yacht."

Ari watched as the man climbed into the limo and, without delay, the limo took off, accelerating a little faster than one would expect.

"Ari, we ID'd the photo; it's Kwok Kong."

"Tom, can you get your eyes-in-the-sky to follow that limo?"

"We are following him, Ari, and we've got a match. That's our guy. Find some wheels; we think he is headed toward the airport."

From his vantage point on the hood, Ari saw a stretch Mercedes limo pulling up with a couple inside. In an instant, he was moving again, jumping down from the hood and running across the plaza to the car. As the chauffeur got out, he left his door open to go around to open the passenger curb-side door for the couple inside to disembark.

Ari jumped into the driver's seat and slammed his door, gunning the accelerator. The couple inside were pushed back into their seats, howling in surprise and protest.

The chauffeur, standing on the curb in frozen animation with his hand out to open the door, was left totally mystified as his car screeched away up the street.

Ari pressed the button to pull up the privacy shield, separating himself from his screaming passengers. The howls of protest from the couple died down as the shield closed, and he again pressed his headset. "Tom, I need directions. How far behind am I?"

"We are sending a map to your phone now, Ari. You are about seven minutes behind him. Confirmed, he is headed to the airport."

Ari drove like a madman north for the airport. His concentration was broken for a moment by the male passenger hammering on the privacy shield with his shoe. Ari ignored him, continuing at breakneck speed.

The traffic along the airport road was heavy in both directions. As Ari's driving became even more erratic – weaving in and out of the oncoming cars – his male passenger slipped back, ceasing his incessant banging on the window, apparently deciding the crazy man driving their limo probably didn't need any added distraction.

The airport came into view, and Ari barreled into the departure terminal, tires squealing. Two police motorcycles took up the chase behind him, sirens blaring as he screeched to a halt in front of the terminal, the car skidding noisily to a stop at a 45-degree angle to the sidewalk. As the limo came to rest, Ari pressed the button controlling the privacy shield, allowing it to slide down, and tossed the keys to the man in the back.

Ari smiled as turned around to look at his passengers saying, "Scusate."

He jumped out of the limo and ran into the passenger terminal, looking back over his shoulder to see his passenger arguing with police and being led off in handcuffs.

Ari ran into the private plane terminal, tapping his microphone as he went. "Where is he?"

"Ari, he is on the runway now."

He ran over to the large windows overlooking the runway just in time to see a private jet taxiing out and gaining speed. The plane was already wheels up. Ari could imagine Kong inside removing his cap to reveal cold, oriental eyes staring back at him.

Ari was furious. He found a quiet corner to talk on the phone with Burke. "Tom, I don't get it. The Raven just had the Italian Finance Minister killed?"

"You know almost as much as we do, Ari. The Italian Finance Minister was scheduled to meet the Chairman of our Federal Reserve."

"Do you think there is a connection?"

"I don't know Ari, but I've got a real bad feeling about this one. I want you back here ASAP, I've checked the flight plan for Kwok Kong's charter and he is on his way to Washington D.C."

♦ ♦ ♦

Ari had been in Naples as a guest soloist for the Tel Aviv symphony, but one call from Tom Burke at Athena headquarters had changed all of that. He went back to the concert hall to listen to a recording of his last rehearsal -- the final practice before he performed the most challenging solo of his career. With a pained expression on his face he removed his headset, walked out of the concert hall and flagged down a cab to return to his hotel.

Only minutes later he walked back into his hotel room, the same wistful look on his face. He crossed the room to the closet and moved back some hanging clothes to reveal a safe. He removed a well-worn case from it, opened the case and lovingly stroked his beloved Stradivarius. "Ah, my lovely, we were so close ..."

For almost a year, his Stradivarius had remained locked in a safe room at the Lowry Concert Hall in Tel Aviv. That was 1999, when he had first been "loaned" to the Eyes of Athena – a secret organization created by America's founding fathers at the birth of the nation.

Ari had been Mossad then, called in to aid Athena with the downing of a Stealth fighter in Bosnia because he had been on assignment in the area. When he had flown in to Bethesda to be debriefed, they had asked him to continue the mission with them and capture the Iranian madman bent on turning American stealth technology against the U.S. and the world.

He stayed on with Athena and the special friends he bonded with on that mission. Ari never liked being separated from his Stradivarius, it was how he handled the stress of his occupation and had become almost a part of him. But caution prevailed, and he decided to let it remain in Tel Aviv until he was sure he had planted roots in Maryland.

After a year of training on base – playing a less expensive violin to help relieve job-induced anxiety – he had moved to a townhouse in Georgetown. He was rarely there, but after another year, he had been unable to resist any longer and had gone back to Tel Aviv to retrieve the Stradivarius. He often remarked that a non-musician could never comprehend the love a master held for his favorite instrument.

He carefully returned it to its case and began to pack up his gear for the return flight home and yet another mission. Ari had been after the Raven for years. A high-level white-collar criminal with ties to the Sicilian Mafia, the Raven had recently been taking credit for some more brutal crimes. If he had surfaced in Naples, there had to be a good reason for it.

Still, there was bitterness. Ari had rehearsed his solo non-stop for a month – a rendition of Jimi Hendrix's "Purple Haze" that he had reworked for violin. It was an unusual and complicated piece, but Ari was determined to push himself.

"I wonder how the symphony audience would have received it," he said, chuckling at the thought of it.

I have now mastered the most difficult piece of my career, he thought in retrospect. I know that. For me it is enough. Ari didn't need the audience's encores to satisfy his ego, but he did smile secretly to himself, knowing – and only he knew – that he carried a recording of his last private rehearsal.

It was enough. It would have to be enough because Ari was going after the Raven; he owed some of his comrades that much since they hadn't made it back from Athena's last confrontation with that madman.

2 FINANCIAL PERIL

October 25, 2014
Government Plans for Financial Crisis
Associated Press

GENEVA — According to an anonymous source with the Swiss Bankers Association, the U.S. government is considering contingency plans in light of its inability to cover FDIC deposits at U.S. banks.

With government debt in the United States approaching $18 trillion, and each depositor insured up to $250,000 for covered deposits, sources say the U.S. government is considering changes to the program as part of emergency planning for "a complete financial meltdown."

According to the source, the Federal Reserve is studying options to reduce the level of insurance to more manageable levels of $25,000 maximum per account. Economic advisers suggest that such a move could precipitate a national crisis of proportions not seen in decades. Educated investors would likely sell dollars in favor of more solid investments like gold and silver, while more conservative retirees, who have their life savings tied up in low yielding CDs could face a complete loss of all savings in the event of another Wall Street meltdown.

♦ ♦ ♦

White House Oval Office
October 26, 2014

Morris Winters, U.S. Secretary of the Treasury, was a nervous man. With the Reuters release crumpled in his hand and a worn-out briefcase tucked under his arm, he hurried down the hall to the Oval Office.

The President's Aide ushered him in quickly, but the President barely looked up from a stack of papers he was signing, a bored, almost angry expression on his face.

Winters waited respectfully until the last pen stroke. The secretary standing beside the President's desk took up the stack and scurried out, and the President finally acknowledged his visitor.

"What can I do for you, Mo? You look awfully flustered."

President Richard Klein leaned back in his chair, rolling his writing wrist to relieve the cramping from an hour of solid signing.

After exhaling in a showing of nervousness or anxiety, Winters handed him the release. "We've got an issue, Sir."

Klein glanced over the paper Winters had given him. "Yes, I heard this earlier," he said, sliding the release aside dismissively.

"Sir, that kind of news could start a real panic."

"Oh, I don't think so, Mo," Klein said, rising to take up his putter and a golf ball from a stand beside his desk. He moved over to a small practice green to putt while the two talked. "Most of the voters don't pay much attention to the market or announcements like this. We need to be sure the big boys know that we've got them covered – don't want any of my major players getting worried about their investments in the U.S. government."

The President stopped his putting, stood up as if contemplating his last statement, then shaking off any self-doubt, he tried to reassure Winters.

"They know better than to take this sort of release at face value."

Winters' mouth fell open; the President's lack of concern and understanding troubling him greatly. "Sir, I don't believe you understand the gravity of the situation."

He moved to try to get in the President's line of sight. "China holds a quarter of America's foreign reserves, $4 trillion – that's TRILLION with a T. What is China going to do if there is a run on the dollar? They are going to sell, and sell fast."

Klein looked up at Winters, his face a mask of placation. "No one is going to make a run on the dollar, Mo. The only people who understand the importance of that release are the major players, and they know enough to bide their time and turn the market to their advantage."

"You don't understand, Sir. It's not about forces within our nation."

Now Klein was losing his patience. "Mo, what the devil are you talking about?"

"Someone killed the Italian Minister of Finance, Sir."

"And you think that has something to do with the U.S. economy?"

"Mr. President, the United States of America is the wealthiest nation on earth – and the most despised because of her wealth and her charter to protect the innocent against the bullies of the world. Most of this hate is instigated by nations trying to steer their people away from looking too closely at their own governments; it is safer to encourage hate against the 'Big Satan'."

Winters was pacing frantically around the room, nearly apoplectic with the intensity of his need to make the President understand.

"Most of these countries also realize they cannot win a conventional war with the U.S. Still, all of these countries share two advantages – if you look at them that way – over America. They have NO freedom of the press and NO Congressional oversight committees."

Klein was totally lost watching the little man pace the room, his face bright red and perspiring.

"Unfettered, the objective of these countries is the destruction of America through non-conventional means. These include destruction of the power grid; poisoning our food supplies, poisoning our water supply and destroying our health care system…"

He paused to look at Klein hoping to see true understanding dawning on his face.

"Even holding one quarter of our national debt could be one heck of a powerful weapon," he said pointedly. "And now, a MANIPULATED meltdown of the world-wide financial system."

"Manipulated?" Klein asked.

"We all know the United States government spends on average 50 percent more than it takes in, and what we don't have, we borrow from other countries. If all the central banks that own our dollars start to sell them, the U.S. government will be forced to live within its budget. No one will lend us the money to continue deficit spending, and drastic cuts in the government budget will have to be made – that means social programs.

"So, on top of a failing economy, the loss of jobs that comes with it and the inevitability of the working class becoming more and more impoverished, those poor who may have once turned to the government for income will be out of luck.

"Soon, food stamps will be obsolete because it takes too long for the Washington bureaucracy to reimburse American stores so they can pay their bills. Next comes the demise of Social Security, already being paid in a deficit. The end result is the poor – and there will be more of them than we have seen in decades – will become desperate.

"The paper dollar will be worthless. You know those middle- and upper-class folks who have been buying gold and silver for years? When the cow dung hits the fan, there will be two lines at the check-out counter: one for people with REAL money – gold, silver, Euros, Swiss Francs, Bitcoin and the like – and one for everyone else. And when closing time comes and there's nothing left to offer those with paper dollar IOUs from a defunct government? That's when it gets ugly, Sir.

"That's when people start turning on one another for a loaf of bread – that now costs three times what it used to. And the 'crazies' hoarding canned goods and growing veggies in their greenhouses will look pretty darned smart, especially if they've got a good gun and a stock of ammo to protect it all.

"We have borrowed so much money, the bankers own us, Sir. But these money lenders we have allowed to control our future are potentially our most dangerous enemies – China and the Middle East, radical Islam – they own us. And someone is setting the stage to hand us over to them."

3 BRINGING IN THE CHIEF

White House
Later that Day

White House Chief of Staff Ed Gonzalez was not a man to trifle with.

A pre-dawn riser, he intentionally got to the office early. The first reason, he liked to be there before any of the staff so he could have some quiet time. The second, in the privacy of his office, he could make a cup of tea the way he liked it – the way his mother had taught him, the way it was made in the "old" country – none of this microwaved or lukewarm water business.

The definition of a good start to the day was when none of his staff – or anyone's staff for that matter – arrived until they were meant to.

Gonzalez thought today was going to be a perfect day. He was sitting at his desk, both elbows firmly planted on the mahogany top, delicately holding a freshly brewed cup of his preferred orange pekoe tea. His nose was centered over the slightly steaming china, taking in the perfect aroma of a cup of cha made properly.

He leaned in to sample the delicate scent, and that was when he knew his day was going to be a challenge. He heard his young, impulsive assistant arrive in the outer office, clattering loudly, ruining the sanctity of the silent morning.

Before Gonzalez even had time to open his eyes to this sudden intrusion, Brett Carter burst through the door, slamming it back against the wall with a cantankerous thud.

Without an "Excuse me" or "Good Morning, Sir," Carter launched into his reason for the unceremonious interruption.

"Sir, I have the Vice President on the line," he said in a brazenly loud voice.

Gonzalez raised his head slowly. To a perceptive person, the look of near-explosive anger would have been obvious. To a brand new, over-eager White House staffer, it was invisible, his excitement too intoxicating.

When Carter saw there was no response coming from his boss, he inhaled for another attempt to get through.

"Sir, you don't understand; it's Jade McQueen, herself! It is so cool. I have been talking to Jade McQueen personally."

Gonzalez simply sighed, hoping the new would soon wear off of his newest staff member. "Did she tell you what she wanted?"

"Oh, yes, Sir, this is so cool, she would like to make an appointment to see you this afternoon."

"I see," Gonzalez said, making a mental note to have a discussion with the lad later about his professional language skills and abundant use of the word "cool."

"And did she mention what she could possibly want that is so urgent?"

"She didn't say, Sir. She just asked me in the sweetest voice to make sure I did her the favor to get her on your schedule this afternoon. Oh, my gosh! Jade McQueen asked me to do her a favor."

If his mother could have seen the face Gonzalez made after his assistant's outburst. She would probably have advised evacuating Washington, D.C.

Under considerable duress, he just responded, "Very well, fit her in."

◆ ◆ ◆

McQueen entered every room as if she owned it, a quiet aura of power encircling her decidedly feminine form.

"Hello, Ed," she said, her Southern charm sweeping in before her as she took a seat in front of the Chief of Staff. She may have been the Member from New York at the Eyes of Athena, but she had never lost her Arkansas roots.

McQueen, had been elected Vice President in 2012, but had filled the position for more than a year before that. Gentle urging by the Athena Board had convinced President Klein to select her when his current VP was forced to vacate the position due to health issues. She had been a member of the Athena Board for not much longer than that. She was now rumored to be a sure bet for the higher office in the next election.

Gonzalez looked a little mystified. The Vice President had direct access at all times to the President and rarely had need of the Chief's services. His mind raced ahead wondering what she wanted from him.

McQueen wasted no time with pleasantries, "Ed... You don't mind if I call you that, do you?"

She waited for Gonzalez to shake his head.

"In my position, I am sometimes privy to information that is not even known by the CIA." She watched Gonzalez for his reaction; he was leaning forward listening intently.

"You see, sometimes in my travels, I am approached by characters that... Let's just say, they would not be welcome in the White House."

"I don't understand, Madam Vice President, you are heavily protected at all times –" Gonzalez began, but McQueen cut him off.

"Jade, please, Ed. I have found it useful to make myself available to some of these characters in the interest of national security. Many I know from my time as Secretary of State, and my Secret Service agents have been with me since that time and know the drill. They keep me safe and guarded but not isolated from these... contacts."

Gonzalez nodded.

"Ed, one of these contacts has gone to great lengths to let me know that a certain colleague of his is involved in a plan to derail the U.S. economy – to compromise the Federal Reserve and initiate a type of financial Armageddon on the U.S.A."

"That is a tough nut to swallow, Jade."

"I agree, Ed, but this person told me what the first steps of the campaign would be. He told me there were two international central bankers this man could not buy. They would have to be silenced... forever. You get my gist?"

"I'm listening." Gonzalez was totally intrigued, knowing McQueen wouldn't waste her time if she felt there was no merit to the information.

"One of the bankers he told me was in danger was the Italian Minister of Finance."

Now she really had his attention. "But wasn't he killed in Sorrento yesterday?"

She nodded her head.

"Why are you telling me this? Why not go straight to the President or even the Secretary of State?"

McQueen cleared her throat. "Well, we both know the President does not always have his mind on matters of state, and I have found we do not work as well together as I would have liked. As for my replacement, the Secretary of State tends to be wary of information I bring to him – especially when it comes from one of those... contacts."

"I see. So you thought I could bring it to the President from another source and get some action taken?" Gonzalez asked.

Again she nodded. "My understanding is that Mo Winters had already planned to brief him on the impending financial crisis."

"Who was the second target they wanted to get rid of?"

McQueen shrugged her shoulders.

"Can you tell me anything about who's doing this and why?"

McQueen took a deep breath. "I can't tell you who and I don't know why."

4 THE WORLD GONE MAD

FLASHBACK – April 28, 1975
Saigon, Vietnam

Alex Stangl was furious. Only last week the city outside his window was filled with hope and determination having chosen the RIGHT side in this war of Capitalism against Communism. Tensions had run high with the enemy advancing, but children still played in the streets, and neighbors still called one another friend.

Even as Americans had quietly fled the city over the last month, relations had remained good, but with the North Vietnamese at the gate...

Alex looked at the crib holding his newborn twins, Pieter and Wolfgang. His wife, Heidi, watched from the doorway. She saw anxiety replace his usual happy-go-lucky smile and started to panic when that look turned to one of, "What have I done?"

Dry heaves rose in her gut with the fear of an impending disaster and she ran to the bathroom, hand over mouth, adrenalin and bile rising in her throat. Some minutes later, she was able to look over her shoulder at Alex. He had not moved. She wiped her mouth, walked cautiously back into their living area, and found him still staring at their two miracles.

Teary eyed, Heidi hesitantly mumbled out between emotional deep breaths, "Tell me."

Alex looked at his bride, "I'm so sorry Heidi; I never dreamed they would abandon us."

Anger replaced fear on Heidi's face, but in her husband's eyes, she saw only defeat.

"I spoke with Ben. The final evacuation of all personnel is imminent. It will be a madhouse, and I thought the CIA would protect us – assure us safe passage home – but that is not the case; it's every man for himself."

Heidi and Alex had been married for 18 months, but she had already begun to learn his expressions. She knew he was thinking he should have sent her away weeks ago. Before she could soothe him, one of the twins cried out, waking his brother.

Heidi picked up Pieter. "Feeding time." She busied herself with Pieter's diaper before turning to Alex. "Check Wolfgang's diaper, then I'll feed them both."

This was more than Alex could bear; he walked out onto the porch and sat in a small chair. He lit a cigarette then turned around to watch his family. Heidi had finished cleaning the boys, and when she had firmly put one boy to each breast she looked up at her husband.

With determination she said, "We will go to the Embassy first thing. We will get out."

Alex nodded his agreement, but the loving smile on his face disappeared as he turned his head toward small arms fire breaking the spell of their denial somewhere in the distance.

He thought back to earlier that day, he had waited anxiously for word from his handler. As a member of the CIA stationed in Saigon, he had remained entrenched within the city long after it was safe – for him or his tiny family.

Tensions were rising. If only he had been able to get Heidi and the boys to safety sooner. It seemed the whole world had gone crazy in an instant, just when his brand new sons were drawing their first breaths – as if the twins' birth was synchronized with the North Vietnamese advance.

The NVC crept closer each day to the city of Saigon, until they sat primed for the final push to take control of the city and declare a victory and an end to the war.

"Do not fret, husband," Heidi said as she walked toward him, placing her hand on his shoulder. By now, they were both nearly immune to the constant noise of the city with the enemy so close.

Alex looked up at his wife – his selfless wife, the woman he adored – the guilt bringing tears to his eyes. He knew better, he should have sent her back to Switzerland weeks ago, before the twins had been born. Alex knew his own selfishness and desire to have her close by had resulted in this situation. He looked up into her bright blue eyes. How I adore her, he thought, noticing the pain there and the weariness in her demeanor. The labor and the past few weeks had been hard on her.

He chided himself, I should have known and forced her to leave months ago. The U.S. government thought the South Vietnamese could hold Saigon through the dry season – into the next year – but they had been wrong, and everyone was caught off guard.

When it became obvious Saigon would soon fall and the evacuations of dependents and non-essential personnel began quietly in March, he begged her to go. She refused; she could not bear to leave him behind, and he could not abandon the assets in his care as double agents with the NVC. The CIA held out a flicker of hope for a South Vietnamese turnaround until Da Nang fell early that morning.

And as of that morning, Alex had escorted all of his assets across enemy lines and on to more secure locations – a job made infinitely easier with that line drawn seemingly inches from his living room window.

Alex looked back to the crib where the boys slept. Both bore his darker, Sicilian coloring, although they had their mother's piercing blue eyes – a gift of her Swiss lineage. Pieter was the stronger of the two, while his identical twin, Wolfgang, was weak and sickly.

He is so frail still, little Wolfgang. Alex worried he was too weak to make the journey ahead of them. It had only been a few weeks since Heidi brought the boys into the world, and not under the best of conditions. The tropical climate of Vietnam was hard on his wife since she was accustomed to the crisp mountain air of Switzerland. He glanced from one to the other, his worry showing on his face. Heidi was watching; she leaned down and kissed his wrinkled forehead.

Alex turned his face into his wife's side and held her tight. He could not bear the thought of losing his little family – this incredible gift he had been given in the middle of his hellish assignment. Just when life had seemed its darkest, he met Heidi, a Red Cross worker from Switzerland, and love found a way to bloom.

Alex had not only given Heidi's name to his sons, but he had taken it as well. As a long-time operative with the CIA, he was used to adopting and living under many assumed identities. To make sure his past never came back to hurt his family, he had assumed Heidi's family name. It not only wiped away any connection to his spotted career with the CIA, but also any connection to his family's darker past.

It was his family's history that first brought him to the attention of the CIA. They could trace their ancestry back to Sicily, where they were enforcers for the Cosa Nostra – the Sicilian Mafia. The mere mention of his family name in Sicily still evoked fear – the Vitale's reputation for brutal domination was legendary.

But his boys would be safe; gone was the connection to the Clan. From now on, his family would be Stangl.

His thoughts were interrupted by the shrill sound of the telephone ringing, increasingly rare as the conflict near Saigon had escalated. The sound woke the twins, and Heidi moved to soothe them as Alex answered.

"Yes?"

"Good evening, Alex, it's Ben."

"Hello, Ben." His tone was cold after having already spoken with his handler earlier to be told there was no plan for his extraction.

Alex was an NOC – Non-official Cover – operative for the CIA. He knew when he signed on that the danger he would be putting himself in was just part of the job, and it was an acceptable risk to him, but that was before Heidi.

Now Heidi was tied to his lack of cover, and if caught by the North Vietnamese, they would both be on their own with no official help or diplomatic immunity forthcoming.

Alex didn't beat around the bush; he answered his agency contact with harsh frustration, "Ben, do you have our new passports?"

"Yes. I have them for you and the twins in your new name. I'm still waiting on Heidi's."

Alex tried to suppress his anger, he was getting close to losing his cool. "You still don't have a passport for my wife?" he asked through clenched teeth. "You've got to be kidding me. Can't you get a 'special' one from Covert Affairs?"

Alex had changed identities frequently and knew he could get a complete set, including credit cards and passport, within two hours. Now that his wife needed a genuine passport, one that she was legally entitled to, they waited.

Covert Affairs was the CIA department that handled the needs of undercover or NOC operatives. It had contacts in U.S. state licensing departments – often called the License Integrity Unit – where licenses were procured for agents going undercover. In this confidential driver's license program, the agent would get a valid driver's license with a fictitious name, birth date and address. Once the false ID was issued, a passport and credit cards could be requested – all genuine, but with fake names.

After several moments of silence, Ben said, "Our local CIA agents have all cut ties and pulled out, Alex, they've gone. Take your family to the Embassy first thing in the morning. I'll have someone with an envelope waiting for you at the ground floor security desk of your apartment building before you leave. I'll include an authorization for Heidi signed by the Ambassador."

"We'll be leaving first thing."

"He'll be there. Thank you, Alex. You did good work there."

Alex moved to hang up the phone, but heard Ben add, "And Alex ..."

"Yes, Ben?"

"Take care, my friend. I'll see you on the other side; my evac flight leaves tonight."

Alex did not bother responding; he had that knot tightening in his stomach, acid building. It felt like he was playing a deadly game of musical chairs, but he was the one running in circles and there were no chairs to be found.

5 THE PRESIDENT'S BOOK

White House
October 26, 2014

President Richard Klein was born to sit in the Oval Office, or so he and his father thought.

Since birth, he had been groomed by his parents to put the family name on the list of America's First Families. Due to his family's vast business interests – mostly inherited from his grandfather and massively expanded by his father – he never had to struggle financially.

The downside to his upper-class upbringing was that he had gained no street smarts. His grooming had included annual vacations to all the trendy international vacation spots but he always saw the world through the windows of the family's private jet. He never had to face the reality of a canceled flight or sit in the waiting room of Bangkok International, exposed to the pungent aromas of people who had been traveling by bus for three days – quite often with no facilities – many who had never been close to an airport before.

The challenging theme in his first run for the Oval Office had been his privileged upbringing, and his attitude that the country owed him the Presidency was a characteristic he still tried to hide. He spoke "Bostonian American" – the local version of English that included an R at the end of every word – and so pervasive was this habit that winning the southern vote had been a constant struggle even in his second campaign.

His father had managed both of his presidential runs and his first term in office, from behind the scenes. One of his father's last acts before he died at the end of the last campaign was to insist his son appoint a Chief of Staff with street savvy. That's where Ed Gonzalez came in. Gonzalez grew up in the Spanish Harlem of Boston. A rough and tough street fighter, who had struggled for every nickel he ever earned, his view of the outside world was formed by looking out the window of a Hercules military transport plane on his frequent overseas assignments during his military career. Still, Gonzalez was able to hide his natural vernacular, only occasionally lapsing into street talk.

The Chief of Staff was proud of his achievements, and so was his mother – a Cuban immigrant who had pushed, protected and loved him during his childhood. Her greatest pleasure as she enjoyed her retirement was to receive a telephone call, look at the phone, and recognize the caller ID as the White House. Many retirees develop idiosyncrasies; his mother's indulgence was to pull out her phone for her infrequent visitors and scroll down through her caller list. Any lobbyist in D.C. would have been envious of the number of calls from 1600 Pennsylvania Avenue.

Klein's father had been diagnosed with inoperable cancer just days before his son's second inauguration. His choice of Gonzalez was his final effort to protect the legacy he had built in Richard. He gave his son one last piece of advice before he died – more in the form of a threat. "Leave a blemish on the family name and hell won't be able to protect you from my wrath."

Once Klein no longer had to report daily to his father, he began to actually enjoy the presidency. What was more dangerous was that he began to believe he was capable of making the day-to-day decisions required of the occupant of the most powerful office in the world.

♦ ♦ ♦

Gonzalez walked along the White House corridor for his daily briefing with the President. As he reached the Oval Office, he knocked on the door, and to his surprise, a loud voice boomed from inside, "Just a minute, Ed!"

Gonzalez waited outside, an uneasy feeling spreading in his gut. Who's with the President? Strange, there's nothing on my schedule. Perhaps it's the First Lady, but she's normally not out of bed at this hour... Humph?

Moments later, Gonzalez could hear laughter from inside approaching the door, and he stood back. The door opened to reveal the President warmly taking his leave from one of the most notorious lobbyists in D.C.

As Gonzalez entered the office, he said, "I didn't know you had him on your schedule this morning..."

The President ignored the implied question as they both sat down on the sofa. "What do you have for me in the daily briefing, Ed?"

Gonzalez watched Klein, worried. Having a lobbyist in the Oval Office and not on the official agenda didn't pass the smell test. The motive in D.C. always came back to money, but Klein had inherited the entire estate of his father, Gonzalez reminded himself ... Or did he?

Gonzalez made a mental note to check on the President's finances to see if he had in fact inherited the estate. Beyond that, he knew Klein had business plans and the speaking tour in mind for life after the White House and that would take financial backing. Gonzalez had hoped to keep the President on the straight and narrow financially until the end of his term, but Klein had been acting lately like he had lost his rudder. He had gotten progressively less controlled since his father died, and Gonzalez didn't like it.

He decided to leave that for the time being, returning to the subject of his daily briefing. As he had just finished meeting with the Vice President, he saw this as the best opportunity to bring her concerns to his boss.

"Mr. President, I have received a tip that someone is trying to tamper with the European Central Bank and perhaps even the Federal Reserve, blackmailing some of the members of the Board of Governors."

Klein seemed more interested than Gonzalez had expected.

"A tip?"

"Yes, Sir. The source is confidential, but credible. The plot may be linked to the murder of the Italian Finance Minister yesterday in Sorrento."

"Yes. Mo Winters briefed me yesterday on the Reuters release," the President said, rising to get his putter from beside his desk and take a few strokes as he talked. "I'm not convinced the sky is falling, Ed, but Mo had the same theory you are suggesting now. Do you have proof of the link with Sorrento?"

Gonzalez shook his head. "No, Sir. We have nothing solid on any of it."

"Well," Klein said, suddenly not as concerned as he should be, "why don't you ask the FBI to look into it?"

"Yes, Sir," Gonzalez said placating. "I thought so, too, Sir, certainly, but in the meantime, as I'm sure Winters told you, the economy is at a critical point right now even without the Reuters release causing any rumors. One wrong move could wreck the recovery, even bring down your administration, and devastate the country."

The President puffed up like a peacock in spring, and Gonzalez watched his demeanor change. The mere mention of something that could impact his administration or reputation had the desired effect; he had to leave the Presidency with a solid foundation for his retirement plans in place.

"You don't think the FBI can handle this, Ed?"

"Of course, Mr. President. I have every confidence. I just think we need to keep some oversight of this project, Sir. We need to be sure something is done quickly and quietly before there is any chance for such a plot to succeed.

"Even at the lowest end of the spectrum, Sir, if someone were able to manipulate policy decisions, they could force those decisions to go in directions that would reduce the flow of money into the system and cause business contraction that would lead to mass unemployment."

That word had Klein's eyes back up from the putting green.

"That could happen faster than you imagine, Sir. No jobs, Mr. President, and this nation turns against you; your name is ruined. It could even lead to a complete financial meltdown."

Gonzalez was tempted to laugh. Just minutes ago, the President was conducting a private meeting with a lobbyist who had a somewhat dubious reputation, and now he was getting his crow up over the thought that HIS reputation might be harmed by a scandal at the Federal Reserve.

The President walked around the Oval Office in deep thought, his manner totally serious. "If this is as serious as you say, we need real action."

As he continued to think things through, Klein said, "If the press gets hold of this... No, no, no. It would be disastrous."

The President turned to look at Gonzalez.

"Yes. Yes. We need help looking into this, but if we use the FBI or the National Security Agency, there could be a leak. That would be self-defeating," he said. "We need anonymity and speed."

His face lit up with an idea. "That leaves me with only one alternative saved just for the President."

Klein walked over to the recessed bookshelf to the left of his desk.

Gonzalez watched the President with curiosity. The shelf was empty other than a few books and a vase, certainly devoid of anything to use as a reference in the predicament they were discussing. Klein hesitated and took a deep breath as Gonzalez watched. Then the President pressed a hidden button. Gonzalez leaned forward, fascinated. What in the world?

The built-in bookshelf, with shelves flush with the wall, started moving. Gonzalez was totally surprised as the bookshelf inverted itself until what was behind it turned to face out. The case and books had disappeared, and a secret cavity was revealed. Judging from the dust, it had been hidden from the world for some time.

Klein reached in with two hands to pull out a dusty book. He pulled a handkerchief out of his pants pocket and proceeded to wipe away the grime, finishing by blowing off the last remaining specks before turning to Gonzalez, who sat stock-still and wide-eyed.

"Ed, have you heard of the Presidents' Book of Secrets?"

Gonzalez stuttered his reply. "Yes, Sir, a fairy tale I assumed."

The President was holding the book reverently like the ring bearer at a wedding. He took the book over to his desk, wiping away another light layer of dust as he opened the first page.

Gonzalez watched Klein. It was the first time he remembered the man showing true unfettered emotion. The tenderness, the sense of history that Klein expressed was a first. Gonzalez made a note to give the guy a break; anybody this moved by a book had to have his heart in the right place.

"No. The book exists. Written mostly by Thomas Jefferson, himself," Klein said, gently stroking the first page. "He and the other founding fathers created a secret organization – the Eyes of Athena -- so secret, even I don't know where to find them."

Klein began to get his emotions back under control. He started thumbing through a few pages looking for something.

"Ed, this is for the President's eyes only. Your total discretion is expected, right?"

Gonzalez nodded his agreement. The President began to read the preface to his Chief.

"What you now hold in your hands is the Presidents' Book of Secrets. This book has been created by founders of the United States of America to help you maintain the freedom of our new Independence.

"We have called ourselves the Eyes of Athena, formed to protect the vital principles of our new nation.

"This book will be handed down to you after your confirmation in a private ceremony by the retiring President. Guard it with your life. We ask you – nay implore you – to pass on this manuscript in the same manner.

"From time to time, Athena or yourself will deem that certain events, as yet unknown, might be of such a sensitive nature that they should be included in this book. Only time will tell.

"One final request we have of you – as of your first acquaintance with this book you will not know who we are, and if your term in office is blessed with peace, you will never know us, but if our suspicions are justified, it might become necessary that you make acquaintance with us or our envoy.

"Please make provisions so that your staff should know that if a special dispatch is received with the Athena Eye that access be given to you. If you deem it necessary to contact us, please have the same printed on the front page of any newspaper published in the 13 Colonies."

The Oval Office was totally quiet while Klein read; even the office telephones respectfully maintained their silence. After he finished, the men – two of the most powerful men in the world – savored the immensity of the moment they shared.

"Is that Thomas Jefferson's handwriting?"

The President nodded affirmatively. Gonzalez was still having a hard time wrapping his head around this. Unbeknown to the world, the founding fathers had created a secret society – a private special branch, a watch dog for the government – managed totally outside the control of Congress. The more he thought about it, the more he liked the idea of an organization that couldn't be bought by lobbyists.

"This is quite some piece of history," he said. "My old university roommate is the Managing Editor at the Philadelphia Daily News. I'm sure I can get him to run an ad tonight."

Klein thought about it a moment. "Ed, we can't have every crackpot threatening the stability of the U.S. like this. Take care of this, and send them a strong message, capiché?"

"Understood, Sir."

6 DON'T CALL ME SWEETIE

Philadelphia Daily News
Dawn, October 27, 2014

In the dark, pre-dawn of the early fall morning, steam hissed up through manhole covers. Garbage trucks ground around their route to clean up the dregs of the previous 24 hours, and the only other real activity was the hustle of the newspaper delivery trucks and vendors opening up their street stalls to sell the latest headlines to morning commuters.

The first shift of morning employees shuffled down the wet sidewalk, ever mindful of the traffic screeching by and sometimes approaching the curb to saturate an unwary pedestrian. Just visible on the front of the Philadelphia Daily News building, which occupied an entire block of downtown Philadelphia, was a sign beside the revolving door that read in a large faded limestone block, "Philadelphia Daily News EST 1925".

An unimaginative drab concrete awning sat above the office entrance. The building looked cold, impenetrable, unfriendly and slightly intimidating. Even during the morning rush hour, the sidewalk in front of it was quiet, its revolving doors seeming strange as they sat motionless.

As Jasmine Cooper arrived, the door began its tortuous rotation to admit her, but as soon as she was swallowed by the spinning glass and spit out again on the other side, the door resumed its lonely vigil in silence, waiting.

To Cooper, the sound of her heels on the marble floor of the lobby thundered around her, making her try to step more gingerly each time until she was almost tip-toeing by the time she reached the elevator doors.

The night shift of a morning paper consists first of reporters, photographers, editors and other similar production crew that may work various daylight hours into the evening and night. From there, it moves into print crew and then assemblers who work into the wee hours of the morning. Delivery takes its shift until the day crew comes on – business, administration, advertising and special section production -- which overlaps back into that day/night shift creative staff.

Somewhere between the print crew and delivery, the cleaning staff sweeps in, and between cleaning and 8 a.m., comes the day-shift go-getters.

Cooper was one of those. A young new employee who had to dress down in order to minimize unwanted male attention, she was an eager beaver and a shining light in the drab cubicles that made up the Daily's advertising department. She got to work before the seasoned vets showed up, looking for extra time to spend tweaking her copy and making notes for her graphic artists – honing her ads to be sure they were top-notch.

Since she beat the old, gray guard to work, she was the first person ready and available to start taking calls when the phones started ringing, and that meant she got THE call. When she hung up, she looked at her boss – her whole face a question mark.

"Hey, Gary, I just got a call from a guy who wants us to run an ad on the front page, top left corner."

"That's against policy," he growled.

Gary Beam was the kind of boss who growled most of his replies. He took great satisfaction in berating Cooper despite her excellent work and made fun of her at every opportunity. She found out he had not wanted to hire her for his department but was overruled. He never had a simple smile or kind word for her, and she had had her fill. She was ready to put a stop to his attitude problem … after all they had taught her well in the CIA how to deal with trouble-makers.

Instead she sighed. "I told him that."

"And?"

"And he said to tell Charlie that it's for his old roommate."

Beam thought that was hilarious. Hardly unable to restrain his snickering, he responded, "You go up and tell the Editor."

Cooper's sigh deepened. "I thought you said he was cold and heartless and that everyone is afraid of him."

Beam didn't have a sympathetic bone in his body. "I did. Your call, your problem. Could be your chance to get promoted, Sweetie."

Cooper was not impressed.

"Yeah or canned. Thanks for nothing." She turned to leave, calling back over her shoulder at the door, "By the way, Gary, could you give me a hand in the coffee room?"

Cooper walked toward the coffee room with Beam following close behind. She knew what she planned but the poor sap walking in behind her had no clue. It amazed her how quickly her close-combat training re-asserted itself. Her walk tightened, she felt her adrenalin making her senses more acute, all her muscles tensed.

The wall connecting the coffee room to the office was a solid four feet thick. Over the top of it, windows stretched to the ceiling, designed to allow the boss in the office above to watch employees abusing their coffee break privileges.

Cooper had decided her best course of action was to teach Beam a lesson he would never forget, but with no witnesses. As he strolled into the room, still wearing a sneer on his face, she grabbed his wrist with one hand, closed the door with the other and spun him around against the wall with his arm tugged up against his shoulder blade, all in one smooth motion. She heard the pop as his shoulder dislocated with the sudden movement and the pain knocked the wind out of him.

"Why?" he gasped.

"You have been the bane of my existence since the day I walked into this place, making every moment a living hell not just for me, but for most everyone who works for you. You are a miserable person, and that makes you a lousy manager who takes out your misery on every other living being.

"Understand this," she said, still whispering closely into his ear as he wept silently. "You ever talk to me in that patronizing manner again, I'm gonna invite you back in here for another cup of coffee."

She released him then, turned him around and straightened his shirt, as he cradled his limp arm. She smiled with sugar-sweetness and with dripping sarcasm, said, "Okay, Sweetie?"

◆ ◆ ◆

My boss wouldn't last five minutes in the CIA, she thought as she walked back out and toward the stairs to the Editor's office.

As much as she tried to dress down, she couldn't help but notice the volume of room chatter diminish and the male eyes turn in her direction as she glided past the Press Room door. She ignored the lecherous stares. Men, she thought, so predictable.

By the time she reached the elevator, she had calmed down. She rode to the top floor, spotted the Editor's office and headed that way.

Cooper stopped outside the smoky glass window, looking at the sign on the door. "Editor" was printed in large, plain, bold font. His assistant was away from her desk.

Cooper looked down at the front of her dress, flicked off some imaginary fluff, straightened her already immaculately pressed clothes and tugged her belt to line it up, then brushed the bangs out of her eyes. She took a deep breath and thought back to her days before the CIA. Air Force boot camp had her crawling through the mud, a barbed-wire barrier suspended two inches over her body. She had to smile at her foolishness as she remembered. That was much more frightening than standing outside the door of the Editor. That thought always helped her put things in perspective.

She knocked on the door, and Charlie Stafford bellowed his response from inside. "In!"

Cooper nervously opened the door. Uneasy, she peered around the corner and waited for her employer to acknowledge her presence.

Without looking up, he asked, "What is it?" Then he looked to see a face as bright as sunshine as Cooper beamed a smile across at his desk, her green eyes accentuated by her bronze-colored locks. On seeing who had entered his office, he moderated his tone. "Who are you?"

"I'm Jasmine Cooper, Sir. I'm in the Advertising Department."

"What do you want up here?" Try as he might, Stafford could not maintain his usual gruff manner. At the sight of the well-dressed Cooper, he subconsciously became aware of his scruffy clothes. He looked like he had slept in them and without realizing it tried to palm down his shaggy, uncombed hair.

In contrast, and despite her inner turmoil, Cooper radiated confidence.

"Come to think of it, I do remember authorizing your hiring. What do I call you anyway?"

"Nobody calls me Jasmine here, Sir. Everyone calls me Cooper."

"How can I help you, Cooper?"

"Well, Sir, I had a call from someone who wants us to put an unusual ad in the paper."

"Why didn't your boss pick up the phone and call me?"

"I don't know, Sir."

"OK, Cooper, what is this about an unusual ad?"

"Well, Sir, I received a call from a customer who wants to put an ad on the top left-hand corner of the front page."

"That's against company policy."

"I know, Sir, that's what I told him."

"So what's the problem?"

"When I told him it was against company policy, he said, 'Just check with old Charlie, your editor.'"

"He did, huh?"

"He said, 'He'll do it for us; tell him to send the bill to his old roommate on Pennsylvania Avenue.'"

Stafford smiled knowingly. He looked over at Cooper, beginning to warm to this new employee. "Cooper, do you know why your colleagues sent you up here to talk to me?"

"I have a good idea, Sir."

"I have a reputation as a dragon around here. They wanted to see if I would terrify you, eat you up and spit you out. Do you think they would mess with you if they knew about your combat training and connections with the CIA?"

Cooper was surprised he knew so much about her. She hadn't listed all of her previous experiences on any resume and had assumed he wouldn't have seen her resume even if she had.

"Why did you come to work here at the Daily?"

"I want to be a journalist, Sir, and I figure you have to start somewhere."

Stafford cocked a brow, not the first time he had heard that plan, but he thought there was more. Always a reporter, he knew a story when he smelled one. He'd come back to that later.

He smiled. "You know, kid, you kinda remind me of me... but a much prettier version! I mean when I started out in this business."

Stafford looked hard at Cooper, then nodded his head at the chair in front of his desk. "Grab a seat."

A few moments later, he looked up, his decision made. "This is what we're gonna to do."

7 COOPER GETS A NEW DESK

As soon as Cooper returned to the Ad Department, she felt the charged atmosphere of expectation. She had spent the morning in Stafford's office, and now her colleagues turned to stare, anxiously waiting to see how she had fared upstairs. A few openly snickered.

"Gosh, I'm going to be so glad to be out of this juvenile place," she said under her breath. She tried not to let their games get to her as she headed for Beam's office. He wasn't there.

"He left in a hurry. Left me in charge," Sam said.

Uh oh, Cooper thought. That's probably not good.

"The ad is a go. Charlie wants an invoice for five times the inside page rate and a draft ad layout on his desk in 10 minutes."

She could feel the disappointment run through her co-workers and heard one ask incredulously, "You mean you call the editor, Charlie?"

"Well, Charlie told me, as the new Editorial Department Apprentice, we should be on first-name terms..."

The silence was unnerving. Out of the corner of her eye, she observed the looks of shock, jealously and bewilderment.

Cooper walked over to her old cubicle, gathered her personal possessions and her coat and swaggered out of the office, purposefully exaggerating the swing of her hips and enjoying every moment. As she approached the exit, she turned to look back over her shoulder. "Ten minutes. I want that ad and invoice upstairs in 10 minutes."

In the meantime, she had left her new boss upstairs baffled. Stafford was a reporter at heart, and so his biological make-up included too many curiosity genes. He was pacing his office; walking, that's how he liked to think. He returned to his desk to write a note, and then resumed pacing. So far, he had written down four simple bullet points:

White House Chief of Staff

Cryptic ad on the front page

Why?

Call Ed?

He shook his head in frustration, looking at his notes. None of this made sense, but at least he had made one decision. He leaned over to pick up his telephone; his assistant answered.

"Yes, Sir?"

"Get Cooper back in here."

By this time, she was back upstairs in the Editorial Department. She had just finished slinging her coat over the back of her new chair and emptying out her few possessions when Stafford's assistant called her over. As Cooper approached, Jane pointed with her head at Stafford's door. "He wants you."

She didn't alter her stride but kept going, knocking and entering his office. He glanced up and pointed a finger to the seat in front of his desk.

"I can smell a great story here, Cooper. I want to know why the White House placed that ad."

"White House, Sir?"

"Yes, that's where Ed works," Stafford said distractedly.

"Your roommate, Sir?"

"Yes, yes. Chief of Staff." Stafford was pacing again.

"I see. Well, why don't you ask him?"

Stafford appeared to give that thought some time again, but shook his head, as if he remained undecided.

"I might, but I'm not sure he would tell me the truth, and then he would also know I was looking into it."

He was still obviously uncertain. "But I do know I want you to look into it. I want you to go see my old roommate at the White House. Ask him to approve your White House press pass. Sniff around quietly, see what you can find out."

Cooper was astonished. "Me...You're going to give the assignment to me?"

Stafford looked up pleased; he wanted to give this kid a break. "You mean you don't want it?"

Cooper couldn't help but sound as eager as she felt. "You are kidding aren't you? I'd love the opportunity. I'd break a leg to get it. A chance to do my first story with the President's Chief of Staff?"

"One and the same."

"Sir, are you sure? I mean, you know nothing about me –"

He cut her off then. "I've got a nose for people, Cooper. You want the chance or not?"

She looked seriously at him almost regretting what she was about to say. "There's something you need to know. Before I came up here this morning, I nearly broke Gary's arm, you know my boss in the

Advertising Department..."

Stafford had been focusing on his list again. He looked up now with a sly smile. "What do you mean nearly?"

8 WHITE CHRISTMAS

FLASHBACK – April 29, 1975, Pre-dawn Hours
Saigon, Vietnam

Alex and Heidi slept little. The fighting had grown louder during the night just beyond the city proper. As they gathered their few things and prepared the boys for travel, they listened to Armed Forces Radio, learning about the attack on Tan Son Nhut Air Base in the dark of the night.

Although nobody thought it could happen this quickly, they had been prepared for the various stages of the evacuation plan:

Option 1 – Evacuation by commercial airlift from Tan Son Nhut and other airports as required.

Option 2 – Evacuation by military airlift from Tan Son Nhut and other airports as required.

Option 3 – Evacuation by sea lift from Saigon port.

Option 4 – Evacuation by helicopter to U.S. Navy ships in the South China Sea.

With the damage to the airport, Alex had to wonder if Option 4 was coming into play soon. They had received no further instructions since the call last night, so they took along the battery-powered radio in case the final option became necessary. The American Embassy had distributed a 15-page booklet "SAFE" (Standard Instruction and Advice to Civilians in an Emergency) that gave them instructions for Option 4. The booklet included a map of Saigon with assembly areas for helicopter pick-up and designation of the "evacuation signal."

Alex shook his head as he re-read this portion of the booklet.

Do not disclose to other personnel. When the evacuation is ordered, the code will be read out on Armed Forces Radio. The code is: "The temperature in Saigon is 112 degrees and rising." This will be followed by the playing of "I'm Dreaming of a White Christmas".

Once the code went out, buses would begin to pick up civilians and take them to the Defense Attaché Office Compound, which had also been hit during the early morning hours; killing two Marines.

Heidi wrapped her favorite silk scarf over her head and tied it under her chin. Alex simply wore a pullover and a scarf against the early morning chill. The tiny twins, Pieter and Wolfgang, were peaceful. They both had their breakfast and had fallen back to sleep. The gentle rumble of their stroller swaying from side to side enhanced their rest.

Alex and Heidi had gotten up early. They had packed lightly. Their package had been waiting for them, as promised, and as they left the apartment building, Alex searched the sky. He could hear the faint sound of helicopter rotors turning, as if they were slapping the air. The vibration was almost palpable, each rotation feeling like a blow to the face for those close to them. In the distance, beyond the embassy, he saw two dark specks in the sky, getting larger by the minute. Mingling with the sound of the helicopters was the whoompf of mortars being fired in the suburbs.

Heidi couldn't help herself. They had agreed to walk at a leisurely pace down the boulevard in front of the embassy, but as other families headed in the same direction, their steps quickened. Each family pretended to take no notice of the other refugees, but gradually their stride lengthened, trying to pull ahead, trying to arrive at the Embassy gates before the competition.

The sound of the crowd grew. Heidi looked to her husband in fear. "What is happening, Alex?"

Before them, a throng of thousands swarmed the Embassy grounds, screaming, pleading, desperate for salvation.

"What will we do?"

Alex was resolute. "We will find a way in."

The front of the Embassy was too tightly ringed by the masses, and the little family moved toward the rear to find a way to get closer to the gates.

"They will let us in, if we can get close enough," he assured his wife.

The closer Alex and Heidi got to the Embassy compound, the more conspicuous the sense of hopelessness became. Crowds were already lined up around the block, facing inward, begging to be let inside. Only Americans, Third Country Nationals and those South Vietnamese lucky enough to be chosen were allowed inside the gate.

Once near the perimeter of the Embassy, they could hear a Marine, dressed in immaculately pressed khaki pants and shirt, shout through a bullhorn, "Please do not panic. Step back from the gate. Only those with papers, please!"

A fog of desperation seemed to descend on the crowd, it weighed heavily and shoulders that had been held firm moments earlier now slumped, proud heads seemed to fall forward. Couples did not want to look at each other; to let a beloved partner see the despondency in their eyes would have been an act of betrayal.

One last couple tried shouting to a Marine, "But we have worked in the Embassy for three years, the Communists will kill us!"

The Marine just shrugged, knowing there was nothing he could do, and walked on without a backward glance to the couple pleading for their lives.

Heidi whispered to Alex, "I need to feed the boys." He nodded and began to push the stroller away from the compound along the perimeter fence. The gunfire from the suburbs was getting stronger and they could now hear the constant pop, pop, pop of small arms fire. The rumor spread among the condemned that the Communists were already in the city.

Meanwhile angry soldiers of the Army of the Republic of Vietnam – abandoned by American forces two years before, their financial support slowly drained, and now facing this – took out their frustration on every non-Vietnamese they saw. They mugged them, threatened them, even shot at them. Now some of these soldiers joined the crowds at the Embassy gate.

Alex and Heidi found a spot where she could feed her babies. The doomed crowd was facing the compound, no one interested in watching a mother nurse her twins.

Heidi began to tear up. Through her moisture-swollen eyes, she looked at Alex, "I never thought I would say this, but if necessary, I would rather this be the last time I feed our boys. You have to agree to take them, even if I can't come. Please, Alex.

"Oh, Alex," she added desperately, "if we can just save our boys, I will be so grateful, but inside me I will be dead."

He kissed the top of her head. "We will all be safe at the end of this journey, my love."

He wished he was more certain.

At the rear of the compound, the crowd was still heavy, but Alex could see where Marines were helping some civilians over the locked gates. Heidi finished her brief feeding and burped the boys. She was just placing Pieter back in the stroller beside his brother when Alex reach into the stroller beside her to retrieve Wolfgang.

"Leave everything. Take only the boys," he said. He began to unstrap Wolfgang, who woke and began to cry. Heidi moved quickly to remove his brother and follow Alex into the throng, both of them stepping over their few belongings, carrying only the twins.

He shoved his way into the crowd, making a way for his wife and babies as he went, taking a beating from the angry men he shoved aside, and protecting his tiny family within the safety of his arms.

When he got to the gate he screamed above the noise to catch the attention of a Marine. Through the bars of the gate, he handed the weary soldier the papers that had arrived just as they left the apartment. The man looked them over perfunctorily and then pointed toward the far side of the gate, toward a large debris pile on his side of the gate. On theirs was a parked car against the gate. An armed Marine kept the crowd from climbing over on their own.

"Meet me over there!" he bellowed above the noise.

Alex turned and guided Heidi toward the spot indicated, taking much longer than the Marine at his double-time pace. Once there, they climbed atop the vehicle. The Marine climbed his pile of debris and reached for the babies over the top of the fence. One at a time, he handed them to civilians standing behind him. Next, Alex lifted Heidi, and the Marine helped her over as well and into the arms of another soldier.

Then Alex climbed the fence and nimbly vaulted over the top to rejoin Heidi in the middle of a group of civilian women. She had one boy in each arm and tears streaming down her face.

"Well, that was an adventure," she said with a half-smile, as the women ushered the little family inside.

It was almost 11 a.m. Alex wondered why no other plans had been made in light of the airport strike. Just then, the first strains of Irving Berlin's "White Christmas" began to drift through the speakers of his radio.

9 ANOTHER TARGET DOWN

Washington, D.C.
October 30, 2014

Anacostia Park was a nature lover's haven in Washington, D. C. The Anacostia River ran along the hiking/running trail before it eventually reached the Potomac. As the river provided such a plentiful source of water, cherry trees abounded with lush vegetation everywhere – a haven for nature lovers and an ideal cover for those who did not wish to be seen.

Ari was hidden behind some bushes under a cherry tree. He wasn't enjoying the natural beauty of the park; he was standing with his field glasses – more the size of opera glasses – up to his eyes, watching and waiting.

Across the park, toward the jogging trail on the crest of a small hill, a man dressed in a black sweat suit was cloaked by more bushes. To a casual observer, if any had taken notice of him, he was just another person enjoying the park, although a little off the beaten path. Slowly, he slipped further into the foliage, and Ari watched him pull a balaclava hood over his head as if he were cold before he took a prone position in the deep bushes far off the trail. Then he reached for a rifle with a silencer and proceeded to put it into firing position, nuzzling the stock against his shoulder.

Eyes closed, blinking, he refocused through the scope and centered it on the head of a jogger running along the river path. He didn't fire; he was waiting. Through the scope, the cross hairs centered on another jogger, the scope followed, but again he didn't fire.

Ari watched, deciding his subject was practicing and waiting, as if he expected his target to jog down this path. Ari kept his binocs focused on the shooter; he was waiting as well.

Finally, his cell phone beeped, signaling an incoming text message. Ari removed his eyes momentarily from the shooter to read his text message. "Target unknown."

Ari shook his head, troubled by the text. He keyed in his response. "Intervening. Can't wait."

The body lying prone on the hill overlooking the river track was deathly still. The man was unaware he was being watched; his attention riveted on the view within his telescopic sight as he watched another jogger approach – a bearded man. The cross hairs moved onto the forehead of that bearded face.

Ari took off toward the assassin, running hard. A group of joggers passed between him and the shooter, momentarily blocking his view. His phone beeped again. This time the text read, "Chairman of Fed possible target. Intervene."

But he was already trying to reach Kwok Kong. He increased his speed, having to push some of the joggers out of the way. The commotion he caused as he rushed headlong down the path made enough noise to reach the hill – and the assassin.

Kong looked back to see the reason for the sound and spotted Ari. A flash of recognition interrupted his concentration and then he returned his attention to his scope as his target approached. The cross hairs focused again, and Kong pulled the trigger.

Everything exploded into motion. Ari was closing in on the assassin when he heard the whoompf of a single round exiting the barrel of the shooter's rifle. The sound hit him like a solid blow, but he didn't break stride, trying to speed up his already full-out gait.

Simultaneously, the target's head exploded. It was as if a Twentieth Century modern artist had thrown a bucket full of red paint at a canvas filled with the images of joggers all around the man. Each of them made a sudden 90-degree turn, faces toward the center with looks of sheer terror, as the now headless torso began to crumple in a shower of blood, brain matter, and bone.

Panic spread outside the previously close-knit band of joggers, and the terrified crowd scattered in all directions, screaming in confusion.

Kong lay motionless on the hill overlooking the river track, making sure he had finished his assignment. When he confirmed his accuracy, he dropped his rifle, stripped off his black sweats to reveal a greenish wind suit, and traded his hood for a hat. He started jogging toward the path.

Ari ran flat out, reaching Kong's old position, panting and franticly searching for the assassin. Sixty yards away, he saw someone in green and thought he might have spotted his man. He looked down and saw the discarded rifle and black sweat suit.

Kong was checking his back-trail and slowed his escape, his oriental eyes met Ari's as the agent caught sight of him. Instead of racing away, Kong slowed even more and turned to raise his arm and aim a silenced pistol.

Ari was pumped full of adrenalin; he watched his quarry level the handgun as if in slow motion. Although everything happened quickly, Ari was in control. He lurched just as the shooter fired, and the slug slammed into the tree where moments before Ari had been standing.

Kong took off, moving with incredible speed now as he blasted away from the river and vaulted over a fence. The crowd dispersed in front of him as he ran along the fence line toward the outside parking area.

Ari gave chase, running like crazy in parallel to the shooter. He pulled out his cell phone as he ran, speaking breathlessly. "Tom, Kong shot the chairman, he's running toward the north exit."

Ari accelerated again, passing into the parking area. He was about to break into full stride when he was snatched out of the air and slammed to the ground. In a matter of seconds, he was surprised to find himself in cuffs, lying face down with two federal agents on top of him, one knee each securing him.

Ari was furious and shouting as he tried to wriggle free. "Get off me! I'm chasing the gunman!"

The Feds paid no attention as they lifted Ari off the ground to take him to their car. In the distance, Ari saw Kong at the other end of the lot, slowing to a walk, smiling evilly and enjoying his opponent's struggle.

10 STAR-CROSSED LOVERS

White House Chief of Staff's Office

Gonzalez was deep in thought when his office door unceremoniously banged open, smacking the doorstop loudly and half scaring him to death... for the second time that week.

Carter babbled excitedly, "I checked The Philadelphia Daily News as you asked, and it ran, Sir."

Gonzalez was miffed. "Don't you ever knock before you come bursting into my office?" Carter was again too excited to do anything but ignore the rebuke.

He fired his question at Gonzalez, "What does it mean?"

Even on a good day, Gonzalez would not have given that secret to the perky intern, but angry as he was now, he wasn't even going to be kind about his denial. The young man's intrusion had ruined his train of thought, and he realized the older he got, the more difficult it was to recall a good thought that had suddenly vanished from his mind.

"Sorry, Brett, it's on a need-to-know-only basis," he growled.

As Carter contemplated a response, the phone rang. Gonzalez leaned over to pick up the receiver, cutting off any chance for Carter to question him further.

"Gonzalez."

"Sir, this is the side entrance Marine Guard Post. I have a gentleman here who says you called him."

"What's his name?"

"Won't give it to me, Sir. Just gave me a card with a weird eye on it."

"An eye?"

"Yes, Sir." Gonzalez could hear a man in the background trying to help the guard with his explanation "...surrounded by thirteen rays of sunlight shining toward the center."

Gonzalez smiled. That call had returned him to good humor. Perhaps the Eyes of Athena people could answer the Central Bank riddle that rankled him this morning.

"Escort him to my office."

He didn't waste any time giving his assistant a look that said, Conversation over. In return, Carter gave him the look of a lovable

Labrador that said, Aren't you going to tell me?

Gonzalez ignored him. Defeated, Carter turned to leave the office. As he reached for the door handle, someone on the other side knocked, and Carter withdrew his hand quickly as if he had gotten an electric shock then looked over at his boss in surprise.

Gonzalez just glared at his assistant as if to say, That's how you're meant to knock on my door.

He didn't wait, but instead bellowed out, "Come in!" followed by a dismissive, "Thank you, Brett."

An immaculately dressed Marine escorted a civilian into the Chief of Staff's office.

"The gentleman you cleared, Sir," he said briskly, eying the man suspiciously. "He's been frisked."

"Thank you."

The man who walked into Gonzalez's office was 6 feet tall more or less with intense eyes and medium-length hair, lean and muscular with a slight military bearing. But those eyes – the face was smiling, but the impassioned focus of his eyes was disconcerting; they neither approved nor disapproved, nor did they hint at even the slightest smile, simply examining with an unnerving intensity.

It was as if those eyes had seen too much pain, too much disappointment, too much … darkness. This was clearly a man to tread carefully around – a person you would want in your foxhole, rather than in a trench in front of you as your enemy.

Gonzalez did not know what to think of his visitor. "Athena?"

The man waited, turned around to make sure the door behind him was closed, then nodded.

"Would you mind telling me who you are?"

"Ari Cohen."

"Thanks for coming, Mr. Cohen. How did you know? Uh ... how did you get here so quickly?"

"We had some business in D.C. Did you want to see Athena about the Vice President's visit?"

If Ari had been hoping for a reaction from Gonzalez, he certainly got it. The Chief of Staff did a double-take, recoiled like a fighter bracing for an onslaught and in a low voice, said, "What do you know of the Vice President's visit?"

He started looking around his office, as if he were scanning for anything out of place where listening devices might have been hidden.

"Relax, Mr. Gonzalez, McQueen is an ally of ours."

Gonzalez did relax then, but thought through his next sentence before responding. "I think I might have underestimated her circle of influence. Yes, Sir, a well-connected lady. Why did she have me go to the President when she could have brought you in herself?"

"You both needed to be in the loop, and this was the easiest way."

Ari changed the subject. "I think you need to know the Chairman of your Federal Reserve was shot this morning; he was out jogging in Anacostia Park."

Another double-take from Gonzalez, and his mouth fell open soundlessly. It was the first time that he could remember that he opened his mouth but found no words.

After some time, Gonzalez finally stumbled across a forming rational thought. "That's not possible, we would—"

The telephone rang, and Gonzalez grabbed it tense and angry. He felt he was not in control of the situation and was irritated at being interrupted.

In the most unfriendly tone, he spat out, "Hello."

A Secret Service agent on the other end of the line was, in fact, calling with official word that the Chairman of the Federal Reserve had been killed earlier that morning.

Gonzalez jumped to his feet, and as he stood with one hand on the phone, the other stroked back his perfect hair as if it were out of place. For the second time in less than two minutes, he found himself speechless.

The first time Gonzalez heard this from Ari, he did not believe him. Hearing it a second time he had no choice.

"What?" He looked at Ari, put his hand over the phone, and trying to regain control of himself and the situation, whispered loudly, "How in the name of all that's holy did you know before us?"

Just then Ari's cell phone beeped with a text message. Before Ari answered Gonzalez's question, he read the text, "Shooter located."

The Secret Service agent continued his report. "He was out jogging this morning. Took D.C. police a while to positively ID him after he took a head shot."

Gonzalez was taken aback by how impersonal the agent sounded.

He looked up as he heard his office door slam, looked around his office and then out his window to see that Ari had not only run out of his office exited the White House, but was walking briskly across the grounds, leaving Gonzalez in a state of bewilderment, not quite sure which way was up. He replaced his phone in the cradle as he slumped back into his chair, shaking his head, overwhelmed by the sudden turn of events.

◆ ◆ ◆

First White House Checkpoint

Cooper made the trip to D.C. and was trying to verify whether her press pass had been approved at the White House checkpoint when everything erupted in chaos.

The Marine Guard was taking his time, going through the protocol to issue her a physical pass. Inside the small checkpoint, an alarm went off and not only did the guard checking Cooper's ID jump to attention, but all members of the security team assumed a full-alert posture.

Cooper tried to maintain her calm. "Not a problem I hope?"

The Marine on duty had just gotten off the phone with his command post.

"No, Ma'am," he said simply, his posture incongruent with his response.

Secret Service black Suburbans, bringing more troops to the alert, screamed into the White House secure zone, sirens blaring, tires screeching as they took the turn into the area at maximum speed.

Cooper's body flew into a heightened sense of awareness, her military training snapping to the forefront. Almost as soon as she presented her ID to the Marine on duty, things had gone totally mad. Beyond her military training, her mind slipped back to her time with the CIA, training for a terrorist attack.

At about that moment, her radio broke in with a news flash alerting her to the shooting of the Chairman of the Federal Reserve. She looked hard at the Marine, then from the corner of her eye spotted someone almost running across the grounds – a flash of the tail of a raincoat trailing a briskly moving figure, the face leading the raincoat vaguely familiar.

The Marine had not seen him. He turned back to Cooper after checking his computer monitor, "Yep, you've been approved. Go to the Press –"

She wasn't there. He scanned the area to see the woman from his checkpoint chasing someone across the grounds. She turned to shout over her shoulder, "I'll come back later!"

It sounded pretty lame to her in retrospect, but her surprise was so total – the sight of that man in the raincoat so disturbing – that she didn't know what else to say. Instead, she left the White House compound in hot pursuit with her car sitting at the checkpoint and the Guard sounding yet another alarm with his superiors.

♦ ♦ ♦

Ari was making good ground now, but not fast enough to have aroused attention on his own. He had acquired the skill of moving much faster than the people around him without appearing to be in a frenzied rush to escape the scene, and he used that now to blend in with tourists on the sidewalks outside the White House to escape the unwanted attention he had garnered when leaving.

He assumed the first alarm was linked to the death of the chairman, when the second alarm sounded and response heightened, he was surprised.

Cooper was sure she recognized him. She tried to run after him, but her quarry was so good at evading detection, she lost sight of him. She guessed where she would go if she were him and followed that hunch, running into a parking lot. There was still no sign of him. Trying to regroup, she stopped alongside an SUV to look around, still uncertain. Not sure which way to go, she relaxed, stood upright and looked around, accepting the fact that the trail had gone cold.

She began to doubt herself, not sure she had seen what she thought she had seen. Something didn't feel right; her senses were picking up something, telling her she should be on full-alert again.

Confirming her unease, she felt a hand clamp over her mouth and a sharp knife tip pressed against her back. Then she heard the familiar voice. "Don't look around; don't say a word. Got it?"

Cooper had no choice; she had been outmaneuvered. She tried to nod. At the same time, she was thinking how cruel fate could be.

She had caught a glimpse of a face that haunted her every thought – a face she had never stopped loving. She had started running after him without a thought except that she had to tell him.

But now, he held her immobile and silent, unable to even look into his beautiful eyes.

"I don't know what you want, but by now you realize that if I wanted you dead, you'd be dead. I'm going to release you. I don't have time to play games with you, so you're going to forget you saw me, right?" he whispered harshly into her ear.

In response, Cooper nodded. She felt hot tears beginning to gather in the corners of her eyes and begged them silently not to fall.

"You don't know me, right?"

Cooper was desperate, Ari's grip on her torso and mouth was viselike, but with a last frantic effort, she twisted her head unexpectedly so that his hand was not totally covering her mouth.

Finally, she managed to eke out the words, "Ari, it's me. It's Jasmine."

To Cooper it seemed like an eternity. Slowly Ari's grip loosened, and then he spun her around. He looked into her eyes, his surprise evident, but his gaze was so intent, as if he looked straight into her soul.

He seemed not to believe what his eyes were telling him, and then whispered faintly. "Jasmine? Jasmine, what are you doing here?"

He was overcome, ever the tender-hearted lover, but as quick as that part of him had surfaced, it was gone with the realization he was on a mission.

Ari looked around, the professional again. "The Carlyle. Tomorrow at 8:00 A.M. Lobby."

His change was so fast, Cooper hardly had time to acknowledge the emotion she had seen cross his face. In a flash, Ari was gone and she was left alone, working out the kinks from the rough handling she had received at the hands of the love she had so long missed.

◆ ◆ ◆

Ari moved in a crouch, retreating from the area as fast as he could without attracting attention. He crossed Pennsylvania Avenue, turning to see if Jasmine was following. She was nowhere in sight.

He resumed his pace, and his phone rang. "Ari, we can't touch him; he's got diplomatic immunity as part of the North Korean delegation to the U.N."

Ari was taken aback. "Diplomatic immunity?"

"Roger that, Ari. I need you in the OFFICE."

Ari's demeanor changed, his unsmiling face was now matched by his eyes – all determination and anger. He was furious, struggling to maintain control. He pocketed his phone, rushed to the edge of the street and held his arm up high to hail a taxi.

He was seething. Government bureaucrats are going to let Kwok Kong get away with murder! That assassin already killed two good men and a bunch of politicians are going to let him get away with it just because some quack dictator sanctioned him as a diplomat?

Ari was also mad because this was the reason he had been called away from his violin solo in Sorrento. It was a petty excuse in the wake of death and potential worldwide financial mayhem. Shaking his head, he walked across the road to climb into the taxi, but he couldn't shake his resentment. This murderer is going to pay. I'm not missing the solo opportunity of a lifetime and then let this man – the misery for so many – get away with murder, case closed.

11 PLAN B

Alex and Heidi sat on a worn leather couch in some mid-level office of the Embassy as she finished feeding the twins.

He walked to the window to look out over the courtyard and parking lot. He could see Marines working to remove the huge tamarind in the center of the compound and other debris around the area trying to create more space for a helicopter landing zone.

From the couch, Heidi looked up uncertainly. "The gates are blocked. How will the buses get to us?"

"They won't," he said, deciding to find someone who would tell him Plan B.

As he watched the scene below, a U.S. military transport helicopter approached. Heidi came over and shouted something in his ear but it was drowned out by the noise. The chopper hovered over the landing area of the compound, the whack-whack-whack noise of rotors so loud that everyone on the perimeter turned to look. The strong wind coming from the rotors blew anything not nailed down up into the air, where it danced around in suspended animation, as if controlled by a puppet master.

Alex could see burning paper floating through the air from the roof and decided to head in that direction first. As he made his way upstairs, he wound through more than 2,500 civilians crowded into the Embassy, finding comfort wherever they could.

"Shot?" offered a rather inebriated older Vietnamese gentleman as he swayed before Alex in the hallway. I see they found the Embassy liquor stores, Alex thought.

"No. I think I'll pass. And you are?"

"Billy. Janitor. You need anything, I'm your man," the little man said, jangling a large ring of keys on his belt before stumbling off down the hall.

Alex made a mental note in case those keys became necessary later and Billy was less mobile.

Up on the roof, he found a number of the Embassy staff working to destroy not only confidential documents but stacks of American currency. Now that's a painful sight, Alex thought, cringing as what must have been $5 million sat ready to go into the incinerator. The billowing cloud of paper ash was growing by the moment.

He found the Ambassador's top aide in the middle of the mayhem, and with the noise of the crowd below and the sound of the incinerators, had to tap the man's shoulder to get his attention as he bellowed instructions to his workers.

"Excuse me. I'd like to get a word."

"A little busy here, Sir. If you'll just wait with the others downstairs ..." the aide said, dismissively.

"I don't think so," Alex said turning his tapping finger into a hard grip that swung the man to face him.

"Now that I have your attention," Alex said with as polite a smile as he could muster. "I have a wife and two small babies downstairs – not to mention the other 2,000 people milling around down there clueless – and I'd like to get an idea of what the plan is now. The others may have not yet realized that we're in the soup, but the moment I heard good old Bing Crosby crooning Christmas carols in July, I knew we had a problem.

"Buses will not be getting through that crowd down there. I see our soldier boys making a nice-sized LZ, so I'm assuming the Huey's will be coming in soon, correct?"

The little man wrenched his shoulder free of a grip that had not grown less intense. "Yes, Sir. That is the plan."

"Excellent. Do we have a time-frame on the evacuation?"

"No, Sir. Once they have finished evacuations from the Defense Attaché Office Compound, they will turn the choppers toward the Embassy."

"Good deal," Alex said, mechanically straightening the man's shirt at the shoulder where he had gripped him and patting him for good measure.

"I'm CIA, which means I have some useful training. I can be very helpful in situations like this," he said in a voice just loud enough to be heard over the commotion. "I'll go find some projects where I can be helpful for the moment, but if you need me, find me."

The aid simply nodded and turned back to his staff.

Alex decided his best bet to be helpful at the moment was with the Marines downstairs. He also counted on the fact that he was more likely to get a line on military movement at the DAO from them, as well.

He again made his way through the crowd inside, stopping to update Heidi, but not lingering to discuss their own plans for the evacuation. She looked so tired; he encouraged her to rest with the boys.

Once outside, he sought someone with some stripes, and found a lieutenant working the slash pile. This time, he waited to be acknowledged.

"Yes, Sir? Do you need help?"

"No, Lieutenant, I'm looking to help out. Where do you need me?"

That brought the soldier down to ground level to eyeball his new recruit. "I can always use a good man," he said, smiling and offering his hand. Alex took it to shake. "Lt. Jimmy Slade, please call me Jimmy. If you want to jump in here with me, we're trying to keep this pile stacked high and tight to leave as much room for the LZ as possible."

"Alex," he said by way of introduction as he released Slade's hand. He quickly stripped down to his T-shirt and joined the men on the pile, working close to Slade so that he could question him further on the plan.

"I sure hope you have a better idea of what the plan is around here than the guys on top of the Embassy," Alex said as he grabbed the other end of a tree Slade was trying to shimmy up the pile.

"About an hour left working to clear the LZ, then we've been ordered to destroy about half a dozen cars in the parking lot that the North Vietnamese won't get their grimy hands on," Slade said with a wide, mischievous grin. "There's no way to know when the evac will start, but I sure hope we get some reinforcements soon."

Alex followed Slade's worried glance toward the crowd still growing outside the Embassy gate. Marines assigned to guard the interior perimeter already looked weary and outnumbered.

◆ ◆ ◆

Once the trees were down, Alex decided as much fun as the Marines were having with the cars in the parking lot, he had better make nice with the Embassy staff on the roof.

First, he checked in with Heidi. She was feeding the boys when he walked back into the little office.

"I was beginning to think you had run off," she said with a weary smile.

"I'm sorry, love. I have been helping where I can. There is still no word on when the helicopters will come."

She nodded, moving to put the boys down on makeshift pallets in drawers from the filing cabinets. A few of the women had found some towels for her in some of the executive washrooms.

Alex jumped to help her, and then sat with her on the couch.

"When the choppers come, I believe they will send the women and children first," he said, taking her hands. "You and the boys need to be on those choppers."

She looked steadfastly into his eyes. "The boys and I will wait for you."

Alex sighed. They had had this fight already. This was one reason they were still there.

"Heidi –"

"Alex, I just know – a mother knows – if we are split up, if this family is split up –"

She began to cry and the words were hard to hear between the sobs. "Alex, I just know that if we do not stay together, we will not survive."

She looked so tired, and Alex heard the tiny wheezing in the little "bed" at his feet – Wolfgang.

"Alright," he said, taking her in his arms. "You and Wolfgang need to rest. Just sleep. You can wait until the later choppers for the women, and I will try to go with you then."

She nodded.

It was a lie ... on both their parts.

Heidi was asleep as Alex gently closed the door behind him, taking one last look at his sleeping family, trusting she would come to her senses and get on board one of the choppers when the time came – for Wolfgang, especially.

12 BEE STINGS CAN BE DEADLY

New York City, United Nations Building
October 31, 2014

Window cleaning on a building the size of the United Nations was a full-time job assigned to special people and one of the best paying jobs for a blue collar workers in New York City even if it required an unusual stamina and an "enjoyment" of nature.

The United Nations building in Manhattan is 505 feet tall. In terms of window cleaning, it would not be considered such a high-risk job – that is, if it weren't for the fact that the building fronts the East River, where strong winds blow in from the Atlantic, breeze by the Statue of Liberty and Ellis Island and finally reach the skyscrapers of midtown, where pandemonium hits, as all the tall buildings cause the winds to be unpredictable, sometimes seeming to blow from two different directions simultaneously.

That day, management had determined the wind was calm enough to permit the cleaners to work, but the window washer assigned to the U.N. Building – instead of making his way to his normal position – was stuffed in a maintenance closet, bound hand-and-foot and missing his coveralls.

He was just coming to, looking down at his nearly naked body, and wondering what the Sam Houston just happened. He screwed his eyes really tight thinking back to the beginning of his shift. Earlier that afternoon, his supervisor had given him the all-clear to work and handed him his radio. Then he walked up to his storage room on the roof. And whammy, here I am, he thought.

Then another thought occurred to him. He remembered getting a bee sting on his neck. As he went to rub it, he had thought, What is a bee doing up at this height?

◆ ◆ ◆

Ari walked across the roof in his new outfit. "A good fit," he said to himself, smiling.

He struggled with his emotions, trying to get his mind back to the business at hand. His uniform felt just a little tight. He headed across the roof with his backpack, going straight for the hydraulic window cleaning cradle. Fortunately it was chilly, so it would look perfectly normal to see a worker dressed against the cold with a hat, scarf and a balaclava-like hood protecting his face.

Ari didn't bother with an equipment check before climbing into the cradle. He tied on the belt-safety-harness, took control of the hydraulic controls and proceeded to lower himself down the side of the building. After descending 10 floors to the 30th, he stopped, took out a rag and began cleaning the window. Momentarily distracted by a police siren, he looked away from the window down to the street, and as he looked down, he felt faint and almost nauseated. He clutched the cradle railing to steady himself.

"Crazy fool," he said aloud. "You know you hate heights; get in that office and get out of here."

He turned his attention back to the window. To the casual observer, everything appeared normal. A professional window cleaner would have noticed he was wiping the window with a dry cloth, having not even bothered using a wet rag first. Inside the office on the 30th floor, nobody noticed the cleaner. A plaque on the door identified it as the offices for the North Korean Delegation.

Ari continued to clean the window, paying more attention to what was happening inside the room now that he was committed. Kwok Kong entered the office oblivious to anything outside. Together with an aide, he walked across the room to enter another office. The office area in front of Ari was now empty, so he pulled out a glass magnet and placed it in the center of the window, then proceeded to cut a circle around the magnet with a diamond cutter. He quickly pushed in the tempered glass. As it broke inward, a gust of wind rushed into the office. Immediately afterward, he put his bag through and then followed. He replaced the circular glass he had removed and secured it in place.

Ari decided his disguise was a hindrance now, so he pulled off his hat and mask to reveal a tense, determined face. The room was empty. He stood motionless, listening, alert for any noise. He was all action as he walked across to the door Kong had entered. As he approached, he removed a pipe from his inside pocket and loaded a dart into the breach.

Ari knocked on the door, opened it slowly and, looking inside, saw that no one paid him any attention. Kong had his back to the door, and he and his assistant didn't even look around as Ari entered.

Ari smirked to himself, How arrogant, so assured of his safety in his quasi-diplomatic immunity. He put the blow pipe to his mouth and blew the dart.

A sharp sting in his neck got Kong's attention and he turned abruptly, putting his hand to the spot and rubbing, as if bitten. When he saw Ari, his eyes went wide in surprise. Before he could call out or raise the alarm, Kong clutched his heart, leaned forward and staggered slightly before falling to the floor.

Kong's assistant looked from his boss to Ari in total surprise. By now Ari had hidden his blowpipe. He turned to the stunned assistant, "Must be a heart attack! Quick –"

The assistant was so stunned he didn't know what to do, so Ari called out roughly, "Better call 911!"

The aide turned, glad someone was making the decisions, and hurried out to call for help. As soon as the aide was gone, Ari pocketed the blowpipe and leaned down over the prostrate Kong. He put his hand over the man's mouth, moved closer and whispered in his ear, "No more innocents."

Kong looked fearfully at Ari, then closed his eyes... dead. Ari released his hand from Kong's mouth, searched the man's pockets to find his cell phone and took it. He looked around behind him to the door to make sure he was still alone, then went over to his bag and started removing his window washing outfit to reveal a paramedic's uniform. He stuffed the old outfit in the bag and pulled a hat down low on his face.

Ari looked behind him at the body lying on the office floor, no visible emotion on his face. He left the office, taking the elevator down to ground floor. He was already feeling a great sense of accomplishment. One less injustice in the world, he thought. The elevator came to a stop interrupting his thoughts, but he was relieved.

Stepping through the doors, he was confronted by a real team of emergency paramedics arriving, wheeling in a gurney. Ari didn't miss a beat, with as much remorse as he could muster, "I think we were too late; he's on the 30th floor," he said, coughing and covering his face as he passed them.

The paramedics ran in one direction to try to save a dead man, and Ari calmly walked in the other, exiting the United Nations complex.

13 CLOSE CALLS AND CALLING CARDS

Washington, D.C., Carlyle Suites Hotel
November 1, 2014

Early the next morning, Ari was keeping a close eye on the Carlyle Suites Hotel. As a field operative for many years, he had learned to listen to his instincts. His gut was telling him now that something was not quite right. He was going to do everything in his power to make sure that "his" Jasmine did not walk into a dangerous situation.

This chance encounter had destroyed his willpower to resist her; he just didn't know if he could walk away from her again. But priority one would be keeping her safe.

Ari was in the lobby, holding the classic ruse of a newspaper in front of his face. Classic ruse or not, it works, he thought.

Ari watched Jasmine walk into the lobby dressed in a finely cut trench coat. His lips turned up slightly, as he noted how the cashmere followed the curves of her still slim figure. She moved with beautiful precision, like a dancer, but he knew it was years of martial arts training that had made her movements flow so gracefully.

She had her lips pursed together, her eyes slightly squinting as if looking for a clue from Ari. Her hands were held together in front of her.

Ari stood with his back to the wall, scanning the crowd. When he was satisfied, he nodded for her to follow him to the breakfast room, both still in professional mode, she knowing exactly what he was doing and having total confidence in him.

They found a table on the far side, where he sat with his back to the wall, still on alert. He indicated with his eyes for her to join him and continued to scan the room for danger.

As they sat there, Ari could feel Jasmine searching his face for any clue to what he was thinking or feeling. They sat close to the emergency exit, giving Ari a view of everyone who entered the restaurant and an escape route if needed. Both remained silent, trying to find a way to start a conversation.

"Ari, I've been following your performances. You are a soloist now?"

She seems nervous, Ari thought. Somehow knowing he wasn't the only one helped.

He visibly relaxed talking about a cherished subject. "Yes. You know I have always loved the violin... My new piece, Mozart and Hendrix; it's a difficult combination to understand."

Ari was smiling, thinking of his hobby. If she had wanted to put him at ease, getting his mind off of espionage and the danger at hand, this was the perfect subject.

"It's a hand-and-glove thing. I think it helps me deal with the violent world I live in."

"How do they handle your frequent 'business' trips?"

"The conductor is ex-Mossad; he understands. There are always plenty of volunteers for my solo spots," Ari's smile faded slightly. "But enough about me, Jasmine, what are you doing here? Last I heard, you were still stationed overseas. Has the CIA moved you back to the mainland?"

"Something ... more important came up. My sister's kid is autistic, pretty severe. Her husband died in the Twin Towers... I'm all she's got. Family you know..."

She opened her hands in a gesture of futility. Her lips began to tremble then, and she looked down at her empty hands. "You said you would call..."

She raised her teary eyes to look into his.

As much as Ari had trained himself to control his emotions, a slight tension still ran across his face. He was uncomfortable with the direction of the conversation. He struggled with a response. It was so long ago, and he had managed to avoid her for all these years – even in the interwoven community of American espionage.

He sighed, and the truth came out. "I wanted to... But, but I nearly got you killed."

She looked at him incredulously. "That wasn't your fault. Special OPs is a dangerous business. We all face danger."

"I still feel guilty, responsible. With others, it is just the job, I feel remorse, but I understand. With you –"

"You need to protect me," she said, cutting him off. Anger rose slightly in her tone. "Even if that means from yourself."

Ari wanted to reach out, to touch her hand on the table in front of him, but he felt vulnerable, scared of her possible rejection. He could feel his eyes tearing up. He smelled her sweet perfume mingled with a scent he knew was Jasmine's own – that aura of femininity, the very essence of her being. It was irresistible.

She watched him, and he knew she was looking for a tell-tale hint of his feelings. She had her hand on the table in front of her – an invitation to him.

Why can't I just touch her hand, squeeze her fingers? Give her some affirmation? Show her how much I care?

He knew why. When he let her in his heart, his mind, his need to protect her could get them both killed. And what if I'm wrong about how she feels?

The moment was intense. There they sat, enshrined in a cocoon of impenetrable unrealized desire. Both wanting the other, but neither certain enough to take the plunge and move their hand forward that inch to consummate their feelings.

Finally she broke the silence, the tension too much for her, "Are you still with Mossad?"

Ari sensed he had missed an opportunity, and he hesitated, not wanting to break the spell and return to the reality of his violent life.

"Yes ... On undercover assignment indefinitely in the U.S."

As he spoke, his eyes focused on another guest entering the breakfast area, and without realizing it, he tensed. Something about this man did not add up. He stood close to the entrance, even when an attendant approached him, as if biding his time, waiting for something.

She didn't notice Ari's nervousness. "Indefinitely? Are you stationed here in D.C.?"

Jasmine has been out of field for a while now, Ari thought, her senses are not as acute as they should be.

She continued, not attributing his new tenseness to the scene playing out behind her. "How long have you been here?"

He was paying scant attention to her at this point, his body strung tighter by the moment as he watched the unwelcome guest at the entrance. The man seemed to be searching for someone in the restaurant who was already seated, perhaps someone he was to meet.

Ari recognized a professional. The man's eyes reached Ari, and Ari sensed them pause for a fraction of a second before moving on.

Still, Ari caught the slight reaction, an imperceptible tightening of the man's facial muscles, as if ...

Ari looked quickly at Jasmine, not wanting to alarm her quite yet, not totally sure whether this was a serious situation or not. As he spoke, he took his eyes off the guy at the entrance and scanned the other restaurant guests, trying to spot any unusual reaction.

"No. I live in Bethesda, actually. Not far out though."

Ari finished looking over all the guests he could see, returning to look at the entrance to the restaurant. A bellboy passed the guest, entering the dining room.

He was carrying a small silver tray in front of him with an envelope, and as he walked in looking around at the seated patrons, he called out, "Message for Mr. Cohen. Message for Mr. Cohen."

Ari tensed; he realized his sixth sense had been right.

Jasmine looked around attentive, and Ari knew she would give the bellboy cause to bring the note to their table. Before he could alert her against it, she turned toward the sound of his name and the bellboy assumed the lady in the finely tailored coat with the good looking gentleman must be who he was seeking.

The young man quickened his step. This should be a great tip; romantic couples are always great tippers. It was the bellboy's last conscious thought. He glided up to their table, tray held out in front of him like a deacon in church collecting offerings.

Following his instinct, and to the utter astonishment of the bellboy, Ari jumped across the table toward Jasmine and pushed her and her chair to the floor. At the same time, from behind the bellboy, the suspicious guest materialized pulling his right hand out from under his jacket and leveling a silenced Glock at the location where Ari had been.

The bellboy, alarmed by the action in front of him, turned trying to get out of Ari's way. The breakfasting guests turned to see the cause of the ruckus as chairs crashed, and as they swiveled to look at Ari, they noticed the hit man with his gun toting arm extended and began screaming. From all over the restaurant came the sound of chairs slamming to the floor as guests tried to get away.

A puff of smoke left the barrel of the Glock. In the meantime, the bellboy had turned into the line of fire. He didn't stand a chance, the first shot hit him in the chest, and he went down, mortally wounded. The tray was knocked out of his hands and landed noisily on the floor, as the envelope with its unread message danced like a lazy butterfly through the air, landing in front of Ari.

He had no time to read it now, but pocketed the note. Jasmine was on the floor beside him, wide-eyed and not understanding what was happening.

He turned to her. "You need to get out of here. I'm going after the gunman. GO!"

She didn't move. "NO!" she uttered with determination. "The last time I did that, I didn't see you for eight years!"

He didn't have time to argue. "OK, I promise. Go back to your office, and I'll meet you there early tomorrow morning. Promise."

He was pleading with his eyes. "Please. You're going to get us killed if you don't leave."

He turned to look at the hit man who was bound to take another shot at the target that had eluded him. He was so intent on pursuing his quarry he didn't see what was going on behind him.

The sound of feet pounding on the hardwood floor was like castanets in a Spanish calypso as people rushed in all directions for the closest exits. This noise masked the approach of one brave man – the hotel security guard. He came in stealthily and assumed a shooting posture. An ex-cop, he had years of firearms training but had never discharged his weapon in the field. He was trained but still hopelessly outmatched when paired against a professional killer.

The guard assessed the situation, saw the hit man, leveled his gun at him and shouted out, "Halt! Hands up or I'll shoot!"

You never see a professional hit man hesitate to take a shot or warn his opponent of his intention. The well-intentioned warning had the predictable effect. The hit man was a gun-for-hire who had spent thousands of hours training for all types of assault scenarios, including being surprised by an enemy with a pistol aimed at his back. He had two choices – lift up his arms in surrender or...

He took Option Two. Pivoting to his left, falling intentionally to the floor, in one seamless motion, he lifted his arm, aimed, and shot the security guard. The assassin's training had taught him to aim for the chest in a situation like this. Unfortunately, he couldn't miss such a large target at this distance, and the security guard went down.

Ari's first concern was Jasmine, but he didn't want to start a gun battle with so many innocent people in the restaurant.

"Now go on, out the back. I'll meet you in Philly, at your newspaper, early, before the staff shows up."

They were both on the ground facing each other and she leaned forward to give him a deep, succulent kiss. In spite of the danger, he had to smile. She noticed he had a look of private thoughts on his face before he turned to confront the shooter, and she smiled as well.

She was on all fours crawling out the back exit. He turned back over his shoulder for the few seconds it took to watch her go, and once she was safe, turned back to confront the hit man who was extricating himself from his situation with the guard.

Ari was impossibly angry, more so because of the danger to Jasmine. He wanted to know who put out the hit and why.

The hit man, still only halfway through the restaurant, had decided to beat a hasty retreat after the chaotic demise of his surprise attack and the appearance of the security guard. With sirens already sounding in the distance, he knew he didn't have time to complete his mission and still get away.

So he ran crouched over toward the hotel lobby. As he headed back out of the restaurant, he tried to assume a more normal posture like one of the frightened guests fleeing danger. Once in the lobby, he turned right toward the coffee shop. His pace slowed to a walk, trying to appear normal. He walked through the coffee shop to the exit.

Ari arrived in the lobby just as the hit man entered the coffee shop. He decided to follow him, but from outside the hotel, so he ran out the front of the lobby and turned to the right. He walked along the street-side of the coffee shop, watching the hit man inside, who was unaware he was still being followed closely.

The hit man exited the coffee shop from the side exit to the street, and Ari turned the corner only to see his target get into the passenger-side front seat of a running car.

Ari took off after the vehicle on foot in the middle of the street. The traffic light changed to green, and the hit man's car roared away.

Ari came to a halt, winded. The street was crowded, but Ari got close enough to read the tag as the car sped off. He had his gun in hand but hidden under his coat and decided not to shoot; there were too many innocent bystanders on the street.

Ari's teeth were clamped together with his lips open revealing a forced vengeful smile.

As the car sped away, Ari pulled out the envelope the bellboy had dropped and opened it, still in the middle of the street, oblivious.

He looked at the card stunned.

It read:

Compliments of

The Raven

Ari's face, already cast like granite, now turned to steel – cold, hard and determined. He turned to walk away, wondering how he could love with such passion – Jasmine and his prized Stradivarius – but also hate with the potency of a cobra.

He walked a little distance toward a quieter street corner and pulled out his cell phone to call Athena.

"Tom?"

"Go ahead, Ari."

"There's just been a hit attempt on me; I was with an ex-CIA operative."

"Are you hurt? Damage assessment?"

"Collateral, two victims I think, but it was the Raven. I've got their plates; I think it's probably a rental. Can you find out who rented it? If it's a rental, it must have a GPS locater. I need to know where it goes."

"Will do, Ari. By the way, did you hear about the murder at the United Nations yesterday?"

Ari didn't so much as flinch or even answer.

"Just get me the trace on the plates I just gave you, please, and by the way, can you handle the White House for me? The Chief of Staff wants to chat."

"Will do, Ari, and please stay away from the U.N."

14 EVACUATION

FLASHBACK – April 28, 1975
Saigon, Vietnam

It was nearly 3 p.m. before the sound of the first Huey came to those on the roof still burning documents, bringing in Slade's prayed-for reinforcements.

For the next four hours, choppers brought in another 130 Marines, but that still brought the total to only 175 against what looked like a sea of desperate souls surrounding the Embassy walls.

At 5 p.m., they got word the choppers from the Defense Attaché Office evacuations would begin rerouting to the Embassy, and the civilians inside began a mad-dash of preparations and triaging to determine first-dibs on chopper seats.

When they got word those choppers would stop flying at dark, the Marines hustled up to ring their LZ with the headlights of the remaining cars in the parking lot. A plea from the Marine commander on the ground through the Ambassador to the Oval Office turned things around, and choppers were set to run into the night despite pilot fatigue and low visibility from the darkness, fires and bad weather.

Alex remained on the roof, thinking Heidi would have an easier time getting on a chopper if he wasn't there to say goodbye. He watched as the first load of civilians headed out to the LZ, but she was not among them. He turned back to work, sure that she would be leaving soon.

♦ ♦ ♦

It was 2 a.m., and Alex was on the roof helping to man the LZ there. The choppers were landing every 10 minutes now on the roof and in the parking lot. For the most part, the women were gone.

Inside the Embassy, the staff ran around in a panic. They moved in random confusion, collecting file boxes, taking them to the side entrance, where Marines carried boxes and equipment toward a transport helicopter preparing for takeoff. Above the helicopter on the landing pad was another chopper waiting its turn, the downdraft so strong it blew hats off, flying all over, as if they had been ripped off at a graduation and thrown into the air in celebration.

Military personnel, with standard military haircuts, assigned to carry boxes to the transport helicopters, suffered no ill effect when their hats were blown off. Civilians charged with the same task did not fare so well. The wind blew their hair into tight knots. Loose clothes blew all over; they almost looked like mechanical scarecrows carrying boxes.

Slade was working alongside Alex. He estimated there were still more than 1,000 evacuees left – most of them civilians – and he had no idea how they would get them all out in the 19 remaining lifts authorized.

Alex still had not made his way to the little office – afraid to find Heidi still there. Slade could see the look in his eyes, clapped him on the shoulder and sent him on his way. Now was the time.

As Alex opened the door, he knew what he would see. Heidi still slept on the couch, the boys at her feet.

He fell to his knees and wept.

♦ ♦ ♦

From a side entrance to the Embassy, three marines marched out in solemn formation, hats held in place by chin straps. They looked oddly formal against the backdrop of panic prevalent elsewhere. Their intent soon became obvious.

They maintained their formal march to the flagpole. One Marine stood formally, put his trumpet to his lips and started blowing. No one along the fence could hear what he played, such was the overwhelming noise from the choppers and the crowd. As he finished his rendition, the third Marine broke formation to approach the flagpole and lower the Star-Spangled Banner.

When the flag was removed and carefully folded by the Marines, an audible gasp of desperation rolled into a growl of rebellion and anger throughout the crowd. The Marines doubled their resolve on patrol at the fence, rifles held at the ready.

As another helicopter began to take off, the outside boundary of the compound was besieged in earnest again. The mob was now pulsating, desperate to get over the fence. Angry hands gripped the fence shaking it with such intensity the Marine guards changed stance again – turning to face the fence, rifles held in the repel position, bayonets at chest height, tension filling every move they made.

Not one Marine seemed to remember these same people would have happily invited them to a family dinner the weekend before. All civility was forgotten as trained killers prepared to defend the Embassy from a crowd of mostly unarmed desperate families.

As the tension rose, more people moved toward the front gate area, the only demonstrators not physically abusing the wrought iron fence were the ones holding children.

Inside the fence, some Marines held position, but clearly struggled with the assignment, faces racked with a powerless expression of remorse. They looked at the mob with pity, with concern -- with the impertinence to question the sanity of their orders. One looked as if he were whispering to himself, saying a prayer and asking for strength, praying for forgiveness for his part in carrying out the orders of superiors that had gone mad, forgotten their humanity. How can we leave them all?

Inside the Embassy Compound to the front, stood a Marine. He had chosen a rock in the garden area on which to stand. He stood still, like granite, unmoved, a bullhorn held firmly in his hand at waist height. No smile or indication of human warmth crossed his face; he might well have been a bronze statue. He was emotionless, the perfect soldier, as if he had forgotten that his enemy of the moment were people his country had been sent to protect.

As the frenzied mob seemed to shake the very foundations of the compound, the Marine on the rock lifted his bullhorn to his mouth and pulled the trigger, "U.S. Citizens only, PLEASE. With... your.... passports."

From the outside Embassy gate, the crowd sent up a unified plea, "Please, Oh, God! Please, let us in! The Communists will kill our families – our children!"

From the airspace over the Embassy, another helicopter arrived, hovering overhead, the reverberating blades on the main rotor beating the crowd with their intensity, the sound drowning out any more appeals from the doomed.

The chopper in the LZ prepared to take off. The main rotor turning with more and more intensity, only adding to the charged atmosphere as harried civilians spilled out of the Embassy building to replace those in the compound boarding the chopper.

At any moment when the crowd noticed the guards' attention was diverted, agile outsiders would try to climb the fence, but by the time one reached the top, before he could get half of the his body over, he was hit by the butt of a parade ground rifle, falling to the ground outside the fence, bloodied and humiliated.

Still, the Marines knew, soon the crowd would be too much for the few of them left.

♦ ♦ ♦

Alex had finally gathered himself together and walked through the door into the little office.

He gently shook his wife. "Heidi, my love. We must go."

She woke groggily, and they began to gather up the twins to make their way up the stairs to the rooftop LZ. They were silent.

It was closing in on 5 a.m., and both LZs were still lit bright as day. All of the evacuees had been called outside nearly two hours ago, and any system or sense of justice had been abandoned as every man wrestled for the next seat on each landing chopper. Word had gotten around that each one could be the last.

Alex again shoved his way through the crowd, making a hole for his tiny family, until they reached the front of the crowd. There stood Lt. Slade.

When he turned to Alex and saw Heidi by his side, Slade's face fell. "U.S. citizens only, Alex," he said with sincere sorrow. "Ford just made the call."

Tears welling in Heidi's eyes, she turned to hand Alex his son, Wolfgang, "You must take them both, then."

Alex took the child, and then he turned to the young man standing next to him in the crowd. He had worked with him on the roof, and knew him to be quiet, but good.

"Timothy," Alex said. "I need a favor."

Barely in his twenties, Timothy stared up into Alex's eyes in true fear at what he knew was coming. Alex handed him Pieter. Beside him, another young man reached to take Wolfgang.

"You must take the twins to the evacuation center. We will find you there soon," Alex said with simple determination.

Heidi was trying to turn him to her, pulling at his sleeve, but he would not look her way. "No, Alex! No! You must go!" she pleaded.

"They have been fed and changed. They will be fine." Alex continued speaking calmly to the terrified young Timothy.

"It's OK, Sir," said the young man next to Timothy.

A Marine near the edge of the crowd was bellowing out orders through a bullhorn, "U.S. personnel only. Make your way to the front now!" Alex saw one last person run out of the building, as if the very devil were chasing him.

Timothy came out of his stupor then and nodded his head toward the young man next to him. "This is John."

"Alex Stangl," he said, emphasizing his last name as he shook the young man's hand.

John held Alex's hand a little longer than normal and smiled. "I come from a large farm family, Sir. I have five younger brothers," he said in a reassuring tone.

Then, turning to the bewildered Heidi, he asked in the deepest, most compassionate voice she had ever heard, "How old are they?"

She mumbled something in return, as he took her hand warmly, as well. If he heard her above the sound of the chopper noise, it would have been a miracle, but his smile never faltered and his eyes never left hers.

Alex leaned toward the boys, "This is Wolfgang and Pieter," he said as he kissed each. "Take good care of them."

"I'll try," Timothy said.

Alex had still not looked Heidi in the eye, as he put his arm around her tightly, and Timothy and John carry their babies to the waiting chopper, the twins screaming in fright in the noisy violent downdraft. Alex could feel her sobbing against him as they watched the young men, babes held firmly in their arms, climb into the waiting Huey.

Finally, Alex looked down into her upturned face as she stared at him uncomprehending. "You would not leave me. I will not leave you," he said, kissing her forehead. "We will find the boys."

He turned her back into the crowd so she could not watch the chopper leave.

♦ ♦ ♦

Timothy looked out the chopper opening as it gained height for the short trip to safety. The sense of foreboding among the passengers was oppressive.

"The Communists will march in within the hour. What will become of those still in the Embassy?" John asked aloud. "How many could be slaughtered as American sympathizers?"

Timothy just shook his head and shrugged, feeling the emotional struggle of leaving friends behind to an uncertain fate. He hugged the still terrified twin in his lap even tighter as he could see the communist forces at the edge of the city. In his mind, he pictured them circling the abandoned Embassy, firing point blank indiscriminately at the desperate crowd of loving, deserted, ex-friends of the United States of America.

15 DESPAIR WEARS ARMANI

Ronald Reagan Washington National Airport

George Cass had seen – and overlooked – many things during his long tenure as the precisely pressed, well groomed full-time attendant in the beautifully appointed men's restroom inside the ultra-chic private terminal at Ronald Reagan Washington National Airport.

Standing by while Simon Brooks puked his guts out in the last stall was not the most unseemly, distasteful or most depraved thing he had ever been privy to, but that did not mean Cass would not expect to be well-tipped for smiling through the experience regardless. That is, if the gentleman in the Armani suit survived the incident. At the moment, the sounds emanating from the last stall did not sound promising.

Armani suits are made to be worn in the board room; they are not designed to hug commodes. As Brooks was on his knees – his arms firmly encircling the porcelain bowl, his heaves uncontrollable – he found himself testing the resolve of his beloved suit. Clutched in his hand was a sheet of paper getting more soiled by the moment. As he struggled to control his guts, he lifted the email again, trying to re-read the message,

To Simon Brooks

Subject: 10356   1000022014

If you value your confidentiality, be at Ronald Reagan Washington National Airport private jet terminal on Thursday morning, 10:00 A.M. Pack for five warm days with cold nights. No passport necessary. BE THERE.

Every time he read the message, it had the same result – extreme anxiety leading to an uncontrollable rolling in his gut – and he had tried to read the email so often, there was simply nothing left in his stomach. Brooks couldn't figure out how someone had gotten hold of his Swiss bank account number.

What happened to honor among thieves? Someone must have sold me out, but who and why?

Approaching the terminal from the parking lot was another man in Armani. But this banker wore his suit the way an Armani was meant to be worn – over a pressed shirt, matching tie and kerchief. He walked at a pace that would never generate a sweat. This man in Armani looked at the passengers inside the waiting area as he approached as if he floated slightly above them.

Inside the men's room, Brooks had finally recovered enough to leave his stall.

As he left the restroom, he tried to straighten his crooked tie and smooth out his wrinkled suit. The new gentleman's eyes reached Brooks, and the sickly man's reaction was immediate. He stopped in mid-stride and stared aghast, the fear etched on his face.

The gentleman slowed his pace, unsure, no longer taking the same confidant long strides. He saw Brooks hesitate outside the restroom door, as if trying to decide which direction to go. Brooks pulled out his email to re-read it again for the umpteenth time, as the gentleman watched, and slowly, recognition dawned on his face as he glanced at a similar piece of paper in his own hand. He nodded his head knowingly, and understanding, he walked into the waiting room.

Brooks looked up as the gentleman strode toward him. His face soured as the man drew closer, as if he smelled a skunk. He tried to hide the hand holding the email behind his back.

"Roger, what are you doing here?"

The man continued to walk confidently toward Brooks, who now recoiled as if in fear.

"Ah, Simon," the man said, brightly, "looks like you got one too?"

Brooks furrowed his brow, not answering, not understanding. "Roger, what are you doing here?"

The man lifted his hand showing Brooks a similar printed page. Brooks looked down and saw nearly identical text, but a different number in the subject line:

Roger Pollard

Subject: 10356   1000492611

If you value your confidentiality be at Ronald Reagan Washington National Airport, private jet terminal on Thursday morning, 10.00 A.M. Pack for five warm days with cold nights. No passport necessary. BE THERE.

"It looks as if we have both been caught with our pants down." Pollard tried to make light of the situation.

"Oh, God, help us! What are we going to do?" Brooks blurted.

"Your flight is ready to board, gentlemen." The voice of the flight attendant startled them both.

Pollard reacted first. "Ma'am, what's the destination?"

She laughed nervously, as if not understanding why Pollard wouldn't know.

"Why, Santa Fe, New Mexico, of course."

16 STANDOFF WITH THE PRESIDENT

First White House Checkpoint
November 2, 2014

As Burke entered the White House compound, sirens seemed to sound from every direction. To the untrained eye, it looked like chaos, but Burke knew the emergency plans in place and understood the whirling commotion. At the first appearance of any terrorist or criminal activity in and around Washington, D.C., the White House turns into a mad house of frantic action. Nervous police line the perimeter, Secret Service agents go into overdrive, and the protection of the President becomes paramount.

After the assassination of the Chairman of the Federal Reserve, the White House security teams were extremely sensitive to any perceived threat. Burke had no idea what threat may have been detected around the perimeter, but as he waited to be taken in for his appointment with the Chief of Staff, he saw no immediate, obvious danger in the current hub-bub of activity, so he tried to be as non-threatening as possible and just wait.

As he watched the lock-down response, two Secret Service agents swooped down in front of him. "Are you Colonel Tom Burke?" Their tone showing not a hint of friendliness. As soon as the Secret Service confronted Burke, the people on either side of him acted as if he had the plague, shuffling away from him, pushing others in their haste.

Burke acknowledged with a slight nod. "You need to come with us."

Without waiting for a response, they stood on each side of him and manhandled him toward the White House. Burke didn't resist.

"What's the problem?"

The Secret Service agents didn't seem to be in the mood for conversation; treating him as if he were the threat.

"The President wants to talk to you... in the Oval Office."

As Burke was shown into the Oval Office, the President didn't waste any time either. "Sorry for the rough treatment, Colonel. I asked to be alerted of anyone asking to see Ed Gonzalez with that little weird eye calling card. You are Athena right?"

"Yes, Sir."

"I want to introduce you to my Secretary of the Treasury, Morris Winters. He brought me some disturbing news this morning."

Winters and Burke nodded at each other as they were introduced, both summing one another up as the President continued.

"Colonel, three Governors of the Federal Reserve have disappeared. As you know, the Chairman of the Federal Reserve was assassinated yesterday, and now I have the Secretary General of the United Nations calling me constantly because he thinks I ordered the murder of a North Korean delegate, who incidentally happened to have Diplomatic Immunity and happened to be the chief suspect in the Chairman's murder. This is a mess."

The President shook his head in consternation, truly agitated, watching Burke to see if there was any reaction. Burke didn't flinch.

"Yes, Sir. Sounds like someone could draw a connection between these events," Burke said simply.

"Colonel, the country cannot afford even the whiff of a scandal at the Federal Reserve," Winters emphasized the word scandal, and as he spoke, the President nodded his head to agree with every word.

The President continued, "We have to get out in front of this, find out what is going on Colonel, I need your help; I need to know what is happening." Before continuing, the President's posture hardened, trying to look as seriously as he could, "By the way, isn't Ari Cohen one of your agents?"

Burke had spent years in the field, undercover. If the President thought he might let something slip, accidentally, the man was mistaken. "Yes, Sir, he is; he's a loaner from the Mossad. We were working on a joint OP in Italy when their Finance Minister was shot."

The President continued, not realizing he was out-matched by the head of Athena's Op Center.

"Did he kill the North Korean delegate at the U.N.?"

Burke hesitated only a moment before answering the question in a measured tone. "That is an unusually direct question, Mr. President. Do you have reason to ask it?"

"Just answer the question, Burke."

Burke hesitated again as if giving his next answer great thought, "I have no evidence that that is the case, Sir." His stare didn't waiver as he responded, and then decided to add, "The information we received from the coroner's office was that Kong died of a heart attack."

"Yes, well, lucky for you, we don't have any evidence to the contrary, but as you said someone sure could draw a connection between these events, and your man is right in the middle of it."

Burke remained silent, unblinking.

Winters now understood the friction between the two men. The President thought one of the Colonel's men had violated U.N. diplomatic immunity and killed the North Korean – an assassin and a diplomat. Burke was either lying or covering up for his man, and the President wasn't sure whether Athena had sanctioned the hit.

"What a mess," Winters muttered just quietly enough not to be heard.

The President stared back at Burke, uncertain. "If I find out that you ordered the hit, Burke, there will be hell to pay... but I must admit, Ari Cohen is lucky to have a man like you to back him up."

Burke was tempted to give the President a piece of his mind but bit his tongue, just adding demurely, "If you say so, Sir."

Even as Burke responded, he was inwardly cursing the fact that his administrative position required him to be so polite.

"With regard to the disappearance of those three Governors, we'll look into it, priority one, and let you know as soon as we have something concrete."

The President and Secretary of the Treasury turned as if dismissing Burke, but he decided to let them know about yesterday – that this wasn't a game.

"Mr. President, Sir, there is... something... I need to add."

The President looked up, suspicion furrowing his brows, clearly not comfortable with this interjection.

"Do I want to hear this?"

Burke hesitated only slightly, thinking to himself that these politicians just didn't have a clue. "This should be OK, Sir. The North Korean that you were so worried about was a hired assassin. Yesterday, another assassin tried to take out Ari Cohen in a D.C. hotel. The calling card left behind was for The Raven – an international criminal we've been tracking for some time."

The President's face grew stern in thought. "Was that the affair at the Carlyle?"

"Yes, Sir."

"And is that tied to the other deaths?"

"We believe so, Sir."

"So you think they tried to take out Cohen?" The President smiled, and for the first time Burke thought the President just might be beginning to get the picture. "From what I've heard, I think they may have ticked off the wrong guy."

Burke nodded in full agreement. "If only you knew, Mr. President, if only you knew."

"On another matter, Burke, how did your man Cohen know about the assassination of the Federal Reserve Chairman before we did?"

"We had been following his killer since he took out the Italian Finance Minister in Naples last week. We were following that trail; we just couldn't intervene fast enough to stop the second murder."

"It seems that you are better informed than my people. How do you get all this information?"

"Like the White House, Sir, we find the NSA to be a great source of information; we just analyze it better..."

With a wink at the President, Burke left the Oval Office.

He was in such deep thought he was hardly conscious of exiting the White House to get into his car. Something bothered him; both the murders and the disappearances of the Governors had one thing in common – money. It was time to work on the background of all these characters involved, there must be a common thread.

He picked up his secure phone, calling through to the Athena OPs center.

17 DEATH ON DEADLINE

Philadelphia, P.A.
November 2, 2014

Cooper was tense, still not completely sure if Ari had made it out alive. News sources out of D.C. hadn't carried the story, and she had called the hotel but they acted as if they didn't know what she was talking about. The D.C. police had no open case on the affair, which didn't surprise her.

She walked toward her office and her new position at the Philadelphia Daily News, but she couldn't help feeling anxious. She was arriving early as Ari had instructed, despite her move to the Editorial desk, where most reporters didn't come in until late morning to offset the late nights involved. She knew her department would be mostly vacant except for the Editor's assistant and Charlie, who never seemed to leave.

The smells of a waking city – bacon, donuts, coffee, nicotine and trash – all tried to distract her from her train of thought. She knew if Ari didn't show up she would be bitterly disappointed.

"He promised he would come," she whispered to herself. But that little devil of self-doubt kept raising its ugly head, saying, The last time you didn't see him for eight years. Way to go girl.

Cooper continued her trek, her mind trying to understand her feelings for Ari. On the one hand, he was the most caring, loving, accomplished musician, and on the other a rock-hard, cold-blooded killer. How could God have endowed the same person with those diametrically opposed attributes?

She knew from experience that work in the dirty business of espionage tended to tear apart the tender side of people, and yet his need to protect her remained. She was no closer to solving the riddle when she came to the corner where she had to turn for the short hop to her building.

Just down the block, she saw the normally motionless revolving doors to her office building begin to turn. Two bulky guys in overcoats walked purposefully out at a brisk pace. They could have been twins – same height, same cropped hair style, similar long winter coats. For the first time since getting up, she was able to change her thought pattern from

Ari to something else.

Her military training kicked into gear, her sixth sense telling her all was not well.

She was cautious going through the revolving door and up to her new office. She saw the light on in Charlie's office, the door slightly ajar. Her breath caught. Hesitantly, she pushed open the door and looked around to Charlie's chair. He was leaning over his desk, apparently sleeping.

She tip-toed over, and whispered, "Charlie, wake up. It's me, Cooper."

Seeing no reaction, she walked closer, silently so as not to frighten him. She noticed his new haircut and freshly starched new shirt, and then the spots of blood on his sleeve. She abandoned her attempt not to frighten him as fear leapt into her own throat. Lunging toward him now, she saw the small stiletto pinning his right hand to the desk, blood congealing underneath.

She had seen a lot of death, sometimes abrupt, always agonizing, bodies ripped apart by explosives, or mutilated in torture, and she had remained a professional. Still she recoiled in horror now, her hand to her mouth to silence the scream winding its way up through her chest. She forced herself to continue her inspection of her once lively boss, spotting the garrote around his neck. She checked his pulse, but it was an exercise in futility; he was still warm, but his heart was silent.

She pulled back, seeing under his left hand the corner of a piece of crumpled paper. Trying not to contaminate the scene, she slipped it out from under his hand and head. It was draft copy for the front page he must have been working on before his attackers entered. Why they hadn't taken it, she couldn't guess. Deadly but not very thorough, she thought. Scrawled on the bottom in blood, Charlie had tried to leave a clue with the last of his strength.

He was right-handed, but that hand was skewered to his desk. In nearly unintelligible letters, his bloody message read, "Pink Adobe, Santa Fe, Wednesday 7:00 P.M."

Cooper couldn't help but say to herself, "Oh, Charlie, what have they done to you? What could have been so important that your last thought was a clue to your murderer, not a love note to your family?"

Cooper read the draft.

Central Bankers Assassinated

In the last 10 days, two of the world's most respected Central Bankers have been killed, and rumors have begun circulating about a criminal endeavor to compromise the integrity of the world's Central Banks.

Confidential sources in the White House confirm there is an ongoing investigation...

Angrily, Cooper thought, He must have spoken to the White House Chief of Staff; how else would he know?

Suddenly a voice from the office door had her wheeling for an object of defense. It took a moment to realize it was a deep, caring voice, and her first thought was, He did come.

With the little remaining resolve she possessed, Cooper exhaled in relief, not saying anything. She was visibly shaking, sinking toward the floor, her muscles relaxing in relief, knowing she was not alone.

Ari rushed over, exclaiming "Jasmine, it's me –"

She looked toward him, clearly overcome with emotion, reaching her breaking point. Ari caught her before she hit the floor. She said nothing, just continued looking at him. Her eyes vaguely distant now, not really seeing anything, but seeming to know he was there.

Ari had her in his arms; he was holding her close, stroking her silky hair.

She was in shock; she had left this brutality behind when she left the CIA, but here it was again haunting her. She had been safe, he thought. Why hadn't she stayed away?

He was stroking her pale face, her tears flowing warmly down her cheeks, as she looked up at him and mumbled, "He got a haircut... he got a haircut."

Ari was puzzled, he didn't know what she was talking about, but it didn't matter, he was here, she was in his arms, and he was content for the first time in a long time. He wanted to go away, just escape, with the love he couldn't deny anymore.

◆ ◆ ◆

Schuylkill River Park, Philadelphia

They spent hours with the police as the first to find the body and report it. It had been tricky for both of them – Ari because he did not want his cover blown and Cooper because she didn't want the mission compromised before Ari could bring Charlie's killers to justice.

They told the police just what they knew about that morning – about the men in trench coats and finding the body – but left out the blood-stained paper folded neatly under Charlie's hand. Only Ari shared her secret, now tucked away in her pocket.

Schuylkill River Park was a green area Philadelphians used for jogging, entertainment and often for a piece of sanity away from the hectic pace of modern downtown. Once freed from the police and the reporters that had swarmed into Charlie's office, Ari and Cooper left the Philadelphia News office for the park. Even now, the brutality of the morning was hard to accept, and the tranquility of the river trail was a welcome break.

"Ari, I'm going with you to Santa Fe."

Ari continued as if she had said nothing, but inside alarm bells were ringing. After thinking through the situation, he turned to her look into her eyes.

"Do you how dangerous this could be? My people might want to use you as bait – show the Raven that you know Charlie's secret and are following the story, draw him out and push his buttons. Are you on board with that?" Ari searched her eyes for an answer, his concern evident. "I might not be able to protect you."

Jasmine was equally as thoughtful as Ari, before she nodded, reaffirming her decision. "I just need to put my CIA hat back on; I can't let them get away with this."

"The only way you can come is if my bosses okay it. That way if we get into trouble, we will have back up. And you need to know that I'm really not OK with this."

They walked a while longer in silence, Ari struggling with his intense desire to protect her, Cooper determined to seek revenge.

"Okay, looks like we are going to do this together, my CO is in Bethesda. We are going to need to go there in person."

Now it was Jasmine's turn to quiz Ari. "Mossad has a station in Bethesda?"

"Not exactly," Ari responded slowly, measuring his words.

She searched his face questioningly, but saw he wasn't quite ready to give her the explanation, and she left it alone.

As they walked along, Ari took his hand out from his raincoat pocket. Looking ahead, he put his fingers into the side pocket of her coat, seeking her hand. Immediately, she intertwined her fingers with his. From somewhere, the sound of a string quartet playing a Mozart piece, drifted toward them, a welcome cliche for the lovers.

They walked off the path toward chairs placed in front of a Gazebo and stopped to sit, still holding hands, watching. Ari and Jasmine wouldn't have noticed if there were hundreds of people around them. They were totally immersed in themselves, both watching the string quartet but not really hearing it.

"Ari, why do we do what we do?"

He looked at her, almost teary. "God gave me two gifts, if I had to choose one, I don't know which I would pick. The violin gives me and others so much pleasure, but my need to stop the evil from hurting the innocent is so important. God gave me that talent for a reason. Perhaps he gave me the musical talent to help me deal with the violence."

Ari looked at the string quartet, and asked as if his mind were elsewhere, "Why did you go into Special Ops with the Air Force and then the CIA?"

"My Dad's favorite expression was, 'All it takes for evil to succeed is for good men to do nothing.'"

The music stopped as she spoke, and Ari turned to her. He stared into her green eyes, lifted his spare hand to her cheek. She reached up to touch it, and they sat facing each other for a long while.

"Please wait here a moment."

Ari walked over to the string quartet and its violinist. After a brief conversation, the violinist gave Ari her violin and bow. He turned to the woman he loved, still wearing his raincoat, and pulled out a clean, folded and ironed handkerchief from his pocket to lay against the chin piece of the violin. He raised the bow and gave her a look as if to say, This is for you, Jasmine.

He closed his eyes and played "Jasmine's Song" – that same song that had haunted and soothed him for eight long years, a song she had never heard.

♦ ♦ ♦

Athena Ops
Bethesda, Maryland

Security at the Athena compound in Bethesda was intense. Ari was not sure what Burke's reaction would be to his bringing Jasmine to Athena, so he left her with strict instructions to stay in the car until he called for her.

Ari was apprehensive about his appointment with Burke. As he sat watching the seconds tick by, he was still not sure how he was going to handle the meeting. The Colonel had not expressed any surprise when Ari called him to schedule an off-the-record appointment. As if such a thing ever existed in espionage circles, Ari mused to himself.

As he fidgeted in a chair in Burke's office, wondering where the Colonel was, an OPs Center analyst poked his head in the door.

"Hi, Ari, could you come this way?"

Ari was surprised. "Where are we the going?"

"Room 13."

That certainly took Ari aback. He was expecting to have a confidential conversation with Burke in his office, not be invited into an area that was typically off-limits to 'ordinary' folk. Ari was led past the nerve center of Athena toward the corridor that had humorously been posted as 'No Man's Land'. This was the hall that led to the Board Room where the 13 board members, representing the original 13 founding colonies – now states – had their infrequent meetings.

Being a bit of a history buff, Ari had always wanted to spend some unsupervised time inside this room where many relics of the founding fathers were rumored to be housed, as well as many journals written by the founding members themselves.

Ari was now able to walk down the corridor. On one wall, a framed parchment caught his eye and he stopped to read it.

Sign that parchment. They may turn every tree into a gallows, every home into a grave and yet the words of that parchment can never die. For the mechanic in his workshop, they will be words of hope, to the slave in the mines – freedom.

If my hands were freezing in death, I would sign that parchment with my last ounce of strength. Sign, sign if the next moment the noose is around your neck, sign even if the hall is ringing with the sound of headman's ax, for that parchment will be the textbook of freedom, the bible of the rights of man forever.

John,

July 1776

Ari continued down the mahogany-lined corridor to the door of Room 13. He lifted his hand to knock as the door swung inward away from him. Instead of the conference room he was expecting, he was greeted by a library, within which 13 leather chairs sat around a large table.

The library was surrounded by an expanse of old books. The room smelled old, not in a dusty unclean way, but in a distinctly timeless, distinguished manner. The sense of leather and ancientness gave the room an identity all its own and it was as if the occupants of this room over the years had an eternal life of their own.

Sitting across from Ari were McQueen and Burke. Ari hesitated. It was not that he was speechless; he just didn't know exactly what to say. Burke was no help; he acknowledged Ari's arrival with a curt, "Ari."

To which Ari replied, "Tom."

Ari didn't have long to wait, as he looked over at McQueen, she greeted him with, "I expect you are surprised to see me here."

"Always a pleasure to see you, Jade. Am I in trouble?" A smirk began to play at the edges of his lips for McQueen's benefit. She may have been one of the big bosses as the Member from New York, but she was also a dear friend and his best friend's fiancée.

McQueen smiled back. "I understand you've been up to... Some of your tricks again, Ari. I am meant to scold you, but I just can't bring myself to be upset that an assassin is dead."

Burke put his elbows on the table in front of him, folding his hands in front of his face, but it couldn't quite hide the smile on his face, either.

"Consider me scolded, Jade." Ari bowed deeply in his mock apology.

"Good. Behave yourself," Jade said with a dismissive wave of her hand. "Now, I understand you have brought us company."

Ari looked at her dumbfounded. Even with all his time at Athena, he still thought he could keep a secret.

"And you left the precious thing in the car, Ari, your manners are better than that. Go, fetch!" Jade's smile was wide now, and Burke laughed out loud at Ari's consternation.

"So much for a private life," he said as he jogged out of the room and down the sacred hallway.

He soon returned with Jasmine in tow, trying unsuccessfully to straighten her clothing and un-ruffle her hair as he dragged her unceremoniously into the room at a fast clip -- so much so that she whipped right into the edge of the table, producing an audible "Ooof" of expelled air as she hit stomach first.

"Ari!" McQueen scolded him like a mother.

Jasmine righted herself and smoothed down her disheveled locks before looking up to find herself face to face with the Vice President of the United States.

"Hello, dear," McQueen said, coming around the table to lead Jasmine to a seat. Jasmine took her offered hand, looking from McQueen to Ari questioningly.

"Sorry, Jade. I fetched her as quickly as I could. Wouldn't want to keep such an important lady waiting."

McQueen shot him a look that could scorch plant life as she settled her young ward into a chair and reclaimed her own.

"There now, Jasmine, is it?"

Jasmine took her questioning eyes off Ari and put them back on McQueen. "Yes, Madam Vice President."

"Jade, please."

"Jade ..."

"I can imagine that this is all a bit ... strange to you."

"I am wondering what the Vice President of the United States is doing in a Mossad station. Yes, ma'am."

"Ah, that."

"I told you it was complicated," Ari said.

"I think perhaps you better un-complicate it for me," Jasmine replied slowly.

McQueen laughed, slapping the table. "I like her, Ari! She's got spunk."

Turning back to Jasmine, she said, "Allow me. You are in the headquarters of the Eyes of Athena. For all intents and purposes our dear Ari is on 'loan' from the Mossad to Athena, although I doubt we ever give him back."

Ari added a hardy "Harumph!" to her statement, and McQueen winked at him.

"He joined our little organization in '99 after assisting us with an unfortunate affair in Russia."

Now it was Jasmine's turn to interject. "That was only a few years after we met ... all that time I searched for you overseas, and you were here?" Jasmine said to him, hurt sounding in her voice.

Ari could not meet her eyes, and McQueen carried on, hoping to salvage the moment.

"We've kept him quite busy all over the world. You see, we are an American organization with international ties. Athena was created two centuries ago by the founding fathers of this nation to protect their most precious concepts of freedom – even from the government they created. We operate outside of the U.S. government, although we take full advantage of its resources through our own means." Here McQueen smiled again, knowing full well she was one of those means.

A light went off in Jasmine's head, "The symbol in the paper... That has something to do with you?"

"Yes, a way to contact us," McQueen confirmed. Her face saddened. "I am so sorry that my ruse to keep my cover was so costly for you. I had hoped Charlie would leave the story alone when Ed warned him off."

Jasmine's tears began to fall. "Charlie could never be warned off the scent of a big story."

"Yes, well, we will see to it that his paper tells the whole tale when we're done – at least the tale that can be told. Agreed?"

McQueen posed it as a question, but it was quite clear that there really was no option. Still, even a reporter who wanted to bring the truth to light had to understand when certain truths needed to stay buried for the sake of the people. Especially when one of those "people" was Ari.

"Of course."

"Excellent. Now beyond that, I understand that you wish to be part of this operation. You've been out of the field for a few years now, are you up to the challenge?"

"I am."

"Ari, are you capable of letting her do this?"

Ari looked from one to the other and back again. "To be honest, I don't know."

"Eh. Close enough." Responded Jade.

Both Burke and Ari turned to stare at her. "No man in love would ever willingly put his love in harm's way. I know from experience that you have to be out of your mind enough to go through with it anyway for the greater good. You know that Ari, you saw me and David struggle to protect one another and still stay on mission. It will be hard, but you can do it. I have faith in you."

"I'm glad one of us does," he said, astonished. Then he turned to Jasmine and took her hand. "If this is what you want, we'll make it happen."

"I want the scum who killed Charlie to pay."

He smiled a sad, knowing smile. "Revenge is an emotion I can work with."

18 THE ESCAPE

Alex and Heidi left the rooftop LZ – the helicopter with their tiny sons on board winding its way seaward – as they made their way downstairs. In the Chancery, the Marines were gathered in a semicircle getting their orders. Complete chaos reigned just outside the now locked doors.

Heidi looked at Alex with terror in her eyes, but found only determination looking back. Again, he sought a man with stripes so he could get an idea of the Marines' next move. This time it was a battle-hardened sergeant who looked at the weary little blond woman beside him with total shock.

"What in the Sam hill is she doing still here?"

"Long story, Sergeant. I'd like to remedy that problem, but you seem to have a situation brewing. Care to enlighten me?"

The sergeant paused to take Alex's measure. "I assume that means she is not a U.S. citizen?" he asked.

Alex nodded, and the sergeant nodded resolutely in return.

"Crowd broke through the gate. The Chancery doors are locked, but they won't hold forever. Our next move is to head up those stairs and get our keisters out of here. The Seabees on the sixth floor are locking the elevators, and we'll be locking the gates on each floor of the stairs as we go. I'd suggest you and and the little lady find a sneaky way out the back and fast."

Just as he said that, his group got the order to start up the stairs and into action. Alex could hear the crowd ripping at the Chancery doors. Without looking into Heidi's terrified face – knowing it would be his undoing – he took her hand and headed for the rear of the building.

They made their way out through the service exit. The choppers had stopped landing in the parking lot now. As the couple crossed the open area to the slash pile in the far corner of the compound, they could see around the front where a water tanker barreled through the Chancery doors and the crowd surged inside.

Alex looked to the roof where another chopper was preparing to leave. He prayed that Slade was on it. Turning back, he helped Heidi over the fence the way they had come in what seemed like days ago instead of hours. No one with the crowd paid them any attention, too intent on getting to the roof of the Embassy.

Alex indicated with his head for Heidi to follow him, and once outside the perimeter, they both crouched low, wary. There was no telling how long it would be before the North Vietnamese arrived, and there was always the risk of running into angry rogue Army of the Republic soldiers. They had a lot of empty space to cross before they would reach any kind of cover again.

Alex couldn't get the image out of his head. While the enemy hadn't yet entered the city, his mind was filled with what-ifs -- seeing the Embassy compound full of bodies of those left behind, the enemy carrying bayonet-armed rifles, determined to wipe any trace of the United States from Vietnam.

He didn't have to work hard to imagine the violence within the Embassy walls as they escaped. Inside, the crowd rushed the gates on each floor, crushing those in the front, desperate to reach the top. All pleading had ceased as they charged forward, bursting through the locks in terror of what was about to happen. There was nowhere to run; hiding would be pointless. The only course left to them would be to face their oncoming executioners.

The image of Billy and his jangling ring of janitor's keys came unbidden to Alex's all-too-vivid imagination. Billy had his back to the wall, his happy-go-lucky inebriated smile replaced with abject terror as he watched an NVC soldier approach, his bayonet-armed rifle held before him, walking determinedly toward Billy the collaborator.

Alex nearly lost focus on Heidi, so intent on that image in his mind's eye of Billy, waiting for death as the soldier advanced. A squeal of pain beside him let him know he had gripped Heidi's hand in a vice as his thoughts grew more dark and heinous.

The last frightful image his mind concocted before Heidi's sound brought him around was a desperate, neglected, abandoned Billy holding the barrel of a rifle as its bayonet sunk into his belly. He shook his head as he brought Heidi's wounded hand to his lips and kissed it. Focus, Alex. You can't save them. You must save her.

They used back alleys and dark streets to make their way down to the shoreline. For her part, Heidi never questioned Alex. She followed with total belief that he would see them through.

At the docks, the few remaining junks and sampans floated peacefully while their owners haggled, demanding outrageous prices. Alex found an old man willing to take them out to the waiting U.S. fleet for a very pretty penny.

As they climbed aboard, Heidi all but collapsed into her seat and lay against him, exhausted. He wrapped his arms around her and prayed she had the strength to finish this last leg of their journey.

"I know you're tired, Heidi. Soon we'll be back with the boys," he soothed, kissing the top of her head. Amazingly, she was already asleep, nuzzled into his neck.

It was just as well she slept. Even with the storm wind in their favor, travel on the junk was slow, and it was nearly noon before they came close to the fleet.

"Alex, I wonder which ship holds the twins," Heidi said, quietly. Alex looked at her, his face a mask of worry. She was so pale, and dark circles had formed under her eyes.

"Soon, my love," he said, kissing her forehead. "I'm sure they are fine, and we'll be holding them soon."

A loud crash aboard the nearest ship caught their attention. Someone had stolen one of the International Commission of Control and Supervision choppers and had been circling the deck of a U.S. ship. Unlike the Vietnamese Air Force pilots, he seemed unwilling to drop his evacuees and then ditch his ship into the sea. Instead, he bailed out 40 feet above the ship, and his Huey hit the side of the vessel. Luckily the ship wasn't damaged, but another chopper was.

In the meantime, another VNAF chopper had dropped his evacuees and was ditching his chopper into the sea – too close to their junk. With their attention riveted on the drama unfolding on the ship in front of them, they didn't notice the giant wave headed their way until it was too late.

Suddenly, they were in the water, and Alex felt Heidi's hand slip from his. He struggled to find the surface. Frantic, he searched for a sign of her, but saw nothing. Diving he tried to search for her in the murky sea.

When his bursting lungs forced him to the surface again, the junk captain was back in his drowning ship bailing and yelling for his crazy American passenger to get back on board.

"Heidi! Heidi!"

Alex dove again. He thought he saw the white of her dress and swam toward her. She was floating, barely below the surface, face down. He pulled her toward the top, turned her up and tried to revive her. Breathing into her mouth as the waves crashed over them.

He couldn't keep them both above the surface. He couldn't breathe, but he couldn't let go. He looked toward the ship where his sons may be sleeping, and took another breath to try and fill their mother's lungs – just as a wave crashed into him and filled his own lungs with water instead.

Alex slipped beneath the surface of the sea, still holding tightly to his beloved wife.

19 HERR DOKTOR ARRIVES

The Pink Adobe
November 5, 2014

Cooper walked up Old Santa Fe Trail, the cold desert evening chilling the bones of the most stalwart character. She made a beeline for the Pink Adobe, one of the more infamous and sought-after locations for a toddy and a steak Dundee and less than a mile from the plaza.

The Pink Adobe had been frequented by kings and noblemen as well as drunks and bums, and that was what gave the establishment its charm – never knowing who or what one might see there. The night was in full swing at the establishment with guests foolhardy enough to arrive without a reservation waiting hopefully in the small lobby and spilling out into the frigid street.

Cooper was wrapped warmly in a ski jacket and a thick woolen scarf with matching hat pulled low to help cover her face. A camera swung from her neck. To the side of the Pink Adobe was the Dragon Room Bar where many visitors chose to make an evening of it watching the trendy visitors and the Harleys going by.

The charm of Santa Fe had been maintained in that historic downtown for more than 400 years, forbidding any attempts to build any newfangled structures. Nestled in the Sangre de Cristo Mountains at the southern tip of the Rockies, old world charm often confronted modern-day reality there. In the winter, imported SUV's with roof racks full of skis drove through the Plaza on their way up to the slopes and the 'Après Ski' hangouts around town.

Likewise, many of the older, single males with the resources to buy a Harley brought their bikes out for an evening drag, wagging their pony tails as they arrived at the fashionable Dragon Room.

Cooper was not just sight-seeing; she was looking for someone. While Ari went to the bar to keep an eye out for their suspects (and keep an eye on Cooper), she was trying to take pictures of whoever arrived close to the time of the appointment Charlie had written down.

She had the Pink Adobe in view, biding her time and waiting for the Raven to appear. She moved a little closer so she could see the outside bar area where Ari was supposed to wait. As she glanced into the forecourt, the loud chatter of conversation, laughter and music from the live band wafted out to her. The outside area was warmed by a huge open-pit fire burning piñon and was sheltered from the wind by the tall walls.

Cooper was about to resume her faster pace when she noticed twin redheads saunter into the bar in short cocktail dresses exposing plenty of cleavage under expensive, open fur coats. They laughed extravagantly, wanting to be noticed. In between them stood a tall, dark, handsome escort dressed in a Tuxedo and drinking a glass of champagne. His groomed appearance showed debonair character — a player — but it was his eyes that drew her in.

Those eyes are not on his two dates, she thought, they are scanning the room. The attractive smile on his face hid his true purpose as he sought someone or something, as well. When his eyes landed on her, only for a brief second, she saw them flash recognition – just enough that only a well-trained observer would have seen it.

Cooper had a similar reaction, but her eyes opened wide, showing an unprofessional tinge of jealousy. Trying to conceal her feelings, she immediately bent down as if to pick something up, annoyed with herself.

Darn it! Do his escorts have to be two killer redheads?

She straightened up and was about to continue her walk up the slight incline when a stretch limo pulled up outside the Pink Adobe. The chauffeur literally jumped out of his seat to run around and open the door.

"Mein Herr, the Pink Adobe… Herr Doktor, we have arrived."

As the door opened, expensive cigar smoke wafted out of the car, and three well-dressed, older, slightly overweight bankers climbed out. They turned to wait for their patron almost reverently, Pollard and Brooks were among them.

Herr Doktor was the last to exit, and a slight chill seemed to accompany this trim, dark-haired man. Snake-eyes flicked to his chauffeur but did not echo the smile on his face.

"Danke, Willi."

He carried a wooden baton-like shaft with black animal hair on one end – somewhat like an antique oriental swat. The man turned to his guests using his baton as if he were conducting an orchestra, waving it toward the restaurant. The baton's black hair seemed to flick imaginary flies as he ushered them in.

Herr Doktor turned back to his aide. "Willi, please show my guests the way to our room, I'll be along in a moment."

Cooper continued her walk, trying to surreptitiously click as many shots as possible of the limo occupants as Willi herded them inside. Unnoticed by the arrivals, she was on the street 100 feet behind the limo.

In her ear, she heard Burke's voice, "You've got to get closer, Jasmine. We need a full facial on that guy to get an ID."

Just then, as Willi spoke to his boss, he removed his chauffeur's hat and bowed respectfully. In that moment, Cooper nearly lost it, recognizing one of the intruders she saw leaving the Philadelphia News building on the day Charlie died.

Her first impulse was to forget discipline and walk into the restaurant to find that assassin. Cooper knew if Ari saw her reacting off plan, he would abort the mission to come to her rescue, and Charlie's effort to leave a clue with his dying breath would be in vain. She couldn't do that to either of the men most important in her life. Charlie would understand; he would follow the story, she thought.

Willi, unaware of the recognition, looked to the Doktor's guests, "Follow me, Gentlemen."

She came back to herself a moment too late. They had entered the building without one more photo being taken.

"Jasmine? Do you copy?" She heard through her ear piece.

"Sorry, Colonel," she tried to respond as quietly and nonchalantly as possible. "I, err, got distracted."

"Stay on point, girl. You're going to get yourself killed."

Inside the lobby, people made way for the over-sized chauffeur leading his line of guests to the banquet room. The party of bankers walked single file behind him, as if to their doom.

As they entered, the leading banker asked Willi, "Where shall I sit?"

The big man took great delight in pointing over to each place setting with its paper name tag in front of the place mat. Each tag had only a five-digit number followed by a space and a ten-digit number.

"Gentlemen, please find the number that you recognize."

Willi tried to hide his delight at the reaction of each banker as they realized what he meant. They sought their own tag, and one by one, took a seat behind their Swiss bank account number. A look of complete anxiety set in on each face.

The bankers gave each other only fleeting glances, so flustered they could not look each other in the eye. Comprehension spread slowly, as they all realized they had similar numbers instead of names on their tags.

Brooks was the most perturbed. Pollard was seated beside him. "Looks like we are not the only Governors with Swiss bank accounts."

"We are screwed." Pollard looked over at Brooks and the other banker, then added, "You do know that if the authorities find out we have Swiss bank accounts, we could get 15 years or more? Tax evasion is not pretty."

While Willi took care of the bankers in the restaurant, Herr Doktor slipped around the side to the bar where Ari was enjoying a cocktail with his twin redheads.

When he entered the bar, he was changed. Gone was the wary man with no smile in his eyes; he now had a spring in his step as if he were 20 years younger, eager for an encounter.

At the same time, another individual recognized Herr Doktor and made his way purposefully through the crowd toward him.

Ari recognized the Raven, and carefully, so as to be not seen, he emptied his glass of champagne in a flower pot and moved to the bar for a refill. He had been taught all these years to never put himself at a disadvantage when confronting an enemy — like turning his back to an assailant. He hated to do it, but there was no other way to even attempt to remain unseen and unrecognized and still keep within earshot. He positioned himself at the bar with his back turned to the deadly Raven, who could easily have slipped a knife between his ribs.

His target greeted the new arrival with a big smile and a bear hug, and then they held each other at arm's length.

"How good to see you, Pieter," the other man said. Ari made note of the Raven's first name.

Gone was the act of the eccentric with the baton, and instead there was just a man meeting a long-missed friend.

"Is everything going according to your plan?"

Ari glanced up into the mirror trying to get a good look at the mysterious Herr Doktor and was surprised to see such striking similarities between the two men. His face was familiar. Burke had not yet received any photos to identify him from Jasmine's camera, so they hadn't gotten anything more on Herr Doktor's true identity. He must be a brother, Ari thought. Surely a twin. His mind reeled.

"Yes, I have the bankers inside waiting for me. I can't tell you everything now, but after I have them back at the ranch tonight, I'll update you."

"I'm starving; let's go have dinner. I hear you have a surprise for them!"

Herr Doktor and the Raven hurried off to dine with his guests, leaving Ari relieved they didn't recognize him but none the wiser for having overheard the conversation.

Cooper continued to walk up the Old Santa Fe Trail outside the restaurant.

When she was far enough beyond the restaurant to not be seen, she crossed the street, turned around, and started walking back down Old Santa Fe Trail toward the Pink Adobe, but on the other side of the street.

Inside the Pink Adobe, Outside the Banquet Room

Before entering the banquet room, the twins spoke privately.

"My brother, you are going to get me into a lot of trouble if you keep using my Nom de Guerre for your escapades."

Pieter tried to keep his tone light, but tension sneaked in despite his best efforts.

"A dicky-bird told me you used the Raven's calling card during your attempt to kill Ari Cohen."

Wolfgang's face turned cold and suspicious. He made no attempts at civility in his tone. "How did you know about that?"

Pieter did not answer, just looked with concern at his brother and waited for an explanation.

"I thought it was quite funny, actually," Wolfgang said, waiving away the issue as if it were a pesky insect.

"Our parents died a long time ago, Wolfgang; nothing is going to bring them back. Surely, you don't want them to kill me, too, do you?"

Wolfgang looked venomous, so angry his face flushed scarlet.

"I will have my revenge; they must pay," he said, hissing out every word.

"But the people who made those decisions are all dead. Who do you seek vengeance on?"

"The American people!" Wolfgang spat.

"They are a disease upon the world, my brother. Make no mistake," Wolfgang added venomously as he searched his brother's face intensely, "nothing has changed since they left our parents to die – left them all to face the wrath of the North Vietnamese."

"By the way, Kwok Kong told me you tried to buy him off, stop him from assassinating the Italian Finance Minister..."

The sudden shift in Wolfgang's demeanor was frightening even to Pieter, who found himself pinned to the wall by his twin's cold stare, the sing-song of his flat, even tone grating on every one of Pieter's frayed nerves.

"Wolfgang, I was trying to protect you, to save you before you committed the first murder. You are going to get us killed."

"Yes, well, it did you no good. He was loyal to me, and the money you gave him funded his second assassination," his brother said with a smile of pure evil.

As soon as the smile appeared, it was gone.

"We must hurry," Wolfgang said with a wave of his hand dismissing the subject. "Our guests will be getting impatient."

He was Herr Doktor again, as he started toward the banquet room, but Pieter took hold of his arm.

"You do know who was standing next to us at the outside bar, don't you?"

Wolfgang immediately turned to his brother, growling, "Who?"

"Ari Cohen."

Pieter felt a shiver run down his spine as he watched the reaction from his brother.

◆ ◆ ◆

The Pink Adobe, Inside the Banquet Room

The banquet room was closed to the public with a crackling fire blazing at one end. The bar held a table just long enough to seat three people on either side and for the wait staff to pass behind their guests unhindered.

The dark red walls were adorned with western paraphernalia and old photos that told the story of the Santa Fe Trail and its early pioneers.

Herr Doktor's demeanor had returned to the affable eccentric, he shooed the wait staff out, waiving his elephant hair baton at them. "Come back in five minutes to serve our appetizers."

He joined the bankers already seated around the table drinking cocktails.

"We will not be using anyone's real name tonight. Secrecy is paramount. The three of you might recognize each other, be careful with your tongues. There is danger at every turn. If you need to refer to my special guest, call him..."

Herr Doktor bent to his flair for the dramatic, pausing to look around the room, his audience hanging on his every word. "Call him... Let's call him, Pieter."

The Raven was strangely quiet. As he watched his brother's performance, he wondered to himself how hate could change a man so. How long could he continue to protect his brother without putting his own mortal life in danger?

His brother was almost beside himself, and as if conducting a symphony, he began revving up for a crescendo. "You are probably all wondering why I brought you here." He stopped, laughing quietly at the cliche. "Your name tag should have answered that question. You all have been stealing money from American taxpayers, depositing it in your personal Swiss accounts. You are all thieves -- thieves in suits -- but still thieves."

He continued to play his audience, pausing dramatically as the bankers reflected dejectedly on their predicament. "Before the next meeting of the Federal Reserve, I will send you instructions. You will follow my orders precisely. You are going to limit the ability of your government to borrow money. If you agree, no one will learn of your indiscretions."

At the disclosure of the price these thieves were forced to pay, there was an ominous silence. Simon Brooks was the first to react,

"But.....But that could shut down the government, surely you can't be serious?" Nervous anxiety causing him to almost stutter every word.

Herr Doktor was now openly gloating, delighted as the enormity of the bankers' predicament finally hit them front and center. He relished his next word. "Exactly." The Her Doktor paused again for dramatic effect, eying everyone at the dining table.

Roger Pollard was the first to break the ominous silence. Still refusing to fathom the depth of his predicament, not willing to believe there was no way out, he said, "And if we don't agree?"

Herr Doktor's cold, dark smile returned, and his hard gaze bore into Pollard's. "Ah, well, there are always consequences for our actions, are there not, Sir?" As if Pollard's refusal would be a mere gnat to be swatted with his baton.

Then he picked up a little bell at his side, calling the wait staff to bring in the appetizers. The rapidity with which the Doktor could change his moods was frightening all his guests, but most noticeably his brother Pieter, who was dumbfounded, and getting more worried by the second.

"Gentlemen, let's leave business to the side for the time being. I have ordered a local delicacy for you all to enjoy."

The waiters brought in trays of freshly fried food, the light aroma permeating the air. Three waiters put their trays down revealing individual plates of tiny, battered-fried finger foods.

Pieter remained silent, but the faint buzz from his cell phone broke the spell of the moment and caught his brother's attention. Pieter nodded at him in apology and looked at the number.

He rose, saying, "Excuse me, Herr Doktor, but I have some pressing business to take care of."

He nodded politely to every guest as he took his leave.

"Good evening, gentlemen."

"You won't be coming back?" his brother seemed hurt.

"Afraid not, goodnight." Pieter felt an enormous relief as the cell phone call had answered a prayer for him, "Please God get me outta here!"

The wait staff resumed serving and when everyone had a plate, the Doktor sat back down and, after a moment's hesitation that his brother would miss all the fun, he went on with a theatrical gesture. "I hope you all enjoy!"

"What are these?" Pollard asked.

"That is for you to tell me. I hear that bankers spend half their days at three-martini lunches, so you should all be expert gourmets."

Brooks leapt at an excuse to change the conversation, so as to not dwell on his predicament. "I know! I know! Calamari. Is that it?"

Herr Doktor responded almost angrily at Brooks, "You are not paying attention, Sir. I said local delicacy. Where would one find squid in the middle of the New Mexico desert?"

Herr Doktor and his guests maintained a silence after that, all stoically chewing.

The fire took center stage, hissing as fresh sap was released by the slightly green piñon wood and projecting eerie shadows on the inhabitants of the room.

After everyone had finished and the clatter of cutlery against china plates was over, Herr Doktor rang the bell again.

"Clear the plates, please."

The wait staff tended to his requests with military precision, and once cleared, the banquet room doors were closed again. As soon as the guests were alone, a chorus of curiosity erupted.

"What was that appetizer?" was echoed across the room, the men looking to make light of their dire straits and stall any further discussion.

Herr Doktor looked at his guests, eying his prey with a sense of revulsion and thought to himself, How soft these bankers are, not used to any headwind or controversies in their lives, not really worthy opponents for someone like me.

He took another dramatic pause, his evil smile spreading. Already some of the men were looking pale. Watching for their reactions with eager anticipation, he announced, "Baby rattlesnakes, a local delicacy that the early settlers used to eat."

The Doktor watched with delight as a look of horror spread on each man's face, They are trying not to believe.

"You are kidding aren't you?"

"Actually, no, quite serious. Did you know that baby rattlesnakes are born live? At birth, they have enough venom to kill a man. We tried to remove the poison glands, but you know little baby rattlers... they wriggle so much... Then we drop them live into hot oil. Very tasty, don't you think?"

One banker rose noisily from his seat and rushed out of the dining area, napkin held to his mouth. The remaining men shared looks of shock and revulsion. But all were petrified now and certain of the evil intent of their host.

One tried again, "You are joking aren't you?"

Herr Doktor was exuberant. In a vile mocking tone, he said, "I'm sorry, my attempt at a little humor was not appreciated..."

He looked around at his guests, reveling in their disgust and fear. The Doktor paused briefly as the banker who had rushed out rejoined the table.

"I see we don't have the same sense of humor. Actually, yes, you just ate baby rattlesnakes. Scrumptious don't you think?"

He felt like a spider slinking across his vibrating web as his next meal struggled, held firmly in his sticky plot, unable to escape. His face grew deadly serious.

"Oh, alright. Do be still, will you. You aren't going to die – at least not tonight – but it is possible that you are going to have a severe case of indigestion, perhaps even for 15 years or so."

Pausing again, clearly enjoying his moment, he said, "That is unless you do exactly as I say."

He looked each guest in the eye again gaining strength from their anxiety. "Now that I have your attention ... Shall we have no more talk of escaping consequences?"

Not a word broke the prophetic silence.

Fools, he thought to himself, none of them know the poison is harmless in their digestive system ... unless one of them has ulcers or mouth sores. Hmmm. A banker with ulcers, he smiled evilly, what could be the odds? Oh, and wouldn't that just be a shame.

The men watched an evil smile again spread across the Doktor's face again.

♦ ♦ ♦

Outside the restaurant Pieter Stangl re-dialed the number that had called him in the restaurant.

"Mr. ... Raven is it? Thank you for calling me back," the silky feminine voice purred.

"Happy to oblige, Ma'am."

"The first half of your prophecy has come stunningly true, and I think we may need to talk."

"Yes, I see your point, but phones are... so public, what did you have in mind?"

"I will be having an intimate brunch tomorrow morning at 10:00 A.M. in my Georgetown House. I'd be delighted if you could join me."

"It would be my pleasure."

Without so much as a goodbye for his brother, Pieter headed for his rental car and the airport.

♦ ♦ ♦

Cooper asked for a table on the veranda at the Upper Crust restaurant across the street from the Pink Adobe. No one else was outside, everyone having abandoned the cold, beautiful night for the warmth of the indoors.

She chose a chair that allowed her to see the front lobby of the Pink Adobe and sat down with some obvious relief.

As she began to lower her scarf and ease her hat off to make herself comfortable, she felt the presence of someone coming up behind her. Assuming it was the beverage waiter, she turned to order.

"I'll have a glass of —"

She looked up and stopped mid-sentence, taken completely unaware and unsure what to say next to the two hulking men looming over her. She recognized the first as the chauffeur she identified earlier, and the second was a good fit for his accomplice she had seen in Philadelphia.

"Silence," Willi whispered, his menacing stare boring a hole through her.

They wouldn't dare do anything here, Cooper wagered to herself. She tried to brazen it out. "I've had enough surprises for one —"

"Your camera, please," Willi said, holding out his hand insistently and punctuating his demand by placing his other hand on the back of her neck, applying sharp, intense pressure.

He certainly seems to be the leader of these two thugs, she thought, but as she opened her mouth to object, she felt the pressure at her neck release, and Willi stepped aside. She looked up at him as the other bodyguard delivered one quick chop to the spot where Willi's hand had been. It was so quick and unexpected that no one noticed anything.

Cooper slumped forward, out for the count. Willi picked her up, while Fritz grabbed her camera and handbag. A waiter finally came out of the restaurant to take her order, looking surprised at the two men.

"Too much mountain air for my friend," he said, handing the stunned waiter a hundred dollar bill.

♦ ♦ ♦

Ari had not been able to follow the twins to the banquet room, where a lack of places to hide made it impossible. He had instead turned to look for Jasmine, just in time to see her carried off the veranda across the street. He found it rather incredible that no one had sounded an alarm with local police.

From the shadows, he watched Herr Doktor's henchmen carry off Jasmine into a darkened alleyway — away from any prying eyes — and load her into the trunk of the waiting limo. He stood seemingly emotionless except for the visible tightening of his jaw and the constant knuckle-popping clenching of his fist. It took a supreme effort to stay put and not run to rescue her. Momentarily, he stopped clenching his right hand and reached up to feel his short-distance blow pipe, secured in his inside coat pocket.

It would be so easy to finish off those lumbering beasts, messing with my girl, Ari thought to himself, his face reflecting his rage. But I'm sure not going to let them out of my sight, even if that's not what we agreed with Burke.

The limo pulled around to the front of the building, and Ari slipped around front without being noticed to watch as Herr Doktor and his bankers were ushered out once more. The Raven was nowhere to be seen.

The limo in which Jasmine was imprisoned headed out of town on the Old Santa Fe Trail. Ari felt he had no time to waste and as quickly as possible, he rushed to his rental car parked in an alley across the street.

He slid into the driver's seat and started the car, then pulled out his PDA with the tracking sensor Jasmine had placed under the fender of the limo beeping back strongly. He quickly took up pursuit.

The Old Santa Fe Trail in this part of town is barely wide enough for two horse-drawn carriages to pass, let alone two modern gas-guzzlers. Ari drove recklessly fast through the winding road toward Old Pecos and Interstate 25. As the signal from the trace device beeped louder, he slowed his pursuit in order to remain unseen.

Suddenly, the complete silence inside Ari's car was blown apart by a sound like the bells of Armageddon. The well-trained super-spy jumped in surprise and let out a little squeal. His phone was ringing with an unearthly tone he had never heard before and certainly had not programmed.

Ari picked it up almost afraid of who might be on the other end. "Hello?"

"Taking a drive, Ari?"

"What did you do to my phone, Tom?"

"Not the point, son. In 500 yards, you will see an Episcopal Church parking lot. Pull over and park; we need to talk. We need to stay on plan, Ari. She volunteered, remember?"

"But if they hurt her –"

"If they spot you following them, they will kill her. Pull over. We have an eye in the sky on the car you are following; we won't lose it."

Ari didn't like it. Anguish and concern was evident in his voice, but he pulled over in the parking lot. "What do you want me to do?"

"I want you to go back to your hotel and enjoy those two redheads. We don't want Herr Doktor to know we are watching."

"Yeah. That's not happening, Tom."

"Just go back to Santa Fe, Ari."

As Burke moved to hang up the phone, he heard Ari's voice again. "Oh, and Tom?"

"Yes, Ari."

"You will remove that hellish noise from this phone."

The line went dead as Burke chuckled despite the situation. He watched the GPS tracker also installed on Ari's phone show that his agent was doing as he had been instructed.

21 ONCE BITTEN

Road Outside Santa Fe to Rattlesnake Ranch

It was all that mattered, Ari had come. His eyes were closed in concentration. A loving smile parting his lips into a heartfelt smile. He was playing his cherished violin. It was a love song, and joyful tears rimmed her eyes as she was serenaded by the man she loved.

Pedestrians stopped on the jogging trail to watch and listen, some of them couples.

She saw another woman in the crowd looking at the man she was with, an unmistakable glare of jealousy on her face. Why didn't you think of that? Her sneer seemed to say, but her boyfriend was oblivious. Cooper was gloating, prideful that it was her man – her Ari – playing the melody for her.

Without warning it was all gone. She felt a large crack on the back of her head and opened her eyes to darkness.

"Did that jealous bimbo on the path smack me on the back of the head?" she whined, trying to reach up to feel the rising knot on her skull.

She listened, finally realizing as the fog lifted that she must be in a car. But the darkness, the smells...

"No, I'm locked in the trunk of a car," she said to herself groggily.

Cooper felt another hard knock on the back of her head. It was still dark. As she concentrated, it felt as if she were wedged up against something. Her hands felt the texture and curve of the object as her mind put together that is must be a tire, and the hard edges jabbing into her back were likely a tire jack, and it was no wonder her spine ached.

She paid more attention to the sound of tires bumping over a rocky road. Now she was being thrown around even more violently by the bumps and tried to clear the groggy feeling from her head. She had to concentrate if she wanted to avoid being knocked out. Slowly her memory returned – she was about to order a drink at a restaurant, then the murderer and his accomplice appeared. Realization crept into her mind; she was being kidnapped, taken away by the Doktor's goons.

Then her mind was on fire with questions. Did Athena see my abduction? Did Ari notice what had happened? Was he too distracted by those disgusting redheads someone organized for his cover?

"If I find out who got him two voluptuous redheads, I will personally strangle them," she growled into the darkness.

Her hands were bound behind her back and she was trapped, nearly unable to move. The next bump threw her around so that her hands were over the jack, and she felt the rough edge with her fingers. With great difficulty she edged over onto her side and could now move her hands and the plastic cuff up and down over the rough edge of the jack, shearing it.

Cooper tried to think back to her training, but it was so long ago and her brain was so foggy. What to do if you are kidnapped by the enemy?

At the time, she had cursed her instructors, but now, she thought back to that loud-mouthed sergeant who had insisted she learn and train and repeat until it was second-nature to her. It was that sergeant who had recommended her to the CIA as his star pupil. She said a secret thank-you to him.

The Air Force training hadn't dealt much with being locked in the trunk of a car, but the CIA had taken care of that side. Cooper tried to gauge the speed of the vehicle, asking herself if she could she see any light. She tuned her senses to the slightest clue.

As the limo bumped down the track, every bump jarred the trunk a little, and she saw little glimpses of moonlight. OK then a moonlit night, I should be able to see.

She listened for other traffic but couldn't hear any. Must be a private road.

Suddenly, she felt a little give in the cuffs she was trying to break, and with a supreme effort, they separated. She was feeling better.

The incessant pounding of the tires on the road diminished as if the vehicle was slowing down. Momentarily, the pounding stopped. Must be arriving, wherever the heck we're going.

Cooper tried to calculate how far they had come since she was woken by the smack to the back of her head. About 15 minutes at about 30 miles per hour, that meant 7 or 8 miles back to the highway.

Piece of cake, that is, if I can just get away from these thugs, she thought optimistically. Another thought started to make her fret with anger. I bet they don't rattle their bosses around at this speed when they drive him down this road. They must be doing this on purpose, trying to soften me up. I'll get even with those two thugs if it's the last thing I do.

Unknown to Cooper, the limo had pulled into the Rattlesnake Ranch driveway.

In the trunk, she felt the car slow down and take a slight turn, followed by breaking to a halt. She turned in the trunk so that her feet were facing the back, ready to attack whoever opened the lid. As the car bounced with the passengers exiting, she heard Willi and his accomplice talking but couldn't understand what they said. Sounds like German, maybe?

She heard footsteps approach the trunk, and Willi pushed the lock. He was relaxed, thinking Cooper was out cold and cuffed. As he reached to lift up the lid, he bent over.

Suddenly the trunk lid fired upward, and Willi hardly had time to react before the heavy metal slammed into his head, smacking him hard. He was ejected backward by the force of the thrust from Cooper, his face bleeding, temporarily stunned.

Fritz heard the commotion, but was too surprised and far away, unloading some cases from the car and walking toward the front entrance. Cooper vaulted out of the trunk like a gymnast, landing almost on top of the stunned Willi.

She had armed herself with the tire jack, and as she jumped out, unsure whether Willi was unconscious or momentarily stunned, she took no chances. Landing on top of him, she pulled her arm back and launched a powerful blow with the jack to the side of Willi's head, knocking him out cold.

Quickly she checked him out, reaching inside his coat and pulling out his gun. For good measure, she launched another blow and bashed him over the head again.

Cooper charged away from the ranch house up the driveway, as Fritz recovered his wits. He growled indignantly at seeing what happened to his friend, pulled out his sidearm and began firing at Cooper. The gunshot bursts landed at Cooper's feet, and she increased her speed, starting to zigzag.

The driveway was lit by lamp posts along the perimeter, making Cooper an easy target as another shot landed too close and she ducked for cover behind some rocks just visible in the moonlight.

Someone else joined Fritz in his search for her, bringing a strong flashlight and exposing the rocks where she was hiding. She heard a shout of discovery coming from her pursuers, but couldn't understand what they were saying.

Don't these buffoons speak English? But the searchlight exposed her, and instinctively, she sprinted in the opposite direction and away from the driveway.

Suddenly, she howled in pain. Looking down at her leg, she had run into buckhorn cactus and been lanced by several spines of the painful venom. She continued to run over the rocky, unfamiliar terrain, slowing down considerably now that she remembered she was in a semi-arid desert full of prickly and venomous things.

A noisy volley of gunshots kicked up vegetation and rocks all around her. The pursuit and shots were funneling her back toward the ranch, away from freedom. She sensed movement immediately ahead and veered to one side just as a second thug launched a baseball bat at her middle. The tip just grazed her as she went down, somersaulted sideways head-over-heels and was back on her feet running with that thug in close pursuit.

Cooper sped along the rocky path lit only by moonlight. She slowed again when she realized they didn't know where she was, but she didn't know where they were either. All around her she could hear footsteps echoing and the maddening voices of the unknown pursuers speaking a language she didn't understand. She crept quietly along.

Out of the blue, a giant rock flew at her. Startled, she jumped back and fired a shot in its direction. She had been frightened into giving away her position, only to hear a second thug on the path in front of her. He shone a flashlight on her trail, blocking access.

Another thug was shining a flashlight blocking her retreat. She looked 90 degrees to one side and saw a steep climb up an almost solid rock face. The other direction looked like it headed to the edge of the mesa they were on and a sharp drop.

I'm not giving up; I'd would rather – Decision made. She retreated five paces toward the sheer cliff, then ran like the devil-possessed toward the drop-off. As she reached the edge, she jumped for all she was worth.

Gliding through the air, legs still churning as if she were running, her parabolic accent was soon interrupted by gravity, and as she accelerated toward Terra Firma. It was too dark to see well, but her intention was to keep running on impact.

It was too difficult to judge, and when she hit the ground unexpectedly fast, she couldn't keep her balance. She rolled over, going forward into a somersault-like movement. Quickly, she regained her feet, astonished that she was in one piece.

Another thug appeared to her side, and just as she saw him in her peripheral, his truncheon hit her on the back of the head. Cooper went down, out cold for the second time not even knowing what hit her.

◆ ◆ ◆

Cooper woke the next morning aching all over. She opened her eyes warily, trying to discern where she was. Instinctively, she rubbed the bump on the back of her head, but quickly she removed her hand, wincing and screwing her eyes up tight.

She decided to lay still and asses her situation. She estimated she had been gone at least 12 hours. Ari must be frantic, at least he better be!

She giggled and winced at the explosion of painful color behind her closed eyes. Colonel Burke and the Athena team should have been able to track her location, so that meant her mission was at least half accomplished. They knew where the guy they had called "Herr Doktor" last night was headed, and where he most likely took the bankers.

The only other Intel Burke wanted, as he put it, was to "Find out what this lunatic is really up to!"

Burke also wanted to know what part the Raven played in this venture. Cooper had yet to see the mysterious Raven, but she had been told he was wealthy, although it was difficult to penetrate Swiss privacy laws to find out exactly what his financial interests were. Burke wanted to know who was pulling the strings here and who this Doktor really was.

Cooper tried to get her mind back to the present, hoping the good guys would arrive and Ari would rescue her. That few moments of reflection had allowed her throbbing head to subside; now she could get on with her mission.

She sat up in bed and took a good look around. The first thing she noticed was that she was wearing a man's pajamas, and a faint shiver ran down her spine. She knew she hadn't put them on, so someone had undressed her.

The bedroom walls were decorated with colorful Navajo rugs, way too many of them for her taste. The door to what she assumed was the house was a heavy, weathered, colonial-Mexican style with old heavy hinges that looked like a Nineteenth Century blacksmith made them. Slowly her memory returned and she saw herself taking a risky leap off the mesa trying to escape from Willi and his accomplices.

"Where the heck am I?" she wondered aloud. She sighed loudly, realizing she must have been recaptured and was back at the Doktor's ranch. As she inched up further in the bed, she groaned in pain, her ribs rebelling against the sudden pressure. Now her temporary amnesia was totally gone, and she remembered the leap from the mesa top, running at full speed after she recovered from a hard landing, and the alarm bells going off as someone stepped in front of her. She was moving too fast to change direction, and then nothing, until she woke up in someone else's PJs.

Cooper heard heavy footsteps in the hallway and a guard knocked on her door. "Be ready in 5 minutes... for breakfast."

"I don't eat breakfast."

"You will today, Fraulein. You will today. Five minutes."

Cooper could almost feel the sneer of contempt as he turned to walk noisily back the way he had come.

◆ ◆ ◆

Herr Doktor's office at Rattlesnake Ranch was a huge affair, large floor-to-ceiling bay windows looked out over the mesa that Cooper assumed she had tried to leap the night before.

She had been led into the vast salon by the massive bodyguard, Willi.

He was in a foul mood, handling her roughly as he brought her into the Doktor's office and constantly fingering the massive welt he had on the side of his head, glaring at Cooper every time he winced.

Willi looked like the type of man who was accustomed to handing out rough treatment to women but not being on the receiving end of such violence. And it appeared he didn't like the turn-about.

He led Cooper to a seat in front of the Doktor's expansive, rustic desk. Finally, he looked at her. "Sit, don't move; don't talk."

Cooper looked over at Herr Doktor. He was sitting at the desk watching a cable news channel. His desk was three rock steps above the rest of the room and on top of it, perched two large glass cages, one on each side. From Cooper's angle, sitting back in her chair, she could only see the top of the cages.

The Doktor didn't bother to look at her. A half-moon-shaped wall behind him was covered with floor-to-ceiling bookshelves almost wrapping the man in a coat of books.

In front of his desk and behind Cooper, the line of floor-to-ceiling windows faced out on a small creek running through the property. Beyond the creek was the mesa, its walls lined with large, smooth, red rocks and cacti. As Cooper watched the view, she marveled that she had been lucky enough to miss landing in a patch of that cacti when she jumped.

The Doktor's attention was riveted on the television screen, and Cooper turned to follow his gaze to the news program airing.

"October comes every year. For the U.S. stock and bond markets, that's not always a good thing. October 1987 is a date that many of you will remember. October of 1907 is a date you'll only respect and remember if you've studied economic history.

"In October of 1907, a panic on Wall Street sparked a nationwide run on banks and nearly halved the value of the New York Stock Exchange in a matter of days."

As the speaker finished his discourse, the Doktor's gaze turned momentarily to Cooper. "I hear you have been making a nuisance of yourself?"

He didn't wait for a response before continuing with his eyes focused on the glass cages on his desk. He reached over to the one on the left side of his desk, opened a little access door on the top and reached in to pull out a small white mouse by the tail.

Cooper recoiled at the sight of the frantically scrambling little rodent, definitely not what she expected. He lifted it up in front of his face, as if trying to see into its soul, but the little mouse was moving too much, turning in circles. As its terrified movements caused its body to wind up in one direction, its tail would get too tight and twisted, all of a sudden, reaching maximum torque, the direction would then reverse, spinning the mouse in the opposite direction at greater speed.

The Doktor then opened the glass container on the other side of his desk and leaned over to look at the creature inside.

Curious, Cooper sat up in her seat and strained to peek onto his desk. The Doktor still held the frightened mouse in his left hand as he leaned closer to the container on the right, muttering in a revoltingly loving tone, "Feeding time, my lovely."

Cooper could see inside the glass container, as a darkish shadow began to slink into the light. A thin, slimy tongue flicked forward, sampling the air. With a feeling of total repugnance, Cooper realized it was a Western Rattlesnake. Alarm bells began ringing as she watched, mesmerized. Cooper couldn't help but shiver as her revulsion for reptiles asserted itself, sending electric jolts down her spine. While the snake uncoiled, its dark, soulless eyes appeared to focus on the Doktor.

The rattlesnake's tongue flicked in and out as it uncoiled, sampling the air. The mouse by now was struggling even more violently since it had sensed the snake. But its body was still turning so fast, it only caught a momentary glance once every rotation. The mouse arched its body backwards trying to look at the snake. The snake's infra-red sensors signaled dinner time, but also warned the snake of the human presence around its lair. As a warning, it began to rattle its tail, the rattling becoming more rhythmic and intense and the time between rattles shortening.

Herr Doktor moved his hand with the petrified mouse toward the snake, almost within reach. The snake continued to slide forward. Cooper noted the Doktor seemed as fascinated as she, watching, anticipating.

In a move that shocked them both with its intensity, the Rattler struck, a lightning fast thrust hitting the mouse. The move was so sudden that although they knew it was coming, they both jumped, and the Doktor's involuntary reaction was to drop the mouse and jump back in his chair.

"There you go, my beauty, breakfast. Don't I always feed you first?"

Cooper was repulsed by the affectionate tone of the Doktor. For the first time since she entered the office, she had his full attention.

"I do like a little adrenalin before my breakfast. It does so stimulate my appetite. Now, what is this business about you and your pesky little camera?"

22 THE RAVEN COMES TO BRUNCH

Georgetown, Washington D.C.
November 6, 2014

Georgetown – after the mad morning-rush-hour when residents make an insane dash to the nation's capital – becomes a sleepy, quaint town. Pieter Stangl had decided to have his taxi drop him off a block away from his final destination so he could enjoy the walk.

Never one to take risks unnecessarily, he did his best to case the area, scanning to see if his approach was being watched. He walked past his final destination on the far side of the street before crossing and approaching the address he had been given.

The closer he came, the more he was sure he could smell fresh-baked pastries with a touch of cinnamon, as crazy as it seemed. Perhaps she really is going to serve me brunch, he thought.

He knocked on the door, and was surprised when the Vice President answered it herself.

Surprised, he asked, "Where is your security detail, Ma'am?"

"Ma'am seems so formal and aging," she said, stepping aside to let him in. "Please call me Jade, and as for my Secret Service agents, I have an... arrangement with them."

As she let the Raven into her home, he took a deep breath. "Do I smell pastry?"

"I thought you might get fed up with hotel food; I know I do."

He smiled a genuine smile, the first in many days. Her reception was so disarming.

"Let's go to the kitchen. Good pastries wait for no one."

McQueen took Stangl's coat and lead him down the hall and into a sunny kitchen, where he was surprised by the generous spread that waited.

"Ah, but don't be too impressed..." McQueen said, noting the impressed look on his face. "I don't cook, a fact you would learn all too quickly. This is all the work of a very accomplished member of my personal staff. A lovely man who once served as a personal aide to the Russian President."

Stangl laughed heartily then. "You stole the President's aide?"

"Let's just say that Gregor was quite taken with me during my visits and was truly wasted in President Bronsky's service."

Stangl thought to himself then that her enchanting smile must be her most disarming of all her political skills.

"Yes, I can absolutely see how that could happen," he said, as they were seated.

"Well, Mr. ... Come now, shall I continue to call you Raven?"

"No, of course not. You may call me Pieter."

"Good, good. Well, then, Pieter, now that we have some of Gregor's wonderful pastries in hand, perhaps our distasteful discussion may go down a little sweeter?"

She took a delicate bite of her apple strudel and smiled.

"Tell me, how did you know the Italian Finance Minister was going to be assassinated?"

Stangl was just taking his first bite and hesitated, but only for a second, before continuing with his scrumptious pastry.

It will give me more time to think how best to answer her question. He still had one nagging concern. Is she a lady of honor? Had she kept her word? The one commodity most lacking in my world is trust, he thought to himself.

As he savored his pastry, he watched McQueen, trying to figure her out. It reminded him of his favorite play when he was a young teenager learning English. His adopted family had spoken mostly Sicilian at home, and he had been shielded from public schools out of his mother's fear that someone might take him from her. But he had an insatiable mind and had begged her for an education that he could use to help the family.

His father had seen him as an asset he could use, and in his teens, a tutor had been brought in to prepare him toward a college education. He had a voracious mind and had been a stellar student, eventually earning a place at Harvard.

During those years, he had discovered William Shakespeare and his much acclaimed "Richard III." After being knocked to the ground in the fever of battle, Richard had cried out, "A horse, a horse, my kingdom for a horse!"

Pieter was thinking as he summed up his situation with McQueen, Trust, trust, my kingdom for a trustworthy ally!

He saw her watching him, as well. He smiled to himself. She must be wondering, can I trust this Machiavellian character?

Once he had thought through his response, he replied, "I find myself in a difficult situation, Jade."

With delicate care, he wiped the corners of his mouth, providing another long pause.

She took that moment to reassure him. "We are aware of your... connections with the Sicilian Mafia here. I am sure you are not new to difficult situations."

He merely nodded his head slightly, agreeing with her conclusion and confirming that he was dealing with a shrewd stateswoman.

"Have you kept your word, not revealed my identity to anyone, not even your Secret Service?"

"As you can see, I have even laid myself at your mercy," she said, sweeping her arms widely to denote her empty home. "Your secret is safe with me. So what is this 'difficult situation' you speak of?"

His face took on a faraway look, as if he were watching events play out in his past.

"It is a very long story, Jade. And to tell it would be to lay myself completely bare before you. You would know my deepest secret. But to keep my secret may be to condemn us all."

McQueen reached across the table and touched his hand. She seemed moved by the pain she saw on his face.

"I will do all I can to help you, Pieter, if you truly mean to help us."

He smiled then, but it was a smile of surrender to a fate he could not escape.

"By now your agents have recognized the resemblance between my brother and I. Identical twins, although I have always been a bit heartier. Have they identified him?"

"No. From what I understand, he was able to kidnap our operative before she could transmit a clear photo of him."

"He took Cohen's woman? We have no time to lose then."

23 DANCING IN DREAMS

Rattlesnake Ranch
November 6, 2014

"The Peyote Cactus is a strange little pin-cushion-like plant with wondrous powers that the true people of this region have been using for centuries to truly know themselves."

Cooper was strapped to a chair in the dining room of the ranch house. She was not alone. The bankers were there, too, strapped in and stripped down to the white T-shirts they all wore beneath their now ruined expensive suits. They had yet to be allowed to clean up unpack the extra clothing they had brought.

At the head of the table, the man she knew only as Herr Doktor spoke in a calm, lecturing tone as he worked methodically with what appeared to be some kind of rudimentary chemistry set. If Cooper didn't know better, she would think he was making tea.

"It's fascinating, really, this little plant. Shaman for the native people have used it in their traditions to induce altered consciousness and introspection. Of course the government has now protected the plant, made it illegal to sell or possess or ingest peyote unless you are part of the Native American Church..."

He turned to his captive audience then with his evil smile, "But I trust you won't be telling anyone."

And then he was back to his task. "It can come with some ugly side effects – mostly vomiting – and has a bitter taste, but that of course is a small price to pay for the chance to know yourself better, wouldn't you say, gentlemen?"

Again he turned to the table, this time with a small steaming pot in hand. "Oh, and of course, my lady," he added, bowing grandly.

And he laughed gregariously, fully pleased with himself.

He rang a small bell in the center of the dining table then, and Willi brought in a tea cart with a beautiful antique set on it.

"Danke, Willi," he said, and Cooper winced at noting the same repulsive love in his tone for Willi as she had heard when he spoke to the snake.

"What's your end game here?" she asked. "What's the point of all of this?"

"Yes, Doktor. We've given you our word to do as you say. Why torture us this way?"

It as Pollard again, and his question earned him an icy glare from his host.

"Yes, you have assured me, gentlemen, that I can count on your assistance, but you are not truly men of your word. Today I will see into your black hearts to know if I can hold you to your word."

He walked behind Cooper then, pausing to stroke her tangled hair. "As for you, my dear Jasmine, call me curious."

"You should all consider yourselves quite lucky," he continued, as Willi poured the liquid from his pot into the delicate tea cups and set one before each of the Doktor's guests. The Peyote Cactus only grows in a narrow strip of desert on the border with Mexico and Texas and into the Chihuahua Desert.

"I had to find just the right … contacts to procure the needed amount for our activities today and went to great pains to find a true shaman from whom I learned the ancient art of creating the mescaline tea from the cactus. It is a long and arduous process and does not produce great amounts, so I have been slaving away for some time on your behalf."

He stopped at the head of the table to look over his guests, again soaking up the fear on every face. They had not noticed that Willi placed a delicate cup in front of his seat, as well. "We are in for an interesting evening, my friends."

♦ ♦ ♦

She was back in Pakistan her face covered in greasepaint, her body a perfectly honed machine, every muscle trip-wire tight beneath her black fatigues and bullet-proof vest.

Despite the physical reality of being half tied to a chair in a ranch house in New Mexico, Cooper could feel every sensation, see and hear everything as if she were there again leading a tac team of Rangers to rescue a young Mossad agent who had been captured on his first mission.

Never one to follow men into a dangerous situation, she had been the first through the door after the explosives blew it apart. Her target sat across the tiny room, stunned and confused and more than a little afraid of her, she thought at the time.

"Ari Cohen? Are you Ari Cohen?" Cooper said aloud as she rode the mescaline-induced hallucinations.

In her vision, Ari's eyes flew open wide at the sound of her voice and he smiled. What a strange man, she thought.

"Yes, I'm Ari Cohen," he stuttered.

"We've come to take you home."

He reached up for her outstretched hand then, and when he stood, she noted he was taller than she expected, and his skin beginning to lose the paleness of fear, took on a warm glow, but it was the color of his eyes that struck her most.

And for a long moment, they stood toe to toe and looking into one another's eyes before a gruff voice at the doorway beckoned them forward.

Cohen fell in behind her and they followed the team out. Soon, they were on the beach outside of Karachi, where they had left a lookout watching their inflatables.

"No contact, Ma'am."

It was her tac team leader. The lookout was nowhere to be seen, and they were holding ground outside the beachhead waiting for an all clear.

Suddenly, the Israeli agent threw himself on top of her. "What the –"

Her protest was cut short by gunfire erupting around them from an ambush waiting in the debris along the beach. She was just catching her breath when she felt Cohen pull her boot knife.

She made a grab for him, "Hey, no!" Too late, she watched him charge around behind the pile.

Desperately, Cooper tried to raise her superiors on the sub at sea, but it was no use. They were in the open now, she was refused permission to engage where they might be seen.

She chewed her nails waiting under cover to see if Cohen would survive.

It seemed an eternity before he came across the beach, bloody, carrying the body of their fallen Ranger across his shoulders, and she was the first to reach him.

"You crazy fool! What were you thinking?"

"I wasn't. It was just... instinct. After you risked your lives for me, I couldn't be the cause of your demise."

Don't do it, Jasmine, she thought, watching as he carried the Ranger and laid him gently beside the inflatables. Don't fall for a fool like this.

♦ ♦ ♦

"So you're Cohen's girl? What a delightful turn of events."

Herr Doktor had yet to partake of his tea cup. Once everyone had been settled with a cup in front of him or her, he had announced that this little experiment would work best if they followed a pattern – Ladies first.

He had then had to have Willi and Fritz force the tea down her throat when she refused to drink it herself and had waited patiently for it to begin to take effect. The other men in the room watched with a combination of horror and fascination.

"And, as we have seen, you are or were U.S. military. So someone is on to us, Willi, as we suspected."

"You want me to get rid of her, Herr Doktor?"

"Oh, no, Willi. I don't think that is necessary. But do take her to her room. I think I may join her later to finish our little experiment, but for now…" he said, turning to the other men in the room. "For now, it is time to turn my attention elsewhere."

♦ ♦ ♦

Willi threw Cooper into her room with a little more force than was necessary, still wearing the bruises on his face from her arrival at the ranch.

But in Cooper's mind she was back on the sub with Ari. They had been underway for more than three days and were finally hours from docking. During that time, she had found herself seeking Ari out more and more – bumping into him in the mess or on the conn. They had spent hours talking and playing games, and she knew they both felt a real connection.

It was no accident that they met outside the mess at that moment. "Jasmine," he said with a smile.

"Hello, Ari." She loved the way he had of cocking his head to the side when he looked at her, and how he always seemed to be looking at her so intently, as if he wanted to memorize every line of her face.

"We will be docking soon," he said, looking away from her.

Something hard caught in her throat. "Yes. I suppose you'll be headed back to Israel."

"Yes. And you?"

"Langley wants me to debrief in the home office."

He nodded.

"It's a small community, Ari. This doesn't have to be goodbye."

He ran his hand through his hair. She wished he would cock his head again and look at her the way she loved.

"No. Of course not. I've got your number. I'll call you once I am settled again."

He smiled at her, but there was a sadness behind it she didn't understand – or maybe she didn't want to.

Don't be a fool, Jasmine Cooper. It's been a few days; he can't feel the way you feel.

She was stunned when her thoughts were interrupted by the touch of his hand on her face. Without a word, he kissed her, and he walked away.

◆ ◆ ◆

"Gentlemen, shall we?"

The Doktor indicated that his guests should use their free hands to drink the tea set out before them, but it was a long moment before any of them moved.

"Oh, let's not dawdle, shall we. Surely you are not afraid after seeing the young lady come through her event in the pink of health?"

Pollard downed his tea in one swallow, knowing there was worse treatment to come if he chose otherwise.

"What have I got to lose? If I've got secrets you don't know this seems a better way to share them than have you beat them out of me," he said, glancing meaningfully at the hulking henchmen lurking behind their master's chair.

"Quite true, Mr. Pollard. So sensible." The other bankers followed suit.

As he waited for their tea to take effect, Herr Doktor explained to them that he had specialized the mixture for them.

"I have to admit that I took liberties with your beverages, gentlemen, having worked more closely with a chemist than a shaman to get a balance that will allow for a more ... guided tour of your psyche. It will be so much more productive for my purposes.

"Unfortunately, I cannot promise that the side effects will not be more potent or more deadly," he said, to the gasps of his guests. "Ah, but what we must do for science, no?"

As he watched for the signs he had been given of the hallucinogen's progress in the bankers, Herr Doktor enjoyed their rising distress.

"We will talk of many things tonight, my new friends, and by daybreak, I will know who I can and cannot trust to be loyal to me in all I ask."

Of course, I know the answer to that, he thought with a smirk. Not one can be trusted and not one will, but how I love my games.

24 TALE OF THE TWINS

Georgetown, Washington D.C.
Home of the Vice President
November 6, 2014

"His name is Wolfgang Stangl, but he is known as Anton Mueller. As I told you, he is the Chairman of the Swiss Bankers Association.

"All of this unpleasantness gets its start almost at the moment of our birth," Pieter said, spreading his hands. "It is a very long and complicated tale that leads us to pastries in your kitchen."

"I see," McQueen said, refilling his coffee cup and gathering up the plate of delights. "Then we shall take our little party into the living room where we can make ourselves more comfortable."

As they settled in on her overstuffed couches, McQueen asked Pieter how they had not connected him to Wolfgang before.

"Your people know the Raven under my father's family name – Vitale. When I was brought to America, I became Pietro Vitale, and it was only in my early 20s that I found out who my real parents were."

"I see. Perhaps you should start from the beginning."

"I was raised Pietro Vitale by Carmelo and Adolorata Vitale in Chicago.

"They were older than most parents, but I was kept at home in my childhood, sheltered from school and the kids in the neighborhood. The woman I knew as my mother was terrified for my safety and guarded me ferociously from whatever harm she imagined awaited me.

"The man I called father was gone more often than not, and when he was home, we were surrounded by his 'friends.' As a child, I was kept out of the way, and he really had little interest in me until I became a teenager. I was naturally athletic, and we had a large, fenced property where I swam, ran and was taught boxing.

"I suppose he simply looked up during dinner one day and noticed I had become a good-sized young man. I had already badgered Adolorata into getting me a tutor to learn English since all she spoke was Sicilian. I had learned quickly and was reading everything I could get my hands on."

Pieter paused, leaned his head back on the couch and closed his eyes.

Remembering seemed to make him weary.

"It sounds like a very lonely childhood, Pieter."

"Yes, well, we are all allotted our own trials I suppose."

He sat forward and sipped his coffee.

"From then on, time with my tutor was cut in half, and I rarely saw Adolorata. The man I knew as my father dragged me along everywhere. He wanted me to learn 'the business,' as he called it, to become a man and prepare to take things over. He was a smart man, although not educated. His English was rough street talk he had picked up since coming to the States from Corleone, and he owed his life to the Cosche or Clan, but he saw where things were going and he knew an educated man who also knew the ways of the Cosa Nostra – that man would go far."

"The Cosa Nostra – the Sicilian version of the Mob."

"Mafia, Mob, Bratva, gang – all words for the same kind of thing, I suppose," he said. "Just different incarnations of a group of immoral men gathered together to take advantage of the innocent."

Pieter rose to pace the living room. His face showed the torment of his conscience.

"I saw behind the curtain all the ugliness that allowed us to have our well-off life. That ugliness sent me to Harvard. By then, I was part of it, although I was lucky enough to be kept above the more violent aspects personally. They wanted my brain, my management skills, not my muscle.

"At Harvard, I got the first sense that I belonged somewhere else. My visits home were more and more strained, my calls home fewer and fewer. I felt I was missing something every time I walked through Adolorata's door – that I just did not belong there. So I started looking into my past.

"I could find no record of my birth in the United States – no one by my name born here.

"So I searched for records of my mother giving birth, and I found that she had... 27 years before I was born. She had a son named Alessandro.

"I drove through the night to confront her as soon as her husband and his goons had left the house. We sat at her kitchen table, and she sobbed as she told me the truth."

◆ ◆ ◆

"I could only save one. I beg you, Pietro, hear me."

Adolorata could barely speak as the sobbing rocked her body. She had known this day would come, and still she had not been prepared to hear him ask her.

"Mother, what are you talking about?" He spoke to her in Sicilian, holding her hand across the table, trying to calm her so she could tell him.

She took a deep breath and dried her eyes with her apron.

"My son's name was Alessandro, but he was always so rebellious. We sent him to school with the other boys, and he came back wanting me to call him Alex. Only Alex, that one. He had such fire in him.

"Carmelo doted on Alex. They played ball every evening, went to all the games. No two could be more alike. And Alex went with Carmelo when he did his business, even when he was younger than you. Such love between them.

"But things changed as he got older. He and Carmelo fought more and more, and Alex refused to be part of the business. Carmelo sent him away. He said Alex was dead to us. He told me that was the only way he could protect Alex."

She went to the cupboard then, and standing on a stool reached to the top shelf, behind some old, unused canisters to retrieve a tin recipe box. She brought it to the table and set it in front of her grandson.

"But Alex kept in touch with me. He sent letters to a girl he knew here from school and she would bring them to me. Such a sweet girl, she was. Here, these are the letters he sent. They are yours. They will tell you about your father... and your mother, Heidi, and your brother."

"Brother?"

"It's all there Pietro. Alex joined the CIA," she laughed the kind of laugh that reeks of sorrow and irony then. "He wanted to get as far from this family as he could. He traveled the world on his assignments, and the last place he was sent was Viet Nam."

Pieter held the worn letters in his hands; they had obviously been read many times.

"That is where he met your mother. She was a nurse volunteering there in the hospitals. She was from Switzerland. Her name was Heidi

Stangl, and that is the last name that your father gave to you and to your brother. He named you Pieter and your twin Wolfgang."

"Twin?"

"Yes. Identical."

"But... Where is he?"

"I could only save one of you."

"So..." Tears began to flow down his face.

"I do not know where the boy is now, Pietro. I wish that I could tell you."

"Moth—" Pieter stopped. She wasn't his mother. "Nonnina," he called her instead with great love, choosing a term of endearment for his grandmother, "what happened? Where are my parents? Why am I here?"

Adolorata's heart broke just a little, but it was a sweet heartbreak to hear that he still loved her.

"When I had not heard from your father during the evacuations of Saigon, where I knew he was stationed, I called his handler. Ben told me Alex and Heidi had drowned trying to escape to the waiting ships but they had managed to get you boys onto the helicopters first."

"Drowned..." Pieter stared at the letters in his hands, as if he could see the fate of parents he could not remember.

"I told Carmelo the truth and demanded that we bring you both home. I called the CIA handler back and told him to find you and to bring you to the States, but he told us that Wolfgang was not well. So he arranged for us to come to you. He flew us to Clark Air Force Base in the Philippines.

"He was so small and so pale." The tears began to flow again as her eyes took on a faraway look remembering the boys in their makeshift cradle. "They had you both in the same little cradle, and you were snuggled up against him, both sleeping. I told the nurses that we would take you both, and I would care for you, but Carmelo would not hear of it.

"He said that Wolfgang would stay and wait for Heidi's family. They would care for the runt. His mind could not be changed. He said Wolfgang would never make the trip home. I bundled you up, and we flew back to Chicago. Carmelo changed your name and said we were never to speak of your parents. It was the only way he would agree to help you."

"He left my brother because he was not good enough?"

She could see the rage rising in her grandson's eyes.

"I'm sorry, Pietro. I did all I could."

"Where is the handler?"

"Ben? I don't know. I never spoke with him again."

"I need to know what happened. I need to find him. What was his name?"

"I don't remember, Pietro. But it's in the letters."

"Very well, Nonnina," he said, but she felt no tenderness in the word this time. "Speak nothing of this to your husband."

He kissed her cheek, and he was gone. In his wake, Adolorata felt a familiar emptiness and foreboding.

◆ ◆ ◆

The shrill sound of McQueen's phone ringing broke the spell woven by Pieter's story. They had been locked away in their tete-a-tete for hours, and her fiancé/former head of security was getting nervous.

"Yes, David?" McQueen said, tilting her head toward Pieter to indicate her apologies. "Yes, David. Yes, David. Hush, David. I'm fine, David."

She hung up the phone.

"Secret Service getting antsy?"

"Fiancé getting antsy and jealous," she said smiling. "It doesn't help that you're a handsome internationally wanted deadly killer."

Pieter laughed heartily and the mood in the room was instantly lifted.

"Is that my cue to leave then?"

"No, that's his cue to get a clue. You're not leaving until you finish the story. However, we're going to have company for dinner in half an hour, so you and I better head back into the kitchen and get to work while we talk. I understand you're a true gourmet, which is great because I could burn water."

Another hearty laugh.

"I see, Madam Vice President. At your service."

They gathered the remnants of their mid-morning pastries, which had carried them straight past lunch, and headed back toward the kitchen. As McQueen began to clear away the dishes, Pieter rummaged through her pantry and refrigerator to find suitable ingredients to make a meal for three. He was mildly surprised that he had no qualms about staying for dinner with her fiancé/Secret Service agent. She had gained his trust very quickly.

"So, go on, Pieter. Tell me about finding Wolfgang."

"Yes. First I had to find Ben Carter. By then, of course, he had left the CIA. Luckily, he had retired, rather than getting himself killed."

"And he remembered your father?"

"Oh, much more than remembered. Ben had great remorse over the death of my parents. He felt very much responsible, and for that reason he had kept tabs on me and my brother all those years, which, sadly, only added to his guilt."

◆ ◆ ◆

He found Ben Carter bent over a bed of fragile Pansies, spraying them lightly with a mister. The man looked old and worn down by life and when he raised up, his back never quite straightened all the way.

"Can I help you?"

"My name is Pieter Stangl."

A light of recognition sprang to Carter's eyes. "Yes, I can see him in your face and her in your eyes," he said smiling. "Come in; I've been waiting for you."

Carter never asked how Pieter had found him; he seemed to assume any child of Alex Stangl would be just as bright.

He led Pieter to the living room and pointed to an old worn-out couch. Before he sat in his recliner, he took a cigar box off a shelf and handed it to his guest.

"This is yours. Alex had a package mailed to me the week before the evacuation, here in the States. Those photos were in it, and I retrieved the papers for you and your family from the military when I took your grandparents to Clark. They didn't want them, but I held on to them for you."

Pieter looked at the photos. Carmelo had destroyed all photos of his father and there had been no photos in the letters.

In one picture, the couple stood in front of a tiny restaurant, arms around one another, smiles beaming toward the camera. She held a shabby handful of flowers. The back read "Our little wedding" in what must have been his mother's handwriting. Pieter thought no two people had ever looked happier or more in love.

He heard the grunt as Carter lowered himself into his chair. "I expect you'll want to know what happened."

"Yes. Why were they still there? Why weren't they on the chopper?"

"I wasn't there, son, so all I know about that I know from the young boys who carried you and your brother to the ship. They said your mother had refused to leave Alex, and Alex had not wanted to leave while there was still work to be done – people to help. By the time he had convinced her to go or she had convinced him, they were only allowing U.S. citizens on board, and she was Swiss. He refused to board, so he handed you boys to some young men he had met and said he and Heidi would meet up with them on the ship.

"I expect that was his plan, too, and he came close. They were on one of those god-awful little boats just off the bow of one of the ships when a chopper ditched next to them and wiped them out. The old man who had taken them out said your dad wouldn't leave your mom. She was sick and weak, and he was trying to breathe for her and keep them both afloat. The sea took them."

Carter coughed then, clearing the lump in his throat.

"The old man's boat was sinking and he had nothing left in Saigon, so he found his way on board one of the ships, telling them about the crazy Americans he couldn't save. The young men recognized who it was and reported them to the captain, and that got back to me. I tracked down where you boys were, and when your grandmother called me, I let her know.

"Heidi's parents had been contacted by a Swiss nurse taking care of you. They weren't wealthy, and weren't sure who could take on two boys. While they were deciding who would have to take in both boys, Carmelo left with you. A few days later, Heidi's sister came for Wolfgang. She took him home to live with her family and her parents.

"I kept track of you both over the years," the old man said, rising again to go to the bookshelf. This time he took down two files. He handed them to Pieter, who saw the first was his. He set it aside almost afraid to see what it would say about him. The second was on Wolfgang, and that one he opened eagerly.

And then he almost wished he hadn't. His brother had been in and out of hospitals and mental institutions all through his childhood, from there it had turned to jail cells.

"He was never very healthy," Carter said. After they took you from his crib, he got worse, always a little blue and small. Almost as if he had gained strength just in being near you. Heidi's parents had blamed Alex for her death and they took it out on Wolfgang. Eventually, the constant mental and physical abuse took its toll, and he became quite violent and abusive in his own right, even with his small size.

"The jail time is all minor – brawling, petty theft, vandalism, arson. He's on a bad path, that one."

"Where is he now?"

"Thought you'd want to know, so I had some old friends dig up his whereabouts. Still in Switzerland, mental patient at the University Hospital of Bern."

Pieter gathered the files and the box and rose from the couch. He reached to shake Carter's hand. The old man held his hand firmly for a long moment. "I hope you can rescue him, son. I'm sorry I never did."

♦ ♦ ♦

"What exactly is this green stuff?" Pieter was about to open a plastic container from the fridge when David Gray snatched it from his hands and tossed it into the trash.

"In this house, it is always better not to ask," he said, offering his hand to the startled Pieter for a handshake.

Pieter took the hand as Gray said, "David Gray. Jealous fiancé."

"And Secret Service agent. Yes, I've heard. Pieter Stangl, internationally wanted criminal."

"I was told 'handsome internationally wanted deadly killer,'" Gray said with a smirk.

"Yes, well, I feel most of that is greatly exaggerated."

"Good to know. What's for dinner?"

"Frozen pizza and beer would seem to be about the best option I can come up with at the moment," Pieter said, shaking his head.

"And you said he was a gourmet," Gray said, kissing McQueen hello.

"Even the greatest gourmet requires a stocked kitchen," Pieter said a slightly terse tone.

"And you interrupted his story, David."

"Yeah, I'm good at that. What did I miss?"

McQueen looked at Pieter. "Not my story," she said simply.

"Right. I am to assume that Mr. Gray is a part of your team?"

"Where she goes..." Gray said in answer.

"And he knows your most secret of secrets," Pieter said.

"And then some," Gray said smiling widely as both Pieter and McQueen blushed.

"And he can be trusted... I mean with my secret at this point?"

"David is Ari's friend, if that is what you are asking. So am I. And it's about time Ari is brought into all of this, Pieter. But he will only be told what we need to tell him. So, you only need to tell David what you need to tell him."

Pieter considered this a moment. "Right."

"OK. Recap. I am the Raven, but the list of my exploits have been highly exaggerated. My brother is the villain your friend Cohen currently seeks.

"We are twins separated at birth by circumstances beyond anyone's control. However, my brother was left in rather unsavory conditions, as I was just telling Ms. McQueen."

"Jade," she said, absently, as she slid the pizza into the oven and puzzled over how to turn it on. Gray pushed her aside to work the buttons.

"Don't laugh, Pieter. It's a new stove. I'm not THAT helpless."

"Oh, please. Let's not forget I have seen the contents – or lack thereof – of your kitchen pantry.

"Anyway, as I was saying, my brother and I did not know of one another for most of our lives. In fact, I was finishing my studies at Harvard when I felt the need to find out more about my past and discovered the truth about him."

"After I visited my father's CIA handler," Pieter said, handing Gray a beer and ignoring the raised eyebrow, "I flew to Bern to see Wolfgang – my brother – at the hospital."

"Sick?"

"Mental patient."

"Ah." Gray took another beer from Pieter and passed it along to

McQueen and the three sat at the kitchen island where the day had begun.

"I could not bring him back to the States, not as long as I was still milking my connections with Carmelo and the Cosa Nostra,"

"Carmelo being?"

"My grandfather."

"But of course. Always good to have connections."

"He had disowned my father and my brother. He would have killed Wolfgang rather than have his existence discovered by the Clan. So I set him up there in Switzerland. I got him better care, saw to it that he had everything he could possibly want. And he improved. I had him tutored, and his mind was as much a sponge as mine had been. He learned fast.

"So, I invented an identity for him and used my own connections to set Wolfgang up as the head of a Swiss bank we owned. I think you can imagine how useful it would be for someone in my position to own such a property.

"In my mind, I had put him in the perfect position to be as nearly legit as possible. All he had to do was what any Swiss bank does – handle dirty money.

"Instead, he has taken his education and his position and he has used it to set up his plan for revenge on the people he thinks are responsible for all of his misery – the United States."

"As in the whole country?" Gray asked. "He blames the nation for his personal tragedy?"

Pieter shrugged. "It was a government that abandoned our parents with no exit strategy and abandoned the South Vietnamese to their Northern enemies. In his mind, this nation abandoned our parents and stole them from us. He told me America is a disease upon the world."

"Is it too late to get your money back on all that good help you got him?" Gray asked.

Pieter sighed. "Yes. I suppose he was never really well. And as his antics increased, his ambitions began to be bad for business, and people around me took notice. Carmelo is long gone, so I have no fear of that old man, but the old secret behind all of this could still get me killed.

"Also, it doesn't help that Wolfgang is getting me blamed personally for some of his latest escapades."

"The calling card. It wasn't you behind the hit on Cohen, and yet one of our best agents thinks you are trying to kill him," McQueen said.

"That's a very bad idea," Gray added.

"Yes, very unfortunate. But I must insist you honor our agreement, use this information however best to avert the coming danger, but no one must link me to Wolfgang Stangl outside this room."

25 THE DOKTOR'S DESERT

Santa Fe, New Mexico
November 6, 2014

Come lunchtime on the day after Jasmine's capture, Ari was frantic.

He had been relieved when Burke decided to have her work as a spotter with the camera and plant the tracking device on the limo. She would still be on hand to use as bait if needed, but they would hold that card until the last hand. He had not dreamed the Raven or the Doktor had any notion of who she was and that the simple act of taking photos of people arriving at the Pink Adobe would put her in danger of being stuffed in the trunk of a limo and carried off into the desert.

For the second time in his covert career, Ari had a difficult time thinking, planning his next move in his normal detached and emotionless manner. *Women! Why must they foul up my foolish brain?* And for what – a love affair that went nowhere when he nearly got Jasmine killed and a harmless flirtation with Katarina that only served to make him lose his mind.

"I need to have my head examined," he said aloud, realizing he had said the same thing when he returned from the Russian mission and his brush with the Azerbaijani Bratva – and Katarina Azarov.

Instead of waiting to leave after dark to recon Rattlesnake Ranch, he had left after lunch, driving around the desert roads to get a good feel for the area. There was only one advantage to his zealousness; he realized that an approach after dark without night vision goggles would be foolhardy. The natural obstacles – especially cactus – were everywhere.

Night falls quickly in the deserts of New Mexico. The elevation above sea level is so high it seems as if the sun is always hanging low on the horizon, dazzling in its intensity. Once the sun starts going down, it moves with astonishing speed. Within moments, everything is pitch black, save for an amazing array of stars. In the ensuing darkness, the night belongs to a host of species that have been sleeping all day. They roam, hungry, and using the dark and the rising moon to stretch and get ready for the hunt or prepare to evade being dinner for some other animal.

Ari lay prone on the mesa above Herr Doktor's ranch house, watching unobserved. Finally, he felt like he was doing something. The luminescent glow of a large watch revealed his mask-covered face, eyes glued to telescopic binoculars. As he removed the binocs, his strong, concentrating eyes could be seen. A look of worry crossed his brow and his hand adjusted the magnification strength as his attention moved from building to building in the compound.

Slowly, he committed it all to memory. In the still darkness, there was just the sound of his breathing. He tensed; below him in the forecourt, a bodyguard emerged from the house and walked over to an adobe brick fire pit.

He busied himself preparing to light the fire then arranged chairs neatly around the pit. It was Willi, and Ari had to resist the temptation to pull out his dart gun and take revenge on the sadistic bully.

Herr Doktor's guests walked out cocktails in hand and sat down around the lee side of the fire, all eyes locked on the flames. Ari scanned the bankers, all clean and seemingly in good health. Not exactly under stress, he thought. No longer kidnapped victims, I see.

After some time, one banker pulled his eyes from the fire and spoke quietly, the sound only carrying because of the silence across the desert. "Has anyone seen the girl since last night?"

At the mention of Jasmine, the prone figure lying on the mesa tensed, his face knotting in anger and concern. He reached for a canvas, tube-like like container. Once certain it was there, he patted it lightly, relieved and comforted all was where it should be.

Ari's attention returned to the bankers. Satisfied, he removed his goggles from his eyes, using the soft glow of his watch face to see by until his eyes adjusted. He tensed again as he saw a small insect crawling toward him. He watched intently, not moving lest the sound give away his position. The scorpion approached undeterred.

He watched as the scorpion moved left to right but still came toward him. When it reached his gloved hand, he stilled even his breathing. The scorpion climbed onto his motionless hand, and Ari just watched. He tried blowing gently on the scorpion. The scorpion, sensing something out of place, moved off 90 degrees away from Ari. Ari sighed softly, amusement spreading into his eyes.

His attention focused back on the forecourt as the voices below became more lively, the conversation warming up. He was growing impatient. If only Jasmine would show up, I could charge down the mesa, rescue her and be done with this surveillance.

Watching the bankers getting refills, becoming a little louder, he decided it was perhaps better she didn't show up; he didn't want to watch these bankers flirting with her. As if reading his thoughts, another banker slurred, "Forget the girl. After last night... Just leave him to his toy."

Ari began inching backward, eyes still watching the front, careful to leave no trace. He felt again for his tube-like canvas container he had strapped diagonally across his back and was comforted by its presence. After a five-mile hike across the desert terrain, he came within sight of his rented Jeep hidden behind some piñon trees.

Ari stopped suddenly, something in his gut warning him, and without a change in pace he moved to the side, keeping some brush between him and the Jeep while he evaluated the situation.

A cloud glided over the moon, obscuring any light. Ari rushed past the Jeep and crept around the far side, where he heard a voice whispering.

"Remember, Herr Doktor wants him alive. Don't kill him."

"Did you see where he went? I don't see him."

Ari slid over to the bushes behind the two assailants and saw them crouching low, waiting for him to make an appearance. Creeping closer, he began to gain confidence, knowing they wouldn't shoot him out of hand.

Quickly, he rose up behind the thugs. "Can I help you find something?"

Totally taken by surprise, his would-be attackers whirled around to look at Ari and then at each other.

"How'd you get back there?"

Thug 2 looked over at his friend. "He's trying to trick us."

Ah, thought Ari, not the brightest of Herr Doktor's men.

Thug 1 and Thug 2 moved closer to Ari, knives held out in front of them menacingly.

As they came within striking distance, they assumed an even more aggressive posture, swinging their arms from side to side, their knives held back even further to get more of a thrust.

And that's when Ari leaped in the air toward them, left leg coiled like a spring. As he landed in front of Thug 1 on the left, he released his left leg in a vicious kick to the man's stomach.

Thug 1 shot backward, gasping for air, bewildered.

Meanwhile Thug 2 looked at his friend, then at Ari. He opened his mouth, revealing broken teeth within an evil smile.

He began swinging his arms, moving forward again, a vicious snarl on his face and profanities streaming from his befouled mouth.

Before he could advance farther, Ari charged. He swung around to his right and launched his right hand open like a crab. He grabbed Thug 2's trachea between his thumb and four fingers and squeezed. At the same time, his left hand grabbed the wrist of the thug's right hand.

Ari maintained his grip, and Thug 2 dropped his knife, clawing at the clamp-like fingers around his neck. Unable to breathe, his face turned blue, spittle forming at the corners of his gasping rotted mouth. Ari released him, and his body dropped to the ground.

Ari swiveled back to Thug 1, now sitting up and trying to shake the cobwebs out of his head. Ari moved behind him and put his knee in the man's back. He secured his right arm around the ruffian's neck and began pressing forward with his left arm. Ari was breathing hard, adrenalin pumping through his veins.

"Why did you attack me? Who sent you?"

Thug 1 struggled against Ari's brute strength, shaking his head, refusing to answer, but Ari continued the sideways and forward pressure. He felt the final resistance of the man's vertebrae, knowing one more push would break his neck. Still no answer from the thug, and for a brief moment Ari's thoughts went back to his early days, endless training and classroom teaching, and one sentence Ari learned that stuck with him all these years. "This is not a business for compassion, compassion will kill you."

Ari snapped back to the present, and against his will and maybe his true sense of morality, he pushed a little more, wincing as the man's vertebrae cracked under the pressure. Ari exhaled deeply, letting his tension go and released his grip. His enemy slipped to the ground.

Ari tried to make sense of these brutal killings. Why would these men commit themselves to such a meaningless death?

That was when his sixth sense warned him he was not alone. He couldn't see his antagonist, but he felt him. Ari reached inside his inner jacket pocket, located his blow pipe and felt for the dart with the three little ridges down its side. In seconds, he was locked and loaded. He still had not seen the third villain, but he could feel him coming. Every hair on the back of his neck was bristling.

Slowly, Ari rose and turned. The new attacker increased his speed, charging at Ari and screaming incoherently.

Still 15 feet away and built like a mountain – a very angry mountain – the man crouched low, moving incredibly fast for someone so bulky. Ari waited to confront his attacker, and in one fluid movement, pulled out his short blowpipe, leveled it, and blew.

His attacker was going too fast to change direction, his blood pumping fast through his veins, thinking he had the drop on Ari.

Ari kept a supply of poison from an African frog specifically for this type of situation. The venom from the yellow and orange frog was deadly, dangerous enough to kill 100 men with the poison on its skin, it was so lethal. The dart went into the man's neck, and with his heart rate pumping so hard, resulted in an immediate reaction. In no time, he fell to the ground dead.

Ari waited for the dust to settle, wary of another surprise that might come running after him. As he waited, he reloaded his blowpipe just in case. Finally satisfied there were no more surprises coming, he knelt down, searched the dead man for his wallet and his neck for dog tags, but found nothing.

Ari repeated the process with Thugs 1 and 2 and came up empty as well. He picked up the first man's hand, and looked at his fingertips; all his fingerprints had been burned off. No ID and no fingerprints, just like his run-in with the Bratva.

Ari didn't get it. Sure, there were other professionals who chose such measures of anonymity, but everything about these mountainous villains warned him of a Mafia connection. But what was the mob doing tied up with a Swiss banker? It didn't making sense.

Ari finished his inspection and headed back to his Jeep, a worried look on his face. Once inside, he hesitated before starting the engine, then as if thinking through the feasibility of a new idea, he nodded his head; a decision made.

He pressed the ignition and immediately afterward the Bluetooth button on his services console.

A mechanical voice responded in the car, "Number from memory or new number?"

"New number," he responded dryly, not sure if he liked this idea of talking to a computer.

"What number would you like?"

Ari punched in, 13 07 04 1776.

It wasn't long before he heard Burke's voice on the other end.

"Hello, Ari, I'm so glad you called."

"Curse you, Tom, you put my... I mean that girl in real danger with that psychopath."

"Was that a Freudian slip, Ari? You nearly referred to her as 'my girl.'"

Flustered, Ari bit his lip, "Curse you again, Tom! Stop changing the subject. That girl is in danger."

"I know. It was a calculated risk, and you knew it was possible. We have to find out what they are up to, and she knew the risk. We've got new information that links him to the Swiss Bankers Association and –"

Ari was beside himself, unable to control his temper. "A CALCULATED RISK! That's typical military officer mumbo jumbo for, 'It's OK, as long as it's someone else's butt on the line!'"

Ari hardly hesitated before adding, "I don't care what you think, I'm going in to rescue her tomorrow night."

As if to emphasize his point, he banged his hand so hard on the steering wheel he accidentally honked the horn.

"What was that?"

"A car went by without dimming its headlights."

Ari rubbed the bridge of his nose and tried to breathe.

"I'll help you tomorrow night, Ari."

It took a moment for Ari to process what had been said.

"I don't care what you –"

Belatedly he realized what he had missed. "What did you say?"

Burke repeated himself. "I said I'll help you tomorrow night."

"How can you help me? You're in Bethesda."

"No. I'm actually at the La Fonda Hotel in Santa Fe waiting for you."

"What?"

"Reinforcements have arrived. By the way, if you are that passionate about rescuing Cooper, don't you think you should lose the twin redheads before we bring her back here?"

Ari was momentarily speechless, ignoring the taunt.

"What reinforcements?"

"Gray is here. Meet us in the La Fonda Hotel downstairs bar. Get a move on, Ari, we have work to do."

Ari smiled at the mention of his dearest friend and closest ally.

"Order me a couple of cold Dos Equis. I'll be there in five."

◆ ◆ ◆

Hotel La Fonda

The famed Hotel La Fonda stood on ground that was once a Presidio surrounded by large defensive walls that enclosed all the principal structures of early Santa Fe – residences, barracks, a chapel, a prison and the Governor's palace. It seemed the perfect location from which to launch an attack.

Ari parked his Jeep in the hotel's underground parking on East San Francisco Street and headed straight for the bar. He was relieved to see the smiling face of David Gray seated next to Burke at a table in the back. Gray rose to hug him, clapping him hard on the back.

"I hear you've had a hard week, brother," he said, handing him the requested Mexican beer.

"I filled Gray in on what we know, and he told me a few things he found out through your mutual acquaintance."

"Your nosy fiancée had something to do with all of this?" Ari said with a note of humor in his voice.

"Let's just say one of her... contacts knew a little something about a little something."

"The man entertaining our missing bankers is a Swiss banker himself, Ari, and he is behind all of it – the murders, the attempted hit on you, and the threat to the Federal Reserve Board."

"But the Raven's calling card... And I saw him meeting with Kong." None of this was making any sense to Ari.

"It's complicated, but the Raven has been caught in the middle trying to stop all of this, and his name has been taken in vain, shall we say," Gray explained.

Ari wasn't sure he was ready to let the Raven off the hook just yet, but that was a chase for another day.

"I saw them, David. They've got to be twins or something."

"Good eye, Ari. It's certainly a family issue there, but that's nothing to do with the case at hand, and we've got to focus on dealing with Herr Doktor in the here and now."

Ari took a long pull on his ice cold beer. "I watched the ranch house all afternoon; but there was nothing moving. Then I had to take out three men to get away from there this evening, so they know we're on to them. We better go in fast, hot and heavy."

"We've got the three of us and a crack tac team," Burke said. He spread a topo map on the table in front of them, and Ari began to brief them on what he had seen during his recon of the perimeter.

When they finished, Gray walked Ari back to his room.

He put a hand on Ari's shoulder. "How are you holding up, brother?"

"I'm fine. We've done OPs like this a million times."

Ari focused on opening his door, but Gray turned his shoulder until Ari was facing him.

"Did you forget who you're talking to? You play it close to the chest, but I know you care about this woman. Don't forget I know what you're going through, Ari. You start losing your focus, you look to me to help you get it back, you understand? We'll get her back tomorrow – alive and well."

Ari exhaled a breath he had not realized he was holding. He nodded and headed into his room.

◆ ◆ ◆

Ari went to bed, but sleep eluded him. Every time his brain relaxed enough for him to enter a heavy pre-sleep phase, his mind would play tricks on him. The first time, he woke in a sweat, thinking he was on the beach in Pakistan as Jasmine led his rescue team back to the inflatable. Again he smelled the tell-tale odor of cigarettes, but he was powerless to intervene as his savior walked into a trap. Ari struggled to be able to move in his dream, and watched helplessly as Jasmine headed straight into the terrorists' position. He woke screaming, punching air in his bed at the La Fonda.

Two more times, Ari tried to rest but each time, something horrific woke him. Up with the dawn, he decided to get an early start and go for a jog before returning to meet Burke and Gray to go over the final OPs plan for Rattlesnake Ranch.

By the time he approached Burke's suite, he was back on his game, physically weary but totally alert and ready for Jasmine's rescue.

He had not anticipated running into Burke's sense of humor.

"Did you lose the redheads?" Burke asked by way of a greeting. Ari paused, wiped the sweat off his brow with the hotel towel wrapped around his shoulder and looked disdainfully at his long-time boss and friend. He didn't offer a reply, but looked to Gray smirking quietly behind the Colonel. "Et tu Brute?"

Gray cleared his throat.

Burke had not made a successful career of ignoring the alarm bells when he had made a false step, and handling his Israeli agent had always been a challenge for him. While they were friends, there was still much he did not know about Ari.

Taking his cue from Ari's stony appearance, he changed the subject.

"Let's go over the plan one more time. We'll leave the tac team a mile back and the three of us will make the trek in first."

"Let's leave after dark. It's a five-mile jog over rough terrain to Rattlesnake Ranch; you sure you're up to it?"

Burke was glad to have Ari back to his normal self.

"You'll be eating my dust, son."

♦ ♦ ♦

Rattlesnake Ranch, Herr Doktor's Office
November 7, 2014

Cooper was seated in the Doktor's office, the rattlesnake on his desk resting with a lump in her stomach to show she had been fed.

"I am disappointed that you didn't join me for dinner last night, Miss Cooper."

She hesitated before answering, cutting the fear she felt with a large measure of contempt. "I didn't have anything to wear."

"I was hoping that you wouldn't need to put anything on for dinner in my private quarters."

Cooper ignored him.

"It appears you have not been forth right with me, Miss Cooper."

"What do you mean?"

"The photos on your camera were of my limo and my guests. I believe your interests were aimed in my direction, Fraulein, or would you prefer I call you Agent?"

Cooper glared at him suspiciously. "I have no idea what you're talking about."

"Yes, well. Your little mescaline journey did not leave you with much memory, I'm afraid."

Cooper tensed. What does he know?

"But we'll leave that be, shall we? Tell me, Miss Cooper, wasn't your Editor at the Philadelphia Daily News murdered recently?"

Cooper's head spun to look at the Doktor. "What do you know about his death?"

Her captor laughed. "Quite a lot actually, but you know that of course."

He rose and walked around the desk to lean over her, playing with her hair as she pulled away from him.

"Your friends will be coming soon. I'm afraid it's time to go."

♦ ♦ ♦

The drive to the outskirts of Rattlesnake Ranch was made in silence, all three men mentally preparing for what was to come. Well before the spot where Ari had planned to park his Jeep, he slowed down to a crawl.

Absently, he said, "Reduce the dust trail."

Ari was busy scouting the terrain, on the lookout for an indication of anything out of place. He leaned over the steering wheel, looking skyward, but even over the glare of the sun on the horizon he saw no buzzards circling. He passed the spot where he had parked the night before and dispatched the three villains. There was no sign of scavengers on the ground or in the air.

"Looks like they cleaned up your mess." Burke was also searching the area for any sign of ambush. "I'm surprised they don't have a welcoming committee for us."

The three of them looked at each other and nodded slightly, unsure whether it was good or bad news. Ari rolled to a stop, the Jeep somewhat sheltered from the road by a stand of large piñon trees. Silently they got out of the vehicle. "Check your side for tracks."

Burke and Gray headed off on the passenger side, Ari on the other, searching for a sign. Minutes later, they were back at the rear compartment of the Jeep, silently signing to each other that they had seen nothing.

Ari, dressed in black fatigues, handed a bag to Burke, who in typical Marine style was dressed in camo. Gray, a former Navy SEAL matched him. Each knew what to do as they passed the bag, they armed themselves with their preferred equipment.

After they emptied their bag, they proceeded to run an equipment check, small firearm, water, night vision goggles.

Burke looked over at Ari, opened a hand-size can of facial camo grease, and began applying it liberally as his eyes lingered on the tube-like canvas bag that Ari had secured on his back over his shoulders. He handed the can to Gray.

"We're not going fishing, Ari."

Ari smiled at Gray as he took his turn with the grease can. The bag did look about the right size to hold a rod. "This fella's little brother saved my bacon last night."

Ari pulled out two cylindrical tubes and attached one to the other.

"A modern version of the original Pygmy Blow pipe, a skill I learned in the Congo. They use them to hunt monkeys."

"He's freaky good with those things," Gray said as he checked his Glock and attached a silencer.

Burke was glad for an opportunity to relieve some of the tension, adding sarcastically, "We're not going to hunt monkey's either, Ari."

Ari took no offense. "That FN you're carrying will blow somebody's head off at 100 yards."

"Darn right it will," Burke said enthusiastically, patting his weapon with great regard.

Ari pulled out a small wallet and opened it to show Burke. It had three rows of different colored darts, red, green and yellow.

"My weapon has about half that reach, but none of that noise, and a lot more versatility. If I just want to knock them out, I use the green darts. The red will kill them instantaneously."

"And the yellow ones?"

"A neuro-toxin. It will immobilize the target immediately and result in such pain they will froth at the mouth. I think I might use those on the two goons that kidnapped Cooper, if I can find them."

"Time to head out, Romeo," Gray said, shaking his head.

Gray was fortunate he turned away before he saw the deadly look Ari gave him at that last hook, but Burke made a mental note to lay off the Jasmine jokes.

♦ ♦ ♦

There is no such thing as jogging in a straight line over the wild brush of the New Mexico plains around Santa Fe. The earth is rarely more than a thin layer of gravel-like stones interspersed with many different types of cacti and sharp, prickly, little bushes. Consequently, it was difficult to keep his eyes on anything other than the ground immediately in front of him. Ari knew that one moment without paying absolute attention to the ground at his feet could result in serious injury.

Forty-five minutes later, the trio slowed their approach, puffing and sweating as they neared the location where Ari had lain the previous night. Ari was leading, slightly hunched over.

"There are bunches of scorpions up here; be careful," he whispered back to Burke and Gray.

"Now you tell me."

The three men took prone positions, with Ari and Gray searching the ranch through their night vision binoculars and Burke looking through the scope on his FN. After a few minutes scanning the scene below, Burke voiced what they were all sensing.

"I don't like this; it's too quiet down there."

"I can hear some music, but no voices. This is not good; I can't pinpoint any enemy positions."

They kept scanning, and after a few more minutes of searching, Ari put his binocs down.

"This might explain why there was no reception committee waiting for us back at the road. Man, I hate room-to-room searches. We're going to have to search this place the hard way."

Ari looked over to see Burke nodding agreement as he scanned the layout.

Without taking his scope from his eye, he said, "Ari, take the west side, work your way in to the center living area. Gray and I will start on the east side. Meet you in the middle."

Ari turned to Burke. "Did you bring a silencer for that handgun?"

"Yeah, why?"

Ari pulled out a sheaf of knives from his gear pack. "Thought you might want to borrow one of these."

"Nah, I got it. See you in the middle."

In a few seconds, the men were lost to view as they set off in opposite directions to descend the mesa.

The forecourt was deathly quiet, as they headed in. They stopped at the edge of the brush, still searching for any resistance. This was one combat situation no soldier liked – leaving the relative comfort of a stealthy approach and making a rapid run across open ground to the outside wall of a building.

As soon as their backs were hugging the wall, it was time to peek through windows, crawl under windows, kick open doors and pull back. If they got no response from within, they would dive to the floor, knife or gun at the ready. Soon it became apparent the ranch was empty.

Burke and Gray had finished their search, and Burke tapped his neck microphone twice. "Anything on your side, Ari?"

"Nothing. All clear."

"Me either. Let's meet in the central living area."

"Roger."

Nobody could have been more surprised than Ari.

"They've gone." He agonized over his discovery, pacing, the men still standing on opposite sides of the living room, still armed and ready. "But where in all that's holy is Jasmine?"

Gray looked at his friend's anguished face and said calmly, "Let's check the library."

They cautiously moved along opposite walls to the library. Looking at each other and sensing something was wrong, they felt they were in a spider's web. Suddenly, Ari knew someone had planned this.

As they crept close to the library, they simultaneously pushed back the double doors and stared in front of them, shocked.

♦ ♦ ♦

Deep underground, the spider who orchestrated the absence of anyone on his ranch watched a closed-circuit television feed spring to life. Front and central on the screen were Burke, Gray and Ari as they walked into the library. Herr Doktor smiled smugly as the men stared at a circular table. Around the table sat six leather high-back chairs each holding a body.

He could see that Ari recognized three of the occupants, slumping unnaturally, held in place by a rope around their chests.

Ari turned to Burke as he approached the bodies. "The mystery of the missing thugs is solved."

"You mean someone recovered the bodies and went to the trouble of planting them here?"

Ari shrugged as he took a closer look at the three remaining bodies, their eyes bulging, faces swollen in the agony of breathlessness, a garrote tied, unmercifully tight around each neck.

"Are these your missing bankers?" Gray asked.

Ari nodded that he recognized them.

"I don't think we need to check for a pulse," Burke said.

Ari examined each of the new corpses with particular attention to the garrotes.

"Burke, you remember the murdered editor at the Philadelphia Daily News?"

"Of course."

"These garrotes are the same type as they used on Charlie Stafford."

"The same type?"

"It is a technique first used by soldiers of the French Foreign Legion. The French called it, 'La Loupe.' It's a type of double loop garrote; even if a victim pulls on one of the ropes around his neck, he only succeeds in tightening the other," Ari said.

"We need to take photos and get out of here; we have obviously been set up."

♦ ♦ ♦

Beneath their feet, in a long unused tunnel underneath Rattlesnake

Ranch, ensconced within a large, sound-proof shelter, Herr Doktor watched the screen with Cooper by his side.

"No point in screaming for help; they can't hear you."

Cooper wasn't thinking of screaming for help. She felt a slight shiver run down her spine. It wasn't the oppressive atmosphere that caused her concern, more the poisoned aura emanating from this man. His hatred was so consuming it cast a devilish gloom over the room.

"What makes a man delight in such evil? You are the saddest, most pathetic human being I have ever met."

The Doktor pulled his attention from the TV monitor with extreme difficulty. As he turned his head, the pupils of his eyes shrank, his glance becoming snakelike, almost spitting venom. His hate was so prevalent it radiated out of him.

"Sad you say?" He regurgitated the question with saliva launching from his mouth at every syllable.

"What do you know about sad?" he screamed at Cooper. "You probably had a perfect little childhood with perfect little parents, didn't you?"

Cooper could see she had really gotten to him and decided to taunt him some more.

"Even the most perfect parents couldn't have altered your basic sick nature. You are just using them as an excuse for your self-pity."

Her tormentor could not take any more of this abuse to his psyche. He launched his chair backward as he rocketed to his feet, slamming his hands on the rock wall on either side of her face.

Fortunately, Willi and Fritz pushed open the door to the room.

"Have our guests left yet?" he asked, turning his attention to them with a cold stare.

"Yes, Herr Doktor. They are leaving the ranch house now," Willi looked from the Doktor to Cooper and back, clearly suspicious of what he had just missed.

◆ ◆ ◆

Ari climbed the rocky slope to reach the top of the mesa. After a few steps, he turned around to examine the structure he had just left. He felt he was being watched.

Burke and Gray stopped and turned to Ari.

"Ari? Something bothering you?" Gray asked.

"I can't explain it. I feel like we're being watched." Ari shook his head in frustration. "I don't get it. Why leave those bodies for us to find?"

"If they are watching us, we are somewhat exposed here; we need to move."

Ari seemed to snap to. "Yes, and I need to get back to Santa Fe. I want to find out what other structures have been built around here; something is nagging at me."

◆ ◆ ◆

"I think it is safe to leave now, Willi, Fritz, lead the way, please... to the tunnel."

"The tunnel?"

"One of the reasons I bought this place. It used to be an old silver mine, and there is a shaft underneath us five miles long that will take us all the way to the other side of the mountain."

Turning to Willi, he said, "Why don't you go ahead. Warm the SUV up for me. It is a little chilly for my taste."

Willi nodded and headed off at a more brisk pace.

"Fritz, why don't you go upstairs and bring our dead friends down here? No point in making it too easy for the authorities. Make sure you leave no trace of our little deception."

Herr Doktor then turned to pull Cooper down a cool, musty corridor beneath the underground shelter to the entrance of a deeper tunnel blocked by another hidden door. Old and rusted, it screeched its protest despite having just been opened by Willi, and Cooper felt more cold air coming up from below. At the bottom in the dim light, Cooper could just make out a subterranean chamber.

She heard a faint voice from below, "The SUV is running, Herr Doktor. I'll come and help Fritz bring the bodies down."

Willi appeared out of the darkness and passed the Doktor and Cooper on his way up to help his partner.

The Doktor stopped at a small alcove chiseled out of the rock wall and retrieved an old oil lantern. He lit it and passed it to Cooper.

"Lead the way, Miss Cooper, and watch out for the rats."

They continued down the steps and Cooper could hear a faint scratching sound all around her. Further down, her lantern shone on shadowy dark shapes running in and out of the lantern light. When she recognized them, she shuddered.

"I hate rats."

A little further on, she smelled exhaust then saw the lights of the SUV.

"Where are we going?"

"Raven's Nest."

"Raven's Nest?"

"Yes. My brother's little retreat."

26 THE CHIEF CHECKS IN

The Governor's Mansion, Santa Fe, New Mexico
November 8, 2014

Burke and Ari stood as the double doors to the Governor's library swung open and the President's Chief of Staff entered. Gray had headed back to D.C. to better hide his fiancé's involvement.

"Good morning, gentlemen, let's sit."

Burke could barely contain his anger. "What is the White House Chief of Staff doing out here in the field?"

Gonzalez eyed him steely. "Damage control."

He turned his eyes from Burke to settle on Ari. "Our Mossad contacts won't tell us anything about you other than you are a concert violinist. Are they kidding us?"

"No, Sir. I solo with the Israel Philharmonic Orchestra in Tel Aviv, specializing in Mozart."

"So you just kill U.N. diplomats as a hobby?"

Ari tensed, and Gonzalez caught it.

"We saw the U.N. security footage of Kong's murderer, and facial recognition software puts you at the top of the suspect list."

"That diplomat was a paid assassin, a menace; he deserved to die."

"We can't have the White House involved in murdering a diplomat, even if the murderer does play the violin."

Burke interjected, "The White House wasn't involved in any murders; and we all know if you had more to go on than a list of suspects, we wouldn't be standing here throwing accusations around. Besides, you need Ari, and it's past time we got down to the business at hand. The Doktor has killed the three missing bankers."

That got the Chief's attention. "Why would he do that? He wouldn't have brought them down here to murder them. It doesn't make sense."

There was nothing but blank stares from everyone in the room when a knock on the door interrupted the meeting. Burke, accustomed to command responded, "What is it?"

A Secret Service agent entered. "I have a call from the local FBI, it's urgent, Sir."

"I'll take it; might be relevant."

With a nod to Ari and Gonzalez, he left the room.

In the hallway, the agent handed him a phone. "We searched Rattlesnake Ranch, and there are no bodies there. Everything appears normal."

Burke looked incredulous. "No bodies?"

"Not one, Sir."

"Thanks. I'll get back with you."

Burke hung up and headed back into the meeting.

"According to the FBI, the bodies of those three bankers – and the three thugs – that we saw last night have disappeared. Herr Doktor is covering his tracks well."

"This is insane." Gonzalez was pacing now. "You tell me he killed them all, which didn't make sense to begin with. Why kidnap them and hold them in the first place? Then you say he killed them and left them for you to find, only you have no proof of that?"

"It's a sick game he's playing," Ari announced with finality. "And if he covered his tracks so quickly, he must have known we had been there or he was still there watching. He wanted us to find those bodies. He wouldn't have moved them until after we found them so that he could make you question our sanity now."

"Well it's working!" Gonzalez was pacing as well, and the two found themselves nearly toe to toe.

"We thought his aim was manipulation of the Federal Reserve. We knew he was blackmailing those members – now has the other members scared, if not also under his thumb," Ari said calmly, but with a note of tension in his voice.

"We've gone to great lengths to be sure none of the others know about the kidnapped bankers – no one knows."

"As far as you know," Ari said. "But now that they are dead …"

"It goes beyond manipulating Federal Reserve policy and the consequences of public disclosure… There will be no way to keep this quiet, no way to reassure the public."

A thoughtful silence ensued.

"A worldwide run on the dollar," Ari said.

"Stock market crash," Burke added.

"A complete business shutdown if people have no faith in American currency," Ari finished.

"In short, gentlemen, pandemonium. Mass unemployment, a depression, starvation in the towns of America. The economy is doomed, and our nation with it."

"This man must be stopped." The White House Chief of Staff waited until he saw both men nod in agreement.

"Good. As the President sees it, we have to do two things. First, we need to find Herr Doktor and bring him in, alive. We can't afford to have him talking to the press.

"Second, we need to make sure the remaining bankers do not link this scandal to this administration."

Burke looked disgustedly at Gonzalez.

"Colonel Burke, I want you researching each of the voting members of the Federal Reserve and Senate Banking Committee. Plan to look into their vulnerabilities and special interests, in case they are being manipulated as well."

Burke decided to play along, knowing full well Athena did not answer to Gonzalez but couldn't afford to have him bring their organization into the wrong light. "In that case, I'll need to hitch a ride back to D.C. with you."

Gonzalez nodded affirmatively. Just then, came a frantic tapping at the library door.

"What is it this time?"

Another Secret Service agent stood waiting. "Sorry, Sir, the White House communications room is insisting that we interrupt you. They have just had a Need to Watch alert from CNN."

The agent walked over to switch on the television and turn the channel to a news anchor.

"In an unprecedented move today, the Federal Reserve canceled its two-day meeting in Washington, D.C.

"No Federal Reserve meeting has been canceled since creation of the institution by Congress on Dec 23, 1913. On further inquiry, it appears three of the seven Governors appointed by the President to the Federal Reserve have been reported missing.

"And on Wall Street this morning, the Dow Jones Industrial average sank 1100 points within 20 minutes of the news release from the Federal Reserve. This is the biggest one-day decline in its history.

"Stay tuned to CNN for up-to-date releases as we follow this story."

Ari looked to Gonzalez, "You were saying no one knew? You forget your enemy is well-connected in the financial community, Mr. Gonzalez."

"We're out of time, Cohen; you need to find that madman."

♦ ♦ ♦

White House Oval Office

"Mr. President, thanks for fitting me in on such short notice; we have a real problem."

"I know, Mo, any updates from Santa Fe?"

"No. Our team is working on all angles, and I feel good about that, but somebody leaked the story about the Fed to the press. The Stock Market sank like a rock yesterday. Then the Dow Jones opened this morning down another 800 points after yesterday's losses. This is a real catastrophe."

Winters paused to catch his breath. "Another week of this, and the entire capital markets of the U.S. will be wiped out."

"What is your solution?"

"We don't have one yet. If you tried to reappoint another three Governors without an explanation as to what happened, I think you might precipitate a financial crash."

"Mo, you are telling me that we have to find those Governors, as in the old west... Dead or Alive?"

"Yes, Mr. President."

"Any chance you could have your people run down the source of the leak or rumor?"

"We already did. It came through Reuters from the Swiss Bankers Association. Funny thing though, it came through the wire before the Federal Reserve had even canceled the two-day meeting. Very Strange..."

The President leaned forward, looking from side to side furtively, "Would the Swiss Bankers Association know which U.S. citizens have illegal Swiss Bank accounts?"

"Of course. They are the entity that passed the information to us."

The President went pale, nervously adding, "Could they have withheld some of the names that had accounts?"

"Don't tell me you have –"

The President leaned back suddenly, shaking his head in the negative, "Me, oh, no, no, no."

◆ ◆ ◆

The Raven's Nest
November 8, 2014

Herr Doktor walked from his brother's office to have his breakfast in the forecourt. Passing Willi, he said, "Bring Miss Cooper here, make sure she is adequately restrained."

As the Doktor stirred his coffee, Willi brought in a somewhat disheveled Cooper. "Thank you for joining me, Miss Cooper. I'd like to say how lovely you look this morning, but I'm afraid our adventures are beginning to take their toll on you."

"Well, you playmates here don't seem to like me much, and I can't say much for the accommodations," she said as Willi roughly thrust her into a chair opposite his boss.

"Yes, well, you have not proved to be much of a guest, Fraulein."

"I don't play well with monsters."

Herr Doktor laughed heartily at that. "Yes, I see. Well, everything will be coming to an end shortly, my dear, and it will all be over soon."

"And you'll get what's coming to you."

"Oh, you are quite right about that, my dear, but I doubt you and I agree on what that means."

"Can you tell me why? Why all of this craziness, and why kill those men?"

"Isn't it obvious by now, you daft woman? I'm destroying your ridiculous government by the most beloved of all its resources – its money. The root of all its evil will be its undoing. All I have to do is bring down the value of the precious U.S. dollar, and the whole American society will crumble. As for those men, it was all part of the plan. Not even the White House can manipulate the death and disappearance of three Federal Reserve Governors."

He sipped quietly on his tea. "If I just blackmailed them, they might try to make a deal with the Justice Department. They are thieves –

thieves in suits, not really trustworthy."

"Then why go to the trouble to blackmail them at all?"

"Not even I could kidnap three prominent members of the Federal Reserve in the middle of Washington, D.C."

"You blackmailed them so you could get them down here to murder them?"

Herr Doktor smiled delightedly.

"You are a devious monster."

The Doktor clapped gleefully, jubilant at the chance to share his genius. "My plan to compromise the bankers was perfect. By now, the next Fed meeting will have been canceled. Panic will already have begun – of course, with a little push from me."

"You will pay for this; you won't get away with it."

"I will get away with it, and I will have my revenge. Those bankers were nothing more than criminals, they lived a lie. They promoted policies to lend money to their banker friends, all the while getting bribes deposited into their Swiss bank accounts."

"And you were a banker for the mob. Why are your hands so clean? What revenge will you get?"

"Your America murdered my parents in Viet Nam. Left them friendless after they had done nothing but trusted you and believed in your American lies. My brother and I were left alone in this world, and I swore I would avenge that deadly betrayal."

"Your parents helped the Americans in Vietnam and were left behind in the evacuations? How horrible and tragic. But that was one American administration, not America."

"Semantics!" he screamed at her, inches from her face. The tears that had formed in his eyes were gone, and they were once again cold and dead.

"You will not get away with this," Cooper said through clenched teeth. "They will find you."

"Of course they will; that is why this is so much fun. I have one more ace up my sleeve – or should I say, a politician in my pocket, though he doesn't know it yet."

"You are sick, twisted. So why are you keeping me alive?"

"Wallpaper, my dear," he said with a dismissive wave of his hand. "Wallpaper."

♦ ♦ ♦

Palace of the Governors
Later that Day

Ari walked out the heavy wooden double doors, exiting the museum, under his arm was a 24-inch cylindrical map tube. He pulled off the top of the tube as soon as he walked into his room and pulled out the maps to spread on his room desk. Pinning both ends down with glasses from the ice bucket tray, he studied the map, a smile spreading across his face, before he moved to his computer to contact Athena.

Soon Burke's face appeared on the screen.

"Ari, what have you got for me?"

"I think I figured it out, Tom. Rattlesnake Ranch was built on an old silver mine and some of the tunnels appear to go on for miles. That could have been his escape route."

"Good work. Any chance you can find one of those tunnels, work your way back in?"

"I'm going to do a recon this evening."

Burke nodded, a serious look coming across his face. "Let me know how it goes. Good luck."

Ari saw Burke moving to cut the connection. "There's one other thing, Tom. On the plans for the ranch down at City Hall, there are some architectural notes referring to a Raven's Nest Lodge in Devil's Canyon."

"Right," Burke said, scribbling a note. "I'll check out Raven's Nest on my end; I might have the lowdown by the time you get back from your recon."

Ari spent the rest of the day becoming intimately familiar with every minute detail of the map and architectural drawings. By early evening, he felt he was ready. He had room service bring up a light dinner that he could eat while he gathered his gear. Before dusk, he was headed out.

He started his recon back at the same location where he had been jumped before. Driving down an old dirt road from that area, he passed a historic marker that read, "Wright Mine Discovered 1873".

After a few more miles, he came to an old gate, the lock broken, bearing an "Entrance Prohibited" sign. As he slowed, he could make out fresh tire tracks leading to the old mine.

Ari opened the gate and drove into a mine tunnel large enough for an SUV to pass. The tunnel was dark, humid, almost medieval looking, but the going was surprisingly smooth. Abandoned mining equipment and rocks lined the passageway.

As he entered a cavern, rats scurried around the middle of the rock floor, trigging his revulsion. He stopped to get a look at what had drawn them. Squinting, he could just make out six partially eaten bodies in the corner, partly skeletal, picked clean by rats, hair hanging down over meatless skulls.

◆ ◆ ◆

Athena OPs

"I have a report on Operation Orthus, Sir."

Burke cocked an eyebrow. Thus far, the OP had been called "O" over all channels. This was the first he was hearing of the full name his analyst had given it.

That was, of course, all the opening his exuberant analyst, Sam, required.

"Operation Orthus, Sir? I thought it very apt, us being Athena, and all. You know — a nod to the Greek gods — Orthus, the two-headed dog of Greek mythology? I mean, how often do you get a case with twin suspects?"

"Report, Sam."

He cleared his throat. "Of course. It's coming together, Colonel. We have an anomaly with 17 of those 24 names, Sir."

Burke had his analysts working around the clock running down information on the members of the Senate Banking Committee and the two Federal Reserve Governors.

"And ..."

"Zurich, Switzerland, Sir. Immigration records show multiple visits over the last five years."

Burke detested how the analysts dragged out providing information, as if they expected everyone to make the instant leaps the data had shown them.

"Which means what, Sam? Lay it out for me."

"Two anomalies, Sir, first whenever you return to the U.S., on your Customs declaration, you have to disclose countries visited. None of them listed Switzerland.

"And, on each departure from the U.S., their airline ticket destinations did not include Switzerland, so..."

"They did not want anyone to know where they went," Burke surmised.

"Precisely, Sir. In 2001, the U.S. passed the PATRIOT Act. It was meant to deter and punish terrorist acts in the U.S. by restricting undisclosed money transfers around the world," Sam was excited now, pacing as he delivered his report. "What it also did was make available to the U.S. authorities the names of any Americans who held secret accounts in Switzerland that they hadn't disclosed."

He stood smiling at Burke.

"So if our Mr. Mueller, as Chairman of the Swiss Bankers Association, had that information, he could withhold it from the U.S. and blackmail every one of them. Good work."

Ignoring Sam's beaming smile, Burke moved on to the next topic at hand. "What about Devil's Canyon?"

"Yes, Sir, it has been located. We also have our eye in the sky over the Raven's Nest Lodge. We show four infrared human images, one probably a woman, according to the heat signature."

"Excellent, send the information to Agent Cohen and copy Agent Gray. I want him on a plane ASAP."

♦ ♦ ♦

White House Checkpoint
Afternoon

Burke arrived at the first White House checkpoint, handed his Athena card to the Marine Guard on duty, and waited patiently.

"You've been pre-cleared, Sir. Please go right in."

Once at the White House entrance, he was met by another Marine and shown into the Oval Office.

"Burke, I sure hope you have some good news for me; we are running out of time."

The President looked harried and sounded stressed.

"I think we have figured this out, Mr. President. The short version is that we believe that, as Chairman of the Swiss Bankers Association, Anton Mueller, whom we've known as Herr Doktor, found out 17 members of the Federal Reserve Board and Senate Banking Committee have or had secret Swiss Bank accounts."

Burke noted this information barely raised an eyebrow for the President, so he continued. "If this was made public they would have faced jail time, public humiliation and worse. They were easy blackmail targets."

"And I am to assume that he was privy to a list of everyone in our government who has a Swiss account?"

Burke nodded, more to himself as a light went on at the President's question. "I'm afraid so, Sir."

The President became noticeably more agitated. He came around his desk and began to pace the room, wringing his hands behind his back.

"Agent Cohen has found the bodies of the missing Federal Reserve Governors, pretty chewed up by rats, I'm afraid."

"I can't afford to have them found like that, and I need them officially dead so I can appoint three more governors," the President said more to himself than Burke.

Still, seeing the political chaos that could come making this plot and its near success public knowledge, Burke and the Board at Athena had decided to play along.

"I think we can arrange something, Mr. President. If our plan comes together, perhaps by tomorrow night. Would that be soon enough?"

Finally, there was a sigh of relief from the President. "Yes, I will get my new nominees ready."

Burke rose from his seat to leave, but the President put a hand on his shoulder. "One more thing, Colonel. I need this to be resolved quickly and quietly. Send this Herr Doktor back to Zurich, no waves, no publicity, no more bodies, understand?"

"No can do, Mr. President."

The light touch on his shoulder turned to a hard grip.

"I beg your pardon?"

"Athena was created by the founding fathers to protect the United States of America and the Presidency. We were chartered to uphold those founding concepts of freedom and morality.

"This man kidnapped one woman, who we believe is still in his custody, and killed at least three people by his own hand who – even if they were dirty bankers – deserve justice. He also orchestrated the murder of two others. I'm not going to let him get away with this, period."

The President backed away from Burke, pointing a shaking finger at the Colonel and stuttering in apoplexy. "You mean to tell me that you are going to disobey a direct order from the President of the United States?"

Burke didn't flinch or change his polite smile, except perhaps to make it more granite-like.

"Mr. President, you seem to forget..." He walked to the door then and stood in the open doorway looking at the pale leader of the Free World. "I don't work for you."

He turned face-first into the wall-hard chest of a Marine guard. Slowly looking up, he took the man's measure and contemplated what trouble he might be in.

"If you have completed your business with the President, the Vice President has asked to see you," the mountain of a man said, turning to lead the way without waiting for a reply. Burke followed with no small amount of relief.

As he entered McQueen's office, her face told him she had already heard from the President.

"Busy morning, Tom?"

Burke took a seat in front of her desk and waited to see where she would land on the subject. He may not work for the President, per se, but as the Eye from New York, he could not say the same for Jade McQueen.

She faced him silently, her fingers tented beneath her nose, waiting for an explanation. Finally, he decided he better give her one.

"I may not have handled the situation with the proper amount of decorum, Madam New York."

"Decorum my hind leg," McQueen said. "You insulted the President of the United States, Tom, in his own office. That leaves me with a nifty little mess to clean up, but I'll deal with that later. You were right about the situation, just wrong about how you handled it."

"Yes, Ma'am."

She waved her hand as if to signal that the subject was closed. "At any rate, we have other matters on the table today. I received your morning briefing on the situation in New Mexico. I have a ... twist ... I need to add to the mix."

Burke leaned forward with interest and no small amount of dread.

"I met with the Raven."

"I beg your pardon, Ma'am?"

"I had him over to the house for breakfast to discuss this issue. As Ari told you, your Herr Doktor is the Raven's brother, and he is heavily involved, although this is not his plot and he would very much like to extricate himself from the whole affair."

"So David told us," Burke said, sitting back and giving McQueen a skeptical look.

"Did he also give the man's real name?"

That had Burke back on the edge of his seat. "His real name? Which means you also know who the Raven is?"

She nodded her head. "I know their true family name, but I have sworn not to release it unless it becomes critical to the mission. As I'm sure you are aware now from the reports and photos, the two are twins. They are the sons of Swiss patriots killed in the Vietnam War. Your Doktor blames the United States, and this plot is his revenge being played out against us."

"I see. And the Raven's role in all of this?"

"It seems his brother chose to use the Raven's name without permission, embroiling him in this mess without his knowledge at first," McQueen's expression took on a strange sadness then. "The Raven then tried unsuccessfully to turn his brother away from the whole plan, hoping to save him from his own destruction."

"That's what David said. He told us the Raven is actually quite an interesting character, charming even. So why keep his name secret?"

"Both the Raven and his brother are living under different names than the ones their parents gave them. The Raven hopes to keep that name free of scandal, as his father – a CIA operative – would have wished.

"Tom, they were good people, and some would argue we owe them. That family name was the only thing his father – who had escaped the Cosa Nostra – had to hold on to."

"So you made a deal with the Raven?"

"I believe keeping the Swiss Bankers Association out of any negative press is to everyone's advantage, Tom. They've had a Sicilian Clan plant in charge for years, under an assumed name. Do we really need to open that can of worms? And if we do, how do we keep any of the rest of it from coming to light?"

Burke thought back to the conversation he had just had. "I see your point. I'm not so sure your friend Ari is going to like it."

"I have acknowledged that we have common interests here," she said, her tone warning Burke to tread softly. "He did not go so far as to ask for protection for his brother, and I believe he sees that there is nothing that can be done to save him at this point. It would seem the man is quite literally mad.

"However, the Raven has offered whatever assistance you may need in exchange for being released from suspicion in this caper."

"We've already discovered our route into his little New Mexico lair, where the Doktor is holed up, and Ari is reconning the location now. I don't think we're in need of the Raven's services," Burke said carefully. "And you're quite sure he wasn't involved in the attempt to kill Ari?"

"Quite."

"Very well, Ma'am, I'll follow your lead here."

"I appreciate that, Tom."

Burke rose to leave.

"And, Tom? Do be a dear and stop bullying my boss." McQueen said with a smirk.

Burke nodded in reply, trying to control the grin spreading across his face.

"I'll do my best, Ma'am."

27 RESCUE

Burke walked back into Athena OPs long enough to gather his gear and hand out marching orders.

"I'm headed to Santa Fe. I want two drones around the clock over Devil's Canyon, armed with Hellfire missiles. Be ready for anything."

"Yes, Sir," Sam said, over-eager to take back his Number 2 position. "Gray is on his way, Sir."

◆ ◆ ◆

Raven's Nest Lodge
November 9, 2014

Burke and Gray met up in the airport and grabbed a rental car. They joined Ari at the hotel, and after a short briefing, the three headed out into the early morning light.

They now walked through the New Mexico brush, matching each other's pace, coats flapping in the light wind, locked and loaded. They were in radio contact with each other and Athena OPs.

"I'd feel a lot more comfortable going in with heavy fire, but I get that blowing their heads off would be a dead giveaway. How close do we need to get for you to hit our targets, Ari?"

"In this wind, 100 feet."

Gray put a comforting hand on Burke's shoulder. "Don't worry, old man. I've seen him knock a fly off a watermelon at farther than that."

"Yes, but there was a hundred bucks riding on that one," Ari said simply.

"I wager you've got a lot more riding on it this time," Burke said, quickly changing the subject. "OPs, are you copying?"

"Yes, Sir."

"How many targets do you show down there?" Ari asked.

"We have three in the front of the lodge and one or two more in the back."

As soon as the three men rounded the top of the canyon wall that hid Raven's Nest from their trail, they separated and made for either side of the lodge. Burke and Gray went left, Ari right. Willi was the first to appear outside, carrying piñon wood to the outside fire pit. As he approached the pit, Ari raised his blow pipe, leveled it and blew, watching Willi react immediately. He dropped the wood, grabbed his neck, stumbled and fell forward, immobilized.

Burke signaled Ari to look back at the lodge as Fritz appeared to check on the strange noises he had heard. Worried for his friend, he called out for Willi, but got no reply.

Fritz walked into the forecourt looking for the wayward guard and just as he saw Willi's feet on the ground by the fire pit, his hand jumped to his neck as if bitten and he, too, fell to the ground.

Burke and Gray rushed up to the front of the lodge and met Ari as he came up the other side. The three stood with their backs to the wall, while Ari reloaded.

"How long does the toxin last?" Burke whispered just loud enough for Ari to hear.

"They will be paralyzed for an hour," Ari smiled. "Don't worry if they froth at the mouth."

The three entered the front doors to the lodge one after another, tucking and rolling to the side, before coming up to seek a new hiding place.

"Can you take care of things here?" Ari asked.

"You going after Cooper and the Doktor?"

Ari only nodded.

Gray didn't bother to ask if he needed help. "Right. Be careful, we still may have one more thug on the loose."

Ari headed further into the house, all business, keeping his back to the wall and moving room to room with his eyes and ears alert. As he edged around a corner, a sharp hard poke to his ribs took him to the ground, grimacing in pain. On the way down, he grabbed his attacker's weapon – a truncheon – and held on, forcing the man to bend forward.

Almost as soon as he hit the ground, Ari was back in motion. He kicked both feet off the wall in a circular fashion toward the attacker knocking his legs out from under him.

As the man fell, he released his hold on the truncheon, and Ari pivoted up to land with force on top of his attacker smashing the man's head into the hard wood floor, dazing him momentarily.

Ari relaxed too soon, and the man launched three quick powerful jabs to Ari's gut, leaving him winded and wary. They both got up and circled each other. The man was blinking fast, trying to stop a stream of blood from a cut over his eye. He couldn't keep it from obstructing his view, and unable to help himself, he lifted his sleeve to wipe it away. Ari seized the moment to coil his left leg and release it like a jackhammer on his assailant's jaw. The man stumbled back, dazed again and confused, not knowing what just happened.

As his attacker rocked from side to side trying to clear his head, Ari launched another kick, knocking the man's feet out from under him. In a lightning move, Ari was on top of him with plastic cuffs and secured his hands. More cuffs were placed around his ankles before the man even knew what hit him.

Still straddling his attacker and restricting his ability to breathe, Ari leaned in close to his ear and growled, "Where's the girl?"

The man glared with hatred, refusing to answer, but involuntarily looked off to the far side of the room.

Ari followed his eyes, and smiled with satisfaction. "Thank you."

He picked up his short blow pipe, blew a knock-out dart into his opponent, and headed in the direction he had been shown. As he headed out, Gray and Burke bounded in.

"Ari?"

"All good. Keep an eye on him, I'm going for Jasmine."

As he turned down the corridor, he heard scuffling noises and screams coming from a room just ahead. He rushed the door, putting his shoulder down as he did, and hit it dead on. Out of the corner of his eye, he saw Cooper lashed to a table half dressed, the Doktor standing over her with a snake, taunting her.

Before he had time to react, another thug jumped at him with a sideways knee-kick to Ari's gut, doubling him over and winding him.

Immediately, Ari put all his effort into launching his doubled-over body at the thug, head-first, taking his attacker by surprise and causing him to stagger backward. In a split second, the man was simply gone, and Ari realized he had fallen into a pit.

Gut-wrenching screams of terror ensued from the depths below, and Ari took a moment to peer over the side. The man was writhing in agony on the bottom of the pit with pythons slithering over him, oblivious to the constant strike of agitated rattlers.

In the chaos, the Doktor dropped the python he was holding on top of the horrified Cooper, eliciting a blood-curdling scream as she writhed against her restraints. The Doktor rushed to the side of the pit to grab snake tongs and tried to pick up a rattler, but the angry snakes were moving too quickly.

In his rage, the Doktor bellowed a slew of obscenities at Ari, who flew to the side of the pit before the Doktor could arm himself with a reptile. He pinned the man's elbows together from behind, immobilizing him and pulled him away from the vipers.

In seconds, the Doktor was secured in plastic cuffs, and Ari was at Cooper's side.

"Jasmine, it's me. It's Ari."

The sound of his soothing voice stopped her struggles instantly, and the python on top of her half-clothed body slowly slithered over the side and off of her.

Recognition spread across her face, followed by consternation. "What are you doing here? Why didn't you get that snake off me? What are you staring at?"

Ari smiled, relieved to see Cooper come back to her senses. Still mesmerized, he picked up her clothing and gently laid it on top of her.

"Oh, we just came to watch the snake charmer."

Ari couldn't help smiling, despite the stream of obscenities still coming from the corner where he had deposited the Doktor.

Still bound on the table with her clothing now sitting on her bare stomach, Cooper became fully aware of the situation. "A little help, Ari. Why are you still staring at me?"

He moved toward her restraints. "Gee, that's some thanks!"

"I tell you what, if you stop ogling me and untie these ropes, I won't personally kill you when I can get off this table. Thanks enough?"

Ari sliced through the ropes at Cooper's wrists, and she hurriedly untied herself, grabbed her clothes and slid off the table to get dressed.

Noticing Ari's eyes still on her, she felt suddenly shy. "Um, would you mind turning around?"

He did, and when she had finished, she took his knife from him and released the Doktor's bonds, quickly grabbing hold of him by the fingers of one hand and pushing his hand back brutally so that he was on his tiptoes. She smiled cruelly then as she pushed him, forcing him to walk back toward the snake pit.

Ari moved toward her, but stopped short as she eyed him for only a moment. He never said a word.

"You know you are a miserable example of a human being," she said, emphasizing each word she spat in the Doktor's face. "You are not worth my time."

The Doktor realized what she was going to do to him and began to scream. "No! You can't! I'll do anything. Pieter! Pieter! Where are you? Help me —"

"Who is Pieter?"

"My twin brother. Please..."

She pushed him to the edge, where he teetered, leaning back, losing balance. With just a little push from Cooper he went over into the pit, screaming unmercifully.

She turned without a word and walked out with Ari.

"He had a twin brother?"

"Yes. I thought so when I saw him with the Raven, and in the bar, he called him Pieter."

♦ ♦ ♦

"I found her," Ari said, as he met up with Burke and Gray in the forecourt, glancing around to be sure they were alone and everything was safe. He nodded behind him for Cooper to follow.

"By the looks of you, she got the better of you." Burke said, trying to diffuse Ari's high-adrenaline post-battle anxiety with a little humor. Ari was so overcome with combat fatigue he didn't even realize Burke was trying to make light of the situation.

"She's one tough cookie, Tom, but this came from the other guard I ran into."

Gray moved quickly to wrap his coat around Cooper's shoulders.

"Hello, Jasmine," he said, as he moved in front of her and began to work the buttons, noting she was still rather in shock and that Ari had a grip on her like death. He also noted the rather possessive stare Ari gave him, and he had to smile.

"I have heard a great deal about you from our friend Ari. My name is David, and I think you and I should go sit in the car and rest, what do you think?"

Cooper looked to Ari, who looked at Gray, the only man on earth he truly trusted. Slowly he released his hold on Jasmine and nodded.

"David is my dearest friend. He will keep you safe. I will join you in a moment."

When she still looked unsure, he added, "Promise."

After they had left the room, Burke asked "Where's the Doktor?"

"He resisted capture, Colonel," Ari said with military detachment.

"I see," Burke said, noting the change in tone. "Are all other guards immobilized?"

"Yes, Sir."

"Fine. Help me move the bodies inside."

With hesitation, Ari followed his commanding officer out to the truck, where the half-eaten bodies of the bankers had been transported from their previous resting place. Both men started carrying the severely chewed corpses to the dining room. The thugs' bodies were also in the vehicle, and Ari helped him take these heavy ruffians inside, as well.

"Why are we doing this Colonel?"

Burke weighed what to tell his agent before answering with the unpalatable truth. "Politics and CYA. Before the President can nominate replacements to the Federal Reserve, there must be a plausible, believable reason to explain their deaths.

If the press found out that three governors were found in a cave in New Mexico half-eaten by rats, they would have a field day, and the financial markets could crash."

Within the restricted confines of the dining room of the Raven's Nest Lodge the stench of the partly decomposing bodies was overpowering. Some of the bodies were so compromised they had to be secured to the back of the chairs with hemp rope, a gruesome task.

They finished securing the last guard to his dining room chair and headed back out to the truck. In the back seat of the extended cab, Gray was entertaining Cooper with stories from Ari's recent past.

"What's that stench?" she asked as Ari opened the door.

"You don't want to know," Ari said, climbing in.

As they drove away from the lodge, Burke picked up his satellite phone.

"OPs, you copy?"

"Loud and clear, Colonel."

"Are you picking up the homing sensor?"

"Yes, Sir."

"Let her rip, Soldier."

Seconds later, a mammoth explosion engulfed the Ravens Nest Lodge. Everyone in the truck involuntarily ducked as they looked back to see flames shooting skyward.

28 IT'S A DATE

Hotel La Fonda

Back at the Plaza, the foursome chose to make their way inside the La Fonda Hotel through a staff entrance at the back, their battered, bloodied, dirty appearance sure to raise alarm otherwise. They waited until the coast was clear and sneaked their way back upstairs, where each headed for his or her own room, shower and clean clothes.

Ari walked Cooper down the hall to her door. "You sure you're OK?"

"I'll be great once I get into something clean," she said, pulling at her days-old clothing as if she couldn't stand the reek of it for one more moment. She reached up to his bruised face.

"What about you?"

He raised his hand to cover hers. "I've seen worse," he said smiling. He looked at his watch then. "Still early ... You up for dinner once you're clean and feel more human?"

Her face darkened a little. "It will take more than a shower to make me feel more human, I think." Then she looked into his eyes again. "But I'm ravenous, so dinner sounds perfect."

"Great. I'll pick you up in an hour?"

She nodded, and he handed her the key to her room that he had acquired from the desk earlier that morning.

As the door closed behind Cooper, the tears fell. She slid to the floor in great, heaving sobs with her arms wrapped around her shoulders. She stayed that way for half an hour, the tears slowly ceasing, and then pulled herself up and into the bathroom. Twenty minutes under a steaming shower released more of her tension and left her only ten minutes to dress, dry her hair and at least put on a little mascara and blush before Ari knocked on the door.

"Punctual as ever," she muttered as she quickly applied her lip gloss and slipped her feet into a pair of flats. The image in the mirror still looked haunted, and she wondered how long that would last.

She pulled open the door, and Ari smiled.

"You look lovely," he said. She wondered if he saw what she saw in her eyes, but as he took her hand, she let go just a little more.

They walked down the hall to the elevators in silence, and remained that way as they walked out into the street and down to the Pink Adobe.

Ari felt her hesitation as they neared the spot where she was abducted. He squeezed her hand, and she looked up into his eyes.

He smiled, took both her hands in his and turned her toward him.

"I have found the quickest way to put the past behind me is to make it mine – to own it, control it, rather than letting it control me."

She nodded, and they went into the restaurant and asked for a seat on the patio.

As they were seated, Cooper turned her eyes away from the street view toward the bar and back to Ari.

"Tell me about the redheads," she said with a mischievous grin.

Ari almost choked on the water he was sipping.

"Work, my dear Jasmine. Just a cover."

She laughed then. "I see. You sure seemed to be enjoying your cover."

His smile turned impish then, too. "Well, who wouldn't enjoy being fawned over by redheaded twin swimsuit models?"

It was Cooper's turn to nearly choke. "Swimsuit models?"

She wanted to throttle him. She wanted to go back upstairs and put on more makeup and a better outfit. She wanted to be something she wasn't.

Ari saw the passing glance at her outfit, and immediately reached for her chin. He turned her gaze back up to meet his.

"There is no woman in this world that is more beautiful to me than the one at this table right now," he said, and she just knew he meant it. Cuts, bruises, sadness and all, the man across the table found her beautiful.

And a little more of the hollowness dissipated. Yes. It will be OK, she thought. I will be OK.

The waitress came to take their order and both settled on sour cream chicken enchiladas smothered in homemade green chile. For a while, the two just sat quietly, looking at one another under the twinkling white lights, their hands clasped across the table, fingers gently caressing one another. Both knew there was much to be said, much to be decided, many questions unanswered, but for now, neither wanted to break the spell.

When their meals came, they ate amid light conversation, catching up on the years they had lost. Ari told her about his concerts and his life in Bethesda. Cooper talked about her sister and her life in Philadelphia.

It seemed like hours later that Ari walked Cooper back to her door.

They stood there a long while, still talking, hesitant to say goodnight, both fearful that goodnight might turn into goodbye.

Ari saw Jasmine's eyes begin to droop. His hand moved to stroke her hair.

"You need to sleep," he said.

For her part, she yawned. "I'm so sorry. I don't want to leave, but I'm just so tired."

"Of course you are. You've had a miserable time of it. Go in. Get some rest. We'll regroup in the morning."

"OK," she said, still not moving to open her door.

Ari smiled at her then, he kissed her softly first on her lips and then her forehead, and then each drooping eyelid. He turned her toward her door, took her key out of her hand and opened it. Gently he pushed her inside and handed her the key.

"Goodnight, Jasmine. Sleep well."

He pulled the door out of her hands and pulled it closed. Then he leaned against it a long while, careful to be silent so that she would not suspect he was still there.

He prayed for her then – a peaceful night's sleep, and a lessening of the pain and emptiness he could see in her eyes. It would take time, and love. He planned to give her both.

♦ ♦ ♦

Athena OPs
The Next Day

Ari and Cooper hadn't had a chance to talk about anything other than the case on the ride back to Bethesda with Burke and Gray. They had all met for breakfast, packed up and headed out bright and early. A debrief with the Member from New York awaited.

When they arrived at Athena OPs, McQueen was waiting in Burke's office. She had been in the OPs Center with his crew the day before, had seen his report filed before they left New Mexico, had spoken with David and had seen Ari's report. Now she waited to talk to Cooper.

As Burke rounded the corner, he found the Eye from New York sitting at his desk, using his computer. He stopped abruptly.

"Morning, Ma'am," he said, a bit grumpy.

"Tom," she said, looking at him over the top of her reading glasses. "I hope you don't mind. Your Second let me in and gave me guest access so I could look over my email. Need to keep up with the other job, you know."

She rose quickly from his chair and suggested they all head into the conference room down the hall. As she sauntered out of the room, she paused to kiss Gray lightly in greeting, then they followed her, Ari commenting loudly about a significant lack of coffee.

As they entered the room where Cooper first met McQueen, the Vice President used the intercom system to ask for a coffee service to be brought in, nodding at Ari as if to say, Satisfied?

She noted Ari stayed close to Cooper – protectively so. The woman was much different after her encounter with Wolfgang Stangl. If I had to choose a word to describe her, I'd say haunted, McQueen thought, appraising the cuts and bruises she could see and imagining the ones she couldn't.

An aide wheeled in a cart with coffee, as well as pastries, which Ari leapt at despite his hearty breakfast. McQueen, who knew his strict diet, raised an eyebrow.

"Almost getting myself killed makes me hungry," he said with a shrug and a smile, as half the pastry went into his mouth – also uncharacteristic for the normally genteel man.

McQueen had to laugh. "I see. Well, if anyone else would like something from the cart, I suggest you get it fast."

Since she hadn't yet had breakfast, she allowed herself a pastry and a nice, black cup of coffee.

Cooper made no motion toward the cart. She sat in her chair waiting and watching the others in the room.

McQueen took her seat. "Jasmine, I understand our operation put you in harm's way, as well..."

She saw Ari's face and neck tense, and his hand moved involuntarily to Cooper's armrest, where his fingers entwined with hers.

"Nothing I couldn't handle, Ma'am." Cooper put on a brave face, but she felt anything but.

"Of course," McQueen said, sipping her coffee. "Well, we are in your debt, my dear. But there is a matter we need to discuss – that little press pass nestled in your purse. There are ... elements," McQueen said, setting her cup down and looking intently into Cooper's eyes, "of this incident, which if reported could cause this nation a great deal of harm. It is our duty here to protect this nation from exactly that."

Ari glared at McQueen. "Are you threatening –"

"I understand completely," Cooper said, interrupting Ari. "I have no need to bring this story to light ... in its entirety."

"I thought you might say that," McQueen said, smiling. "You and I will spend some time together this afternoon – just us girls," she looked pointedly at Ari. "And when you leave, you will have one heck of a story to take back with you."

Cooper only nodded. Ari's hand slid from her armrest, and he looked into his lap. When you leave, he thought. There it is. She will leave; I will stay. What then?

Cooper bit her lip. She seemed suddenly alone. "Of course, Madam Vice President."

McQueen had seen it all. She looked at Gray and he shook his head. He knew that look. The matchmaker in her – the woman who loved Ari like a brother – was already scheming.

For now, she turned to the matter at hand. "Gentlemen, I have read your reports. I trust you have not omitted anything I need to know?"

Ari and Burke looked at one another and shook their heads in unison. "All there, Ma'am," Burke said.

"Good. If you don't mind, take a hike," McQueen said with a smile.

Again, Ari and Burke looked at each other and then at Gray who only shrugged. Slowly they all rose from their chairs, gathered their unfinished coffee, and headed out into the hall. As the door shut behind him, Ari heard, "OK, Jasmine, let's hear your story now."

He turned to Burke. "I have no idea what just happened, Tom."

Burke laughed. "We were dismissed," he said, patting Ari on the back. "Don't worry, son. What bad could come of it?"

Behind them Gray snickered. Ari turned pale. He knew Jade's penchant for meddling in his life. He loved her, but he knew exactly what bad could come of it.

Burke pushed him down the hall, laughing with Gray. "Yeah," he said, "that's what I thought, too. Maybe you need a little shot of something stronger in your coffee this morning ..."

"I think I need a sedative," Ari said, shaking his head woefully. "Didn't I already ask you to have my head examined if I ever let another woman back into it?"

Burke stopped and smiled at him then. "Son, you never let this one OUT of it."

29 MCQUEEN THE MATCHMAKER

Cooper sat across from McQueen, a wary look on her face. For her part, the Vice President offered a look of pure maternal affection.

She had listened to the poor girl pour out her heart about the experience she had just been through. There would be a lot of healing needed there, but Cooper was strong.

"OK, Jasmine," she said, patting the younger woman's hand as she leaned back from her hyper-attentive position. "I think that's all I need to hear. Rest assured that we appreciate all you have done for this nation, and we'll do all we can to be sure you come back from this as whole as possible."

Cooper sighed at that. Whole. The thought seemed a long way away.

"On to more interesting subjects," McQueen said, sliding a sheet of paper across the table. "I'm no writer, but I put down the printable facts of the case and the quotable statements from 'reliable anonymous sources' for you. What you do with it from here, is up to you."

Cooper looked over the sheet. "Wow," she said finally. "There's more here than I expected."

"I know it's not everything, and in some respects, it's probably not the truth you wanted to tell, but it's what we've got," McQueen said, spreading her hands before her in apology.

"I think it's enough to do Charlie proud," Cooper said, a tear in her eye.

"Good. I know the Daily News has already written a couple of stories about his death and unsolved murder. You will be able to report on that when you return as well – link it to the conspiracy at the ranch and tell the world that he was on to the story before anyone else knew it was a story."

"Yes. I will. I still have no idea how he got Gonzalez to talk or even how much he knew …"

◆ ◆ ◆

Down the hall, Ari waited impatiently in Burke's office while McQueen and Cooper talked. After a while, Burke had given up trying to talk to him because he was so distracted, and had gone into the

Command Center to debrief his staff.

Gray had recognized that look and not even tried, opting instead to head back into D.C.

As his mind raced with options for life both with and without Jasmine Cooper, he was so distracted he didn't hear Cooper walk into the room and was startled when she touched his shoulder.

He jumped and snatched her hand, and she screamed. Armed guards appeared seemingly out of nowhere.

As Cooper apologized for the commotion and the guards and Burke dispersed, she laughed nervously. "That's what I get for sneaking up on a spy," she said.

"I'm so sorry, Jasmine." Ari's face was the picture of anguish.

"It's fine, Ari. We're all a little jumpy right now."

"Yes. I see you survived your interview with the tigress," he said warmly.

Cooper smiled at him knowingly. "She speaks highly of you. I'd say she is a truly devoted fan."

"We've been through a lot," he said, taking her hand and guiding her to a chair. He sat next to her but did not release his hold.

"She wasn't unbearable, was she?"

Cooper laughed at the real worry she saw on his face. "Jade is a delightful woman, Ari. We had a lovely talk – after I gave her my report on the OP."

"And was that ... Did that go OK?"

She was touched by the worry lines across his brow.

"It was tough. She wanted to hear as many details as I could give her. I think, though, that was for my benefit – kind of a cleansing – and it worked. I feel better about the whole ordeal having really talked about it.

"I have a long way to go," she said, looking down into her lap, "a lot of demons left to purge, but I was trained for that once upon a time. I can deal with it."

Ari once more lifted her chin so that her eyes met his. "There is no reason you should deal with any of it alone."

She smiled. "I won't be alone, Ari. I have family in Philadelphia – my sister, remember? She's going through a lot, but she's good people, as my Daddy used to say. We stick together, us Coopers."

She was putting on her brave face again, letting him off the hook.

Luckily, Ari recognized it.

"And us Cohens stick with Coopers."

He kissed her then.

When he finally pulled back, only inches from her nose, she said, "But how?"

"I have no idea. All I know is that any music worth performing takes work to make it right. You are a masterpiece, Jasmine Cooper, and together, we are a melody I'm willing to work on."

30 MO WARNS THE PRESIDENT

White House
Later that Day

Mo Winters entered the Oval Office clutching a News Release from the Associate Press, holding it out in front of him as if it had suffered a brush with a skunk.

Winters was in such a hurry to get the news release to the President he didn't even realize the President had company. Sitting off to the side was Beau Mullins. A fancy dresser who knew most of the movers and shakers in town, his only problem was that most of the "connected" people in town wouldn't admit to knowing him.

He was the foremost lobbyist in D.C., and his client list was so impressive it included among them some of the wealthiest nations in the world. Dictators of foreign countries who thought their future might be on shaky ground were on a waiting list to buy his influence. He was said to be able to arrange a green card for the most heinous of civil rights abusers in record time, that is, as long as their Swiss bank account had sufficient zeroes to warrant his time.

"Mr. President, I think you are going to want to see this."

Klein reached out to take the news release, glancing at Mullins, and Winters noticed him for the first time.

Winters had not been charged with the protection of the presidential family name as Gonzalez had, so he gave the presence no matter. After giving the President the information, he respectfully withdrew a few paces from the President's desk while Klein read,

Federal Reserve Governors Killed in Scandal

Associated Press

SANTA FE, NM – The Philadelphia Daily News has reported exclusively that three Governors of the Federal Reserve missing for almost a week are believed to have been killed in a weekend explosion on a New Mexico ranch.

The bankers were meeting secretly according to sources speaking on condition of anonymity with Daily News reporter Jasmine Cooper, who upon following a tip, uncovered the grisly remains of the bankers' bodies in the remnants of the ranch house fire outside of Santa Fe, N.M.,

Saturday.

The bankers had been reported missing earlier in the week when they failed to make arrangements for a meeting of the Federal Reserve Board.

Fire authorities on the scene traced the cause of the explosion to the release of a methane pocket beneath the ranch house. The owner of the property has not yet been determined.

The bodies of the Governors were so badly burned that DNA will be used to confirm their identities. However, Cooper reports that authorities are confident in their belief based on evidence at the scene that the three are the missing Governors.

While seeking the cause of the fire in decades-old mine shafts under the property, firefighters also discovered the body of Swiss Bankers Association Chairman Anton Mueller.

Foul play is suspected in Mueller's death, and Cooper reports that authorities believe he was lured to the ranch by the Governors, where he was killed and his body was hidden in the mine shafts.

Fire authorities suspect that opening the shafts to hide the body is what caused the methane release into the structure above, where a spark ignited the gas and caused the explosion.

The suspected motive for Mueller's murder is his plan to release the names of American political leaders and businessmen found to hold Swiss bank accounts through shell corporations.

The U.S. has sought the release of this information for some time now, seeking judicial ramifications for withholding information about these financial holdings.

The Philadelphia News learned the list was sent anonymously following Mueller's death to the Federal Reserve, which has opened an investigation into the names included.

The list did include the names of the three Governors believed killed in the fire.

Klein looked stricken. He turned to Mullins with concern, but the man seemed unfazed, and merely waved a hand at him as if to say, No worries.

The President turned back to Winters unsteadily.

"Forward my appointees to the Senate Banking Committee. I want those names approved this weekend. We can't afford any delays."

"Yes, Sir. But Mr. President?"

"Yes, Mo?"

Winters had taken on a different demeanor, as if he was dreading the President's reaction. He held out a small envelope.

"This came to my office this morning, Sir, addressed to you."

The President accepted the envelope, gradually opened it and pulled out a small card, it read,

National Bank of Switzerland, Account Number 1307041776

I believe you will recognize your Swiss bank account number.

Compliments of

THE RAVEN

The President puffed up like a spitting cobra, turning to Mullins, who quickly turned away as if he wanted to slink off before Klein could launch a barb in his direction. His retreat made the President even angrier.

His face turned beet red, and before he realized Winters should not hear his statement, he said, "I thought you told me that no one would ever –"

31 THE RAVEN LEAVES HIS NEST

Sassafras River, Upper Chesapeake Bay
November 16, 2014

Jade McQueen ditched her security detail for a compact car rental and an hour-long drive to a little marina on the Sassafras River with her fiancé at her side. Waiting at the end of her journey was Pieter Stangl and the promise of a gourmet lunch.

It wasn't often that she made a move without the detail in tow, but Gray was enough of a body guard, and the threat level was low. Besides, Stangl had mentioned chicken scaloppini with porcini mushroom cream sauce and traditional torta de mele (apple cake) among today's courses, and McQueen determined that was well worth the risk.

For Gray's part, the risk involved letting McQueen drive – something else she rarely got to do these days. He sat in the passenger seat with his eyes firmly closed, his seat back reclined, ignoring the speed at which they barreled down the highway toward their destination and the blaring rock music that attempted to alter the very rhythm of his heart to meet its thumping bass.

He peeked at his bride-to-be and had to smile to himself as she sang loudly with the music. Such gusto for someone so tone-deaf bordered on its own type of bravery.

"You're grinning at me, Gray."

Caught. He closed his eyes and feigned innocence. "I was wondering what all the caterwauling was about."

McQueen smiled at him, knowing better, and continued her abuse of what little melody existed in the rock anthem she had chosen. As she pulled into the marina, she turned down the radio and regained her stately composure.

"Long live the Vice President," Gray said, raising his seat and taking a more action-ready position. He smiled at her, capturing a wayward bit of hair and securing it behind her ear. "Do let's be presentable, Madam."

The Raven had given them directions to his yacht slip and instructions to come aboard when they arrived. He awaited them below.

Once they found the yacht, the luscious smells from the galley lured them from the dock. Stangl met them at the galley door and led them to seats around a well-appointed table.

"This looks wonderful, Pieter," McQueen said, giving him her coat as she took her seat.

"My Nonnina taught me well," he said, taking Gray's coat as well. "She had no daughters to teach, so all her Sicilian recipes went to me."

Gray's mouth was already full from the Antipasti course. He looked up sheepishly as he caught his McQueen's icy stare.

"Pardon my manners. I'm marrying a woman who cannot cook. It sometimes gets the best of me."

His response was rewarded with a swat on the arm from his fiancée and a chuckle from his host.

"No apologies necessary, David. Sicilians love to see people enjoy our food."

Stangl fed them a traditional Sicilian coursed meal. Antipasti consisted of two types of salami (one spicy, one not), cheese, olives and peperonata. Then came Primo (first) Course of homemade pasta with ragu (meat sauce) and risotto with porcini mushrooms.

McQueen was already feeling stuffed when he came to the table with Secondo (second) Course of grilled sausage; chicken scaloppini with porcini mushroom cream sauce; chicken involtini, a thin chicken breast layered with cheese, bread crumbs and ham, rolled up, and breaded with seasoned bread crumbs, then fried; and mixed salad.

Finally it was time for Dolce (dessert) and the torta de mele (apple cake). They wrapped it all up with a shot of espresso, which they took up to the deck, where a sunny November day on the water was brisk, but not overwhelming.

"Well, thank you so much for that delightful lunch, Pieter. I'll be paying for it in the gym for a month, but it was more than worth it!" McQueen joked as they looked out over the Marina and the array of yachts around them. "However," she said, taking on a serious tone, "I doubt you brought us here to show David what he'll be missing by not marrying a good Sicilian woman."

Stangl looked into the bottom of his empty espresso cup thoughtfully.

"I want out," he said finally. "Adolorata is gone. Now Wolfgang. Even the old man has been in the ground for years. I have no family to threaten now. Just me, and I'll take my lumps."

"You want my help—"

"No. Nothing like that. There's nothing even the Vice President can do to unmake a made man, Jade. I'm not asking you to help me or to look the other way. I just want you to know that I'm going to get myself out. If I survive, you may run into me again, and I want you to know that when you do, you can trust me to be on the right side of whatever issue that may be."

McQueen looked hard at Stangl for a long moment.

"I think I would have known that even if we had never had this conversation, Pieter. I expect you are telling me there will be some final … activity involved in your process of extraction from the Clan?"

Stangl sighed – a sound so deep it truly must have come from within his soul. "Yes. There will be requirements or there will be consequences. In the end, there may still be a price to pay one way or the other. If you hear … things…"

He rose then and walked to the bow to look over the water, his back to her. "Well, I just wanted you to know why."

McQueen looked at Gray only to see a mask of understanding – the way only men who have had to pay an unimaginable price can understand. Finally she rose, and put her hand on Stangl's shoulder for just a moment before taking Gray's hand and walking toward the dock.

"Don't be a stranger," she said over her shoulder.

32 BACK TO THE BEGINNING

Ho Chi Minh City, Vietnam
April 29, 2015

Pieter stood on the edge of the Saigon River, knowing 40 years before, his parents had run to its shores looking for a means of escape.

While the city had grown and changed in those four decades, clogging the river before him with more boats and human traffic, the color and nature of Vietnam remained very much the same, he imagined.

Pieter spent his first couple of days playing tourist. He went through the War Remnants Museum and the Reunification Palace, which left him sad and oddly lonely. To cleanse his palate, he chose to spend the next morning and well into the midday in the Museum of Vietnamese History, immersing himself in the history of Vietnam and her people. The rest of the day, he wandered the back streets of the city enjoying he color of its people against the darkness of its slums, seeking out its humanness – the same humanness that drew his parents, he thought.

He even made the trek to Cao Dai Temple in Tay Ninh more than 60 miles outside the city limits. The Holy See of Caodaism, which still escaped him as a concept. They explained it as a religion combining elements of Buddhism, Confucianism, Islam, Christianity and Vietnamese animism that espouses the virtues of vegetarianism, anti-sensuality, benevolence and universality. It all sounds a bit confused to me, he thought, but millions of people find their solace in it, so who am I to judge?

During his journey across the sea, he had done some research on sites to see in the area, anticipating his first real vacation, well, ever. He laughed now, thinking of Graham Greene's description of the temple as "Christ and Buddha looking down from the roof of a cathedral on a Walt Disney fantasia of the East." It fit perfectly for the horrendous pink dragons and those yellow and purple whatever they were. Besides, Greene had briefly been a member of the sect, so Pieter supposed he felt entitled.

Today, Pieter wanted to get out of the city and into some quiet. Along the shore, street vendors and sampan owners alike called out to him in their sing-song language, hawking their wares or offering to take him wherever the river wound.

An old, bent, toothless man caught his eye, quietly watching him from the edge of his moored sampan. Pieter had found a young boy from one of the orphanages working the tourists near his hotel. The boy spoke English and Vietnamese and eagerly agreed to a good wage to follow Pieter down to the water and spend the day with him as his interpreter.

Although you'd find English spoken in most of the tourist areas, Pieter wasn't interested in being a tourist today. He could have easily booked a one-cabin sampan cruise up the Mekong

He nudged the boy, "Lanh Sihn, ask the old man if he can take me down river, into the outskirts of the city, away from the tourists."

He watched the exchange as the boy not only relayed his request but haggled with the grisly captain. Soon, the lad grinned up at him. "He'll take you, and I got you a good price, sir."

Pieter smiled at the boy and ruffled his hair. "Then you shall make a good commission on the sale, son."

Pieter wasn't sure what he even sought so many miles from home. After the hardships he had faced since November, his yacht had seemed to steer its own course toward the South China Sea and eventually Ho Chi Minh.

As the three of them sat in the Sampan, watching the tropical vegetation pass along the river's edge, Pieter reached into the bag at his side. Among the usual wanderer's needs, it carried the tin box his Nonnina had given him all those years ago, and he had added to it the contents of Ben Carter's cigar box.

The boy beside him looked at the picture of the happy couple in front of a restaurant.

"She's pretty," he said, pointing at the redheaded woman with the bright smile.

"My mother," Pieter said quietly.

"They were here?"

Pieter looked up at Lanh Sihn, impressed by his intuition. "Yes. A very long time ago."

"They did not come back with you?"

"They died."

The boy looked at the photo again with a sadness in his eyes.

"You miss them?"

Pieter was looking at his parents again. The pure joy of the photo and the sad story of their lives refusing to rest peacefully in his mind. He took a moment to answer. "I don't suppose you can miss what you never had."

The boy sat quietly for a long while, and Pieter was almost startled when he spoke again.

"I think our hearts know when there are pieces missing – even if they never had the pieces in place."

◆ ◆ ◆

My Dearest Adolorata,

I am sorry it has been so long since last I wrote. In all truth, what little extra time I have these days I spend with a lovely woman I have met, and I have neglected all of my other responsibilities save work.

Her name is Heidi, and she is a nurse volunteering with the Red Cross here from Switzerland. I wish so much that you could meet her and see how wonderful she is – so kind and giving to everyone. Her skin is like ivory kissed across her nose and cheeks with the sweetest freckles, and her eyes are the deepest green. She has fiery red hair to match a sometimes fiery temper, but only when it is just.

She has such as passion for the people here – especially the children – and she has brought such a change to me, made me want to be better somehow.

I love her with all I am, my sweet, sweet Nonnina, and I will marry her if she will have me. I'm going to ask her tonight, even though we have only known each other a few weeks now. Time has a way of condensing itself here – of making the moments more important, the time spent together in an hour more like days in the scheme of things.

I'm sending you a photo of my beautiful Heidi so you can share in my joy. I hope all is well there.

All my love, Alex

Why are you crying? You've read this letter a hundred times. Pieter wasn't sure where the tears came from. It was true he had read the letter many times since his Nonnina had given him the box, but somehow it was different reading it here in this time and place. Although he could not remember his father's voice, he heard it in his head thinking those words as he wrote them to his mother so long ago. Pieter heard his father's love pour out in every pen stroke, which he found himself now touching lovingly, before he snapped back to the sampan and the boy sitting next to him.

He had no idea how long he had been sitting quietly, reading through the correspondence and looking at photos in the box. The boy had known somehow that his new friend needed the silence and sat looking out at the passing scenery, but now they were pulling up to a small village along the river's edge.

"It is the captain's home," Lanh Sihn said quietly. "His wife will cook for us."

Pieter put the box away and put on a hearty smile. "Sounds delightful."

33 GREEN EYES AND REMEMBRANCE

The home of Captain Hai Trieu was not what Pieter had expected. Houses in the city had been of more modern construction, small and efficient and not always up to American standards of size and amenities, but nothing like this.

Before him stood a compound of sorts just off the river banks, rising above the water level on stilts. The roof was thatch, the walls wooden planks, and a porch wrapped around the front, inviting them in.

As they climbed from the sampan to the dock, the Captain simply turned toward his home at his slow, intentional pace without so much as a nod. Lanh Sihn and Pieter followed, with plenty of time to take in the view. There was no village near Hai Trieu's home. Pieter surmised that what the family needed beyond the small garden, the river and the cattle and poultry he could see came from the captain's daily excursions into the city. It was a life he could admire.

A woman as withered as the old man came to the porch to greet them, although Pieter could not hear the nearly whispered words between the captain and his wife. He and Lanh Sihn removed their shoes and followed their hosts inside.

At the center of a structure that may have contained at most seven rooms, was the largest, with four intricately carved wooden columns rising to the grandly high ceilings. At the most prominent spot in the room stood an altar decorated with lacquered boards and parallel vertical panels displaying sentences written in old scripts Pieter did not understand.

"It is tradition in our homes for the main room to be for guests and for our ancestors," the boy explained. "Owners put more of their effort into this room than any other. The men will sleep in rooms at the center of the house, the women in the side rooms."

The captain had taken a seat at his table, and Lanh Sihn lead Pieter over to find a seat as well. He guided the clumsy Sicilian through the proper etiquette for the simple meal and explained the conversation and interesting stories the captain told.

As Hai Trieu's wife cleared the dishes, the trio walked out onto the porch, where the old man smoked a pipe and looked out over the river. He spoke lazily to the boy and then waited on an answer from Pieter.

"The captain wants to know if you wish to return to Saigon now or to go further up the river or to stay here tonight and explore inland."

Pieter stood a moment looking out over the quiet river. He relished the peace.

"Do you have to be back tonight, Lanh Sihn?"

The boy didn't miss a beat in his reply. "I have nowhere to be and no one missing me, Sir."

Pieter took his measure for a long moment.

"Well, then, please tell the captain that we would be honored to be his guests."

The boy smiled up at Pieter, and it lifted the dark mood that had plagued him throughout the day.

After a bit, the old man went down to the dock to secure his vessel and Pieter decided to take a walk into the near jungle behind the couple's home. He wondered that they had no children, extended family, no one else living in the big house by the river. He would have to ask the boy about that later, he thought.

The boy … As he trooped through the thick vegetation wondering at tropical plants he had never seen before, the image of the boy niggled at the edges of his thoughts. You let him in, Pieter. Another project for you to work on? Just like Wolfgang. Ah … but this one you can help. Yes, I'll have to do something about little Lanh Sihn when I leave Vietnam.

He was lost in his thoughts, headed back to the farm house in the oncoming sunset, when he ran smack into a young woman carrying a chicken. Startled, he dropped his bag, without thinking, fully intending to catch her falling bundle and make up for the error of the collision. It was not until he had the unhappy chicken in his hands – pecking and clawing at him, while slapping him in the face with both her wings – that he realized this may have not been his best move.

"I'm so sorry, miss, are you—" he stuttered, while ineffectively attempting to subdue the chicken and regain his composure.

Luckily, the pretty woman with the peach skin and the dark green eyes, saved him from his predicament, expertly recapturing her charge and removing it from his inexperienced clutches.

She giggled slightly under her breath. "I'm fine. Are you OK?"

Pieter was startled once more by the sound of English in this remote area and by the American hue of her Vietnamese eyes. Eyes he realized suddenly that he had been staring at for an inappropriate amount of time.

With nothing better to say, he stuck out his hand by way of introduction, and said, "Pieter Stangl, and you are?"

"Holding a chicken."

Pieter looked down at his extended, un-taken hand, and her two-handed grip on the still unhappy chicken.

"Yes. Yes, you are, a veritable mad hen. You're probably wanting to do something with that, and I am probably in the way," he said, noting he was standing in the middle of the path to the house.

She smiled at him as he stepped aside.

"Thank you, Mr. Stangl. My name is Ngoc Thanh, but you may call me Jade if you will come with me to help wrangle the chicken into a pen. She is normally much calmer."

Pieter rushed to her side. "Of course, but I must warn you, I have no experience whatsoever with chickens – at least not the live kind."

She laughed then. "Relax, Mr. Stangl—"

"Pieter."

She looked up at him from her much smaller stature. "Relax, Pieter. All you have to do is open the coop."

◆ ◆ ◆

Wrestling the chicken back into her coop wasn't as hard as Pieter expected, and he came away without a scratch and with most of his pride intact.

As Jade walked him back into the house, she explained that she was the captain's daughter, after a fashion, and worked at one of the mission schools in the city, where she also lived.

"I don't normally come out to my parents' house during the week, but I wanted to check on my mother. She was ill last weekend, and I wanted to bring her more medicine.

"So you are visiting from America? Lanh Sihn told me you seem to be visiting old stories."

"Old stories?" Pieter was again impressed with the boy. "I suppose that is one way to put it. My parents died during the Fall of Saigon. I never knew them, and I guess I felt the need to see where they had met and lived."

"The War is what draws so many Americans," Jade said, as they settled in chairs on the porch to watch the setting sun.

"Yes, I imagine that is true."

"So, may I ask, why Jade?"

"It is the meaning of my Vietnamese name. My mother named me for my eyes."

"Ah. Yes, I can see why. Unusual."

"My father was an American here during the war."

"He left you behind?"

"There were many of us left behind. After the Communists took over the city, even those with American citizenship waited years to get out. In the 1980s, the American government passed a law allowing Amerasian children to come with their families into the U.S., and tens of thousands fled, seeking the American dream.

"Life here for people like me was hard after the war. We were not Vietnamese, but we were not American. We were discriminated against here, but those of us who tried to fit in over there, in your country… it was no better."

"You went to America?"

"Yes, I was there for four years. I learned English, and real Capitalism and that hate is hate all over the world."

"Did you find your father?"

"My mother had a photo of him, but that's all. It was never meant to be. She was lucky. She met a man who loved her and accepted me. He has treated me well, although he is not an emotional man. They encouraged me to seek a better life in America, but understood when I felt a higher calling here.

"I came back to work in the mission school to teach English and math to the orphaned children, to try to arm them with an education and with hope to make the future of Vietnam different … better."

Pieter had a faraway look in his eye. "It must be nice to have a calling like that."

"It is always good to have a purpose for the soul as well as the body."

He smiled, but there was sadness in it. "I think my parents would have liked you."

"You know, I have another … friend named Jade, back in the states. In some ways, she is part of the reason I'm here. Opening up to her about my parents and my past ... digging it all up again ... I haven't been able to stop thinking about them since I spoke to her months ago."

"You said they died during the Fall of Saigon. Who were they? I've never heard of American civilians killed during the evacuations."

"Well, they weren't American civilians, I guess. My father was CIA and my mother was Swiss, a Red Cross volunteer. They married in Saigon, and my brother and I were only babies when the city fell."

"They got you out."

"Yes. At the last moment, when only Americans were boarding the choppers, my father handed us off to two young men and stayed with my mother, planning to help her escape."

"But they didn't make it."

Pieter was quiet a moment.

"No. The story is a bit sketchy. My father's CIA handler got it second-hand from someone on-board one of the ships who heard it from a sampan captain. The old man swore that when their vessel was overturned, my father drowned trying to keep my mother above the water, breathing for her. They were overtaken by the waves."

Two green eyes stared at him in the dimming light. Without a word, Jade took Pieter's hand and all but dragged him back into the house where the captain sat with Lanh Sihn.

She bowed slightly to her father before sitting beside him and touching his hand. She spoke quietly to him, but with a certain level of excitement, looking back at Pieter from time to time.

Without knowing what else to do, he sat beside her and waited. He looked over at Lanh Sihn and wondered why the boy seemed so interested in him and at the shock growing on his face. He was growing more and more uncomfortable.

The old man puffed his pipe for a moment and then began to speak and Jade began to translate.

"Yes. I remember the woman with the flaming hair and her man. The sky was full of choppers, the sea full of boats and ships, and the world was ripped apart. He paid me to take them to the ships, and we were close when the waves hit."

Pieter's eyes flew open, his mouth hung. "He is the captain? But ... he boarded the ship... How?"

"He could not leave my mother. When he stood on board the ship, looking at his damaged sampan, all he could think of was how to get back to Saigon. He leapt back into the sea and swam to an abandoned boat to make his way back."

"So, he saw my parents. He saw ..."

She spoke to her father again, and again translated his words for Pieter.

"He kept crying out to the American to get back in the sampan and help him bail so that they could make it to the ship. There was no way to save the woman. But he would not stop searching the waters.

"Again and again he dove until he found her, and then he put his mouth on hers to try to push the breath of life into her. Even from where I sat, I could see she was as gray as the dark clouds above.

"He burst above the waves to try and gather breath for her again, but the sea hit them with an angry fist, and he was swept beneath with her. They did not come up again. I made my way onto the ship to tell the Americans of the brave couple so that their family would know."

The captain spoke again, this time not in answer to any question from his daughter. Pieter looked quizzically at her until she gave him the translation.

"It was nothing. Superstition from an old man," she shrugged, rising to go with her mother into their sleeping quarters.

"He said theirs was a love too strong for this world," Lanh Sihn said, laying out his own sleeping mat. "The sea must never see your deepest passions or she will take them for her own."

34 FITTING IN

One night had turned to two and then a week. The captain had taken Pieter and the boy back into the city to get his luggage and Lanh Sihn's meager possessions and had brought them back to his home on the river's edge.

Since then, it had been more than a month. During the day, the captain went into the city with his Sampan. Once each week, Pieter tagged along to spend the day connecting on his business matters, but otherwise, he and Lanh Sihn worked on the farm to repair the buildings and pens, feed livestock and generally take direction from Hai Trieu's demure wife.

Pieter had even called a truce with the chickens and learned to pluck their eggs from beneath them without so much as ruffling a feather. It was a sense of peace badly needed by a psyche he had not realized was so damaged.

Jade came out to the farm every night now, and her long talks with Pieter were helping him come to terms with the death of his parents and his brother, although he had not told her the truth about Wolfgang or his own past. It was a situation he intended to remedy.

It was their custom to go for long walks after dinner, before the sunset and they sat on the porch watching the moon rise.

"You're very quiet tonight, Pieter. Is everything alright?"

He smiled at her in the warm glow of the approaching sunset. "I want to talk to you about some serious matters and I'm not sure how to bring it up."

"Why is it hard for you to tell me?"

Pieter thought hard about the real reason before responding. He had no worries about issues with the authorities or problems with her family. He only worried that Jade would no longer look at him the way she did right now.

"I'm afraid that you will see me differently... That you may not like me when I've told you."

"These are things you've done in the past?"

"Some of it."

"Things you are not proud of about your family?"

"Also some of it."

"You know my past. Who am I to judge? Besides," she said, turning to walk on so that he would not have to look her in the eye if he chose to talk, "Vietnam is a country full of the past. My people have had to do many things to survive – my mother. I do not think I will see you differently because of who you used to be."

Who you used to be … Is that true, Pieter? Are you changed? He shook his head as if it would shake away the thoughts beginning to cloud his judgment about himself.

"Do you know anything about the Cosa Nostra? The Clan?"

She looked at him as if trying to understand.

"The mafia?"

"I know the mob. I heard about them while I was in the States. Like the gangs. Bad families."

"Yes. Well, kind of."

"My father's family was Sicilian. When they rescued me, I was raised by a high-ranking member of the Sicilian mafia – the Cosa Nostra – in the U.S. as his own son. I was never told about my parents growing up, and I was brought into the 'family business' in college."

"My grandfather protected me to some degree. Because he was a Mafiosi – a made man in the Cosa Nostra – and I was at Harvard making connections the Clan had not had before, he made them see me as an asset they needed and convinced the Consiglier – that's the counselor for the Clan – that I could be used by the Clan without having to be 'made.'

"This was a kindness to me, I suppose, but I was never told why. To become Mafiosi usually means murder – proof that you are committed to the Clan. He spared me that. Anyway, I was left to finish college and come back to the Clan to act as a kind of financial adviser to the Capofamiglia – the boss – at the time. My father was his Capo Bastone – his under boss, and together they ran things on our end of Chicago."

The two took a seat on a bench by the water, and Pieter looked to gauge her reaction.

"So, you're in the mob?"

"Was. After my brother was killed … No before that. For a long time, and probably even before I really became part of the Clan, I knew I didn't belong in that life. When I found out about my parents and my brother, I had to find him and to rescue him. I needed my Clan connections to keep him safe and to take care of him, so I stuck it out.

"But I played as minor a role as I could, milking what I could from the Clan while doing as little harm as I could. It was a hard game to play because weakness is a trait not taken lightly by the family. I wore a great mask, made good use of people at my disposal and employed a lot of theatrics to build up my reputation as The Raven – internationally wanted killer and white-collar thief.

"The Raven was all me because the Cosa Nostra has a lot of really archaic views on what constitutes the right and wrong of being a bad guy. Anyway, after Wolfgang's death, I was done. I went to Diego Covello, Consiglier to Giovanni Fazello, the Capofamiglia.

"You see, Sicilian Clans are democratic. Our boss is elected. So is the counselor. So I asked Diego to take my request to the members – to release me. My father, as they knew him, was dead. I had no other family ties, and I had purposefully never tried to rise in the ranks of the Clan."

"So they let you leave this Clan?"

"If becoming Mafiosi means murder, you can imagine that refusing it requires a sacrifice as well."

♦ ♦ ♦

Chicago, IL.
December 12, 2014

"Are you sure you want me to do this, Pietro? I knew your father. He would turn over in his grave to hear you talking like this."

Pieter called for a meeting with Diego Covello in the back of a well-known trattoria near Grand Avenue in the heart of Sicilian Chicago. His men waited outside, leaving just the two in a back room to discuss what he saw as a private affair.

"Padrino Covello, you knew my father," the word burned on Pieter's tongue. "You know that he protected me from the ... harsher elements of life in the Clan. He did not mean this life for me, but he knew of nothing else."

Pieter softened his tone and added another dose of respect. "Padrino Covello, I am an honest man and a loyal man. No man can be trusted more with the secrets he has been given. I will do what has to be done to prove that, but I want my life to live."

Covello sighed deeply, considering the dilemma before him. "I will take you before the membership, but the price may be steep, Pietro. Are you ready to pay?"

"For a life outside, I would give everything."

♦ ♦ ♦

Unused Warehouse on the Outskirts of Chicago
December 21, 2014

Two weeks later, Pieter stood in the circle. The membership had met, and he was lucky many had spoken on his behalf calling him a loyal and honest man. A true made man who could be trusted to take the secrets of the Clan to his grave.

For hours he had answered their questions and accusations and judgments on why he wanted to leave. His resolve had not wavered, and the votes had been cast, and he had been called back into the room to hear the verdict.

"Pietro Vitale, you bring a sadness to my heart tonight," Giovanni Fazello said. He was seated at the head of the circle and held two pieces of paper and a dagger in his hand.

The scar on Pieter's palm and the tips of his fingers began to itch as he remembered his induction ceremony – the photo of some saint he could not recall, the dagger and the matches. They had sliced open his palm and bled him over the photo of the saint, then lit it on fire and forced him to hold it as it burned and he pledged his allegiance to the Clan.

"Your compare have chosen to release you, and tonight we will retract the ceremony that brought you into our fold," he said rising with the dagger and one piece of paper. Pieter held out his scarred hand to be sliced again. The same forgotten saint was once again besotted with his blood, but this time carried back to Fazello's seat and placed in an urn beside him to set ablaze.

Pieter looked at him quizzically.

"We require more from you than old traditions this time, boy," he said, handing Pieter a piece of paper. "By your hand. By midnight tomorrow. Your life or his. Complete your task, and we will consider you bound to keep our secrets."

Pieter looked at the paper in his hand. The name listed was familiar, a well-known businessman in the community who had become troublesome for the Clan. His heart sank. He had known the requirement that might be made of him, and even knowing the vile lifestyle of the man he was to target didn't make it easier.

He nodded at Fazello and walked out of the room, hoping never to see his compare again.

◆ ◆ ◆

"You were forced to murder a man to gain your release?"

Pieter snapped to from the memories he had been reliving for her. He would spare her the story of his actions after that point.

"Yes. He was a real low-life – prostitution, drug trafficking, human trafficking – all under the guise of Business Man of the Year. I shouldn't have felt badly about it, but no matter how often you are forced to kill in your own defense or the defense of your Clan, having to kill one-on-one on orders – that's different."

"But you did kill out of self-defense – defense of your life and your chance not to have to kill or steal or any of that again?"

He looked into her green eyes for a long time then. "Yes, I suppose that's true. For a chance to live a better life – to do something better with the life my parents gave me."

He didn't realize he was holding her hand at first and couldn't remember when he had taken hold of it. It simply was. This feels right. Here, now, with her, in this place. I have never felt I belonged anywhere until this moment, he thought. How funny to have come so far – all the way back to the beginning – to finally find where I fit.

35 NEW BEGINNINGS AND DEADLY ENDINGS

Hai Trieu's Farm
April 29, 2016

Pieter looked down into the tiny face, unable to believe what a year had brought. Another anniversary of his parents' death, but here he sat on the porch of the captain's farm with his beautiful wife, holding his own son.

My younger son, he though smiling, as he heard Lanh Sihn call from the captain's boat, coming in from class at the mission. They had taken to calling him Lannie, and he liked it. In just a few months, he had met and married the woman he had not dared to dream of and had adopted his lanky interpreter.

It was such a whirlwind. They had married at the consulate, with a reception at the mission school where Jade worked. Their wedding photo was very similar to the one of his parents in front of the little Saigon restaurant from so long ago, and both were now proudly displayed in a frame in their room.

And then his tiny miracle, Theo Alessandro Stangl had been born.

When Jade had become pregnant, they decided to stay in Vietnam until after the baby's birth so that her parents would be there, but to take their family back to the States soon after. Pieter had begun to make inquiries about schools and mid-sized cities in Maryland, having a fondness for the people there.

He took Jade's hand, loving how the warmth of the sun's rays enlivened the peach color of her skin and put sparkles in her eyes when she looked up at him and smiled.

I understand it all now, he thought, remembering every line he had read over and over in the box of letters from his father. He said my mother completed him and his family grounded him, and now I understand. No man could want for more.

Lannie leapt from the captain's sampan to tie it off, already babbling about the exciting day he had at school and already asking his million questions for the day about what life would be like in America.

Pieter laughed and Jade smiled. He could not wait to take the boy back home – back to the home they would build for him – and give him everything a child could need.

♦ ♦ ♦

Chicago, IL.
May 24, 2016

Anthony Vitale had loved his uncle like a father. He had never understood why he had been willing to raise the traitor's son – and then to have him betray the family by turning tail that way. It could not be tolerated, no matter what his Clan had said.

Uncle Vitale's decina had been weak since the day he died. Anthony had been blessed to lead his own decina, and they were strong, commanding great respect within the Clan. His need to avenge his Uncle's name would be overlooked, he was sure of it.

For a year, he had searched for some sign of the coward, and now word of him had surfaced in Maryland of all places. Figures he wants to be close to the Feds, Anthony thought as he ground out his cigarette in the ashtray on his desk. The PI he had hired to trail his cousin said the weasel was going by Pieter Stangl and had run off to Vietnam, married some woman there and had a kid. He's lost his mind, marrying some dink and bringing home half-breeds. No wonder he won't show his face here.

"Joey!"

His second promptly entered his office, waiting on orders. "They found the weasel coming in to the states on that big yacht of his next week. He's docking in Boston Harbor on the third. Make sure he never makes it to the dock."

"Sure boss. What do you want us to do with the bodies?"

Anthony thought about this one, but in the end his need to make an example of his cousin won out. "I want him found. I want the families to know."

"Sure, boss."

♦ ♦ ♦

Atlantic Ocean, Headed for Boston Harbor
June 2, 2016

It was after midnight, and Theo had been rocked back to sleep with the sweetest Vietnamese lullaby Pieter had ever heard. Now he and Jade sat in the bow of their yacht looking at the moon on the water and dreaming out loud.

"Tomorrow we will dock and make our trek into Boston to see your new house, my lovely wife. Are you excited?"

"I could hardly sleep before your son woke us," she said, playing with his fingers as she lay against him, cuddled into the curve of his arm. "I was in Houston when I came before, and it was so long ago. I cannot wait to see Boston."

"Yes, well, it's sure to be different from Houston. You'll find the accent different at least!"

Jade laughed. "Yes, I'm sure. So many accents come through Saigon. I think I have heard them all."

"Well, you will get to see plenty of Boston as we shop for furnishings and trimmings and … well, everything."

Jade giggled. "Yes. That has me excited."

He hugged her then. "See, you are and American."

The two continued with their banter and their plans, so engrossed in one another that they never heard the speed boat coming along-side their yacht from the other direction.

Pieter, thinking himself free of his past, had finally stopped listening for noises in the dark – other than the cry of his child – and did not hear the bumping against the hull until it was too late.

His body had tensed without him knowing it, his gut telling him something was wrong before his conscious thought kicked in.

"Pieter, what's wrong?" Jade asked, feeling him tense against her just as the first masked man rounded on them.

He threw her toward the open hatch and sprang at the gunman, catching him before he could fire. "Go! Get the boys!"

She scrambled toward the bedrooms below as he fought their attacker, not knowing there were more following behind her.

As Pieter wrestled the gun from the first attacker, two more men followed Jade into the galley that stood between the hatch and the bedrooms. As she stumbled through, she grabbed a large knife from the chef's set and rather than go through the door, she turned and buried it as far as she could in the neck of the nearest man. Screaming with the rage of a mother tiger protecting her cubs.

The knife hit home, and as the artery burst, his life's blood sprayed her white nightgown crimson. He fell forward, and she barely escaped being trapped beneath his dead weight, turning to run through the door and lock it.

"Lannie!" she screamed their pet name for Lanh Sihn. "Wake up! Get your brother! Hide!"

She was leaning against the locked door, putting all her tiny weight against it as the second man threw himself into knocking it in.

"Jade! I must help!"

"Hide! Save him!"

The door gave way, and Lannie ran without looking back. Instead of hiding, he took Theo, wrapped tightly in a blanket and still sleeping despite the noise, and crawled through a window just above sea-level and out onto the deck.

He heard her scream behind him, and his heart burst into a million pieces, but he kept going – into a life boat hanging on the side of the yacht. It was covered, and he slipped beneath with the sleeping child still tucked against him, undisturbed by Lannie's tears.

◆ ◆ ◆

Pieter couldn't manage to turn the tide on the gunman. He had hold of the gun, but was trapped beneath the man's huge bulk and couldn't release the weapon to try to get out from under him. For the attacker's part, he wasn't letting go to save his life – literally.

A woman's scream broke the night, and Pieter followed it with one of his own. It was a scream so guttural and animalistic, he would never have thought it came from him – a scream followed by an inhuman level of strength that hurled his attacker off of him and into the open hatch.

Pieter followed him down the stairs, and threw himself at the man crumpled at the bottom. Feeling a knife at the man's belt, he pulled it and sent it deep into the man's chest, staring deep into his shocked eyes as he did so.

Once dispatched, Pieter looked from his attacker to the carnage in the galley and the battered door beyond. He raced through it to find his beautiful wife viciously beaten and slashed, her peach skin stained with her blood, her green eyes open and unseeing.

Pieter collapsed beside her body, pulling her into his arms and crushing her to him wailing long silent, gasping sobs into her long, soft hair. What have I done? What did I do to her?

Hearing a noise in the cabins beyond, he lay her gently back to the floor and rose to his full height. He turned back to take the kitchen knife from the neck of the man behind him. She fought so hard for our boys, he thought, as he looked once more at his wife.

Silently, he crept around the doorway and into his infant son's room to see a man standing over the crib, talking on a cell phone.

"No. The whore is dead, and Vinnie is taking care of the rat, but she killed Diego, and the boy got away with the baby."

They were the last words the man ever spoke, as Pieter slipped up behind him and slit his throat.

He took the phone in time to hear his cousin say, "At least the rat got what he deserved. The boy won't get far with that half-breed kid. Just make sure you leave my cousin out where the families will see."

"Anthony." The ice in Pieter's voice chilled his cousin's veins miles away.

"So you bested Vinnie. I should never have underestimated you. You are a Vitale."

"No. I am a Stangl."

"Yeah. Well, Mr. Stangl, you better run, you weasel, because I'm not done with you."

"Oh, no, Anthony. You are mistaken." Every word was precise, dripping in venom. "I am not done with you."

Pieter dropped the phone on the dead man's body and turned to look for his sons. He saw the open window and his instinct knew where to look. He headed back to the deck to follow a hunch.

Once top-side, he called out to Lannie, but it was long, agonizing moments before he saw his sons emerge from the life boat. He rushed to hold them, inspecting Theo in Lannie's arms.

"Jade ..." Lannie cried against his chest, refusing to let his brother go.

"I know."

"Why?"

"It's my fault. My past. But I will make it right."

Lannie looked up at him, the street-kid back behind damaged eyes.

"You'll get the man behind this?" It wasn't really a question; it was a command.

Pieter held the boy's face in his hands and looked down at his infant son in Lannie's arms. Revenge was not what Jade would want, not for him or their boys, but the look in Lannie's eyes and the pain in his heart spoke a story only they understood.

"We will make him pay."

OTHER WORKS BY SPENCER HAWKE

The Arrows of Islam, Book 1 of the Ari Cohen Series

The Forgotten, Book 3 in the Ari Cohen Series

Kindle, ebook, paperback and audio versions are available at my website and www.spencerhawke.com and Amazon.com

Mystery of the Dead Sea Scrolls- Revealed

Portuguese Version— http://amzn.to/1yWBPpq
And English-to-Portuguese Translation — http://amzn.to/1BNK3i0

DEAR READER

I hope that you have enjoyed reading The Swiss Conspiracy as much as I enjoyed writing it. For now, our journey with these characters has come to an end, and I, for one, will miss them. If you enjoyed meeting Ari Cohen and company, please let me know! I love hearing from my readers and value your comments.

Please visit my website to leave me a comment or review at www.spencerhawke.com.

Thank you so much for taking the time to join my friends and me on our adventure and for letting me know your thoughts!

~ Spencer

ABOUT THE AUTHOR

Spencer Hawke was born in England and educated in the United Kingdom. He set off as a young boy seeking adventure abroad, and at the age of 21, he and a friend took off for Africa and crossed the continent North to South through the Sahara, sometimes on foot when their old Land Rover did not want to travel as far as they did.

Eight months later, having dodged many conflicts and machine-gun-toting patrols, the pair rolled into South Africa bound for Australia, determined to swim the coral of the Great Barrier Reef. But fate had a different plan for Spencer. In Johannesburg, he met a Brazilian girl who professed undying love for the young Brit. He changed his ticket and flew off to Rio de Janeiro in search of his love.

Once in Rio, she was nowhere to be found, and short on funds, he was forced to get a job. He went to work for General Motors in Sao Paulo. Eight years and two children later, he again had enough money to take off for what he thought would be his final destination.

Spencer landed in Oklahoma in the middle of the 1980s oil boom, and he and his children made a home for themselves in Oklahoma City.

Today he is raising another gift from God, grandson Devon, who is already as avid adventurer as his grandfather.

Find Spencer on *Facebook at www.facebook.com/spencer.j.hawke*. Connect with Spencer, learn more about the Ari Cohen Series and enjoy his blog, the *Weekly Debriefing*, on his website: *www.spencerhawke.com*.

CPSIA information can be obtained at www.ICGtesting.com
Printed in the USA
LVOW07s0928061215

465612LV00020B/877/P